The Long Weekend

by Clare Lydon

Second Edition 2017
Published by Custard Books

ISBN: 978-0-9933212-7-6

Cover Design: Kevin Pruitt
Copy Editor: Gill Mullins
Typesetting: Adrian McLaughlin

Find out more at: www.clarelydon.co.uk
Follow me on Twitter: @clarelydon
Follow me on Instagram: @clarefic

Also by Clare Lydon

London Romance Novels

London Calling

This London Love

A Girl Called London

Other novels

Nothing To Lose: A Lesbian Romance

Twice In A Lifetime

The All I Want Series

All I Want For Christmas (Book 1)

All I Want For Valentine's (Book 2)

All I Want For Spring (Book 3)

All I Want For Summer (Book 4)

All I Want For Autumn (Book 5)

All I Want Forever (Book 6)

Boxsets

All I Want Series Boxset, Books 1-3

All I Want Series Boxset, Books 4-6

All I Want Series Boxset, Books 1-6

ACKNOWLEDGEMENTS

Book two is finally here — yay! As with most books, there are many people who've helped me along the way and you're all fabulous. No, really.

First, muchas gracias to Jamie Cootes, Jeremy Cope & Lola dog for welcoming me into their Spanish home where this story idea was hatched, along with the first 15,000 words in one perfect week. Thanks for the gorgeous paella, vino tinto and afternoon sunbathing sessions.

Gallons of thanks also to my early readers for your very constructive feedback: Suzanne Evans, Rachael Pollitt, Elaine Brown, Rachel Elliott, Sheryl Scott, Rachel Batchelor, Tammara Adams and the legend that is Angela Peach.

Oodles of plaudits to my friend Kevin Pruitt for another creative masterpiece of a cover — you are a star, it's official. Thanks to Gill Mullins for her eagle-eyed editing skills and unfailing enthusiasm. And finally thanks to Adrian McLaughlin for the typesetting and constant encouragement. I simply could not do this without all your support.

Big love & thanks to my gorgeous wife Yvonne who read this manuscript countless times and still has nice things to say about it. I knew there was a reason I married her.

And finally, thanks to everyone who bought my first book, *London Calling*. That encouraged me to write another, so you only have yourself to blame.

For all my university friends.
We've shared some drama-filled times,
but you'll all be terribly pleased to know
that none of them feature in this book ...

THURSDAY

Chapter One

The purple Fiesta hit another pothole where there should have been solid ground and the car slumped to the left like a well-rehearsed drunk.

Vic's nausea rose. However, as she was the one who'd made the call to drive down this particular road/dirt track, she didn't think Stevie would appreciate her sharing the fact that she might vomit any minute now.

Stevie tugged on the black handbrake, her fingers fitting into its ridges perfectly. It made a crunching sound, which fairly reflected the mood in the car.

"I'm not even going to ask if this is the right road, seeing as it's not even a *road*." Stevie surveyed her surroundings. "I'm guessing we should have turned right at that last junction?" Her voice didn't hold the acute anger Vic had been fearing: rather, Stevie curled her lips into a weak smile.

"It's the way it said on the map." Vic wiped her palm across her clammy brow.

"Perhaps if you hadn't been trying to eat a Flake without spilling it all over the car, you'd have been paying more attention." Stevie sighed beside her, then blew a raspberry. She rolled her neck in a semi-circle from left to right. It rattled the whole way round like an old, rusty chain.

Vic ran her hand through her short, brown hair and took off her black glasses to wipe them on the hem of her shirt. Over five hours on the road had taken its toll on both of their nerves. The clock on the dashboard read 16.34. She put her glasses back on but wasn't sure her vision was any clearer.

"What about the sat nav?" Stevie glanced sideways.

"The one that got us into this mess in the first place?"

Stevie stared straight ahead into the late Devon afternoon. There was not a single house or business in sight, just a few sheep in the neighbouring field. "At least it's got a sexy voice," she said.

"A sexy, lying voice." Vic smiled.

The tension in the air silently popped.

"We haven't seen a sign for miles, though," Stevie added.

"Devonians aren't big on signs. But they do make lovely cream teas."

"Great. If we ever get to where we're going, maybe we can have one."

"That's the spirit." Vic stroked Stevie's denim-clad thigh. Her wife's muscle tensed but she ignored it. Instead, Vic flicked on the top light and surveyed the Collins UK Road Atlas in her lap. After a few moments she looked up, renewed certainty plastered across her face.

"I think I've got it," she said. "If we get back onto the

bit that was an actual road, we should hit the main road in, like, ten minutes. Fifteen tops. And babe?"

Stevie turned her head slowly, her short blonde crop hardly moving as she did so. Her skin sagged with tiredness, her complexion the colour of rice pudding. She was too tired to respond.

"I'll buy you a beer when we get there."

"You fucking better," Stevie said. "And you're pushing us out of this ditch if we're stuck, too."

Vic leant in and kissed Stevie briefly on the lips. She straightened up in the passenger seat, trying to ignore the fact Stevie's body had just tensed again at her touch. Vic laid the map on her lap as the Fiesta's engine roared into life again.

"What's the ETA?" Stevie asked, looking over her left shoulder and shifting the gears into reverse as the tension hastily began its reassembly.

"One hour, tops."

"That's what you said last time. We will make it by Easter Sunday, right?"

Vic frowned at her sarcasm but said nothing.

"And any texts from the others yet? Are they on their way?" Stevie asked.

Vic reached into the door compartment and retrieved her phone. "Nope," she said, shaking her head at her home screen, before carefully placing the phone back in its cover. Vic had a habit of killing phones; it was an expensive habit she was trying to break.

Stevie pressed her foot down on the accelerator and looked behind her. They both heard the engine rev but the car stayed still. Stevie pursed her lips and tried again: same result.

Vic screwed up her face as Stevie looked over at her.

"So you know that joke I made a few seconds ago?"

Vic let her eyelids settle, before taking a deep breath and opening her passenger door. "I thought driving your car into ditches only happened in rom-coms?" she said, before disappearing out of the car.

Chapter Two

Geri had endured a shit week and today hadn't been much better. She'd gone into policing because she had a vague notion she wanted to help people but she could just as easily have landed a selfish job with her degree. A job in a bank maybe, just like her mate Kat. Kat worked long hours too, but she got to wear power suits and go to swanky wine bars, *and* pulled in over three times her salary.

Plus, when Kat said she worked in finance, fewer people seemed to sneer than when they caught sight of Geri's police badge. Geri was still at a loss to know why, considering Kat's business had brought the country to its knees, whereas her only crime was to protect the public from criminals and make the world a safer place. Life wasn't fair.

On the plus side, Geri was now a CID sergeant in London. As well as a desire to help others, the desire to be Christine Cagney had always been at the forefront of Geri's life and she'd achieved her dream. A by-product of that dream was that it made her ridiculously attractive to women, something that'd never been lost on Geri. The job had its perks. Also, she now had four whole days off in a row.

Four, including a weekend. It was almost unprecedented.

Today, her boss had been a royal pain in the arse, a stickler for protocol and paperwork which was the bane of her existence. It wasn't what she got into policing for — if she'd wanted an office job, she would have applied for one. She bet Christine Cagney never put up with this shit.

Geri had been looking forward to the weekend away for weeks but she wasn't feeling the love today: she was coming to the end of her period and her body was sluggish, her stomach still bloated. Geri shook her head again at Mother Nature, so insistent that she have the option to breed every month. Geri had no desire to do so, despite what her mother kept hinting. As far as Geri could see, mothers did nothing but irritate your life.

Geri swallowed down two more Nurofen Plus as she zipped up her bag before heading out the door, tucking her brown, freshly straightened hair behind her right ear as she did one final check in the mirror. She'd looked better, she'd looked worse.

The deadlock clunked shut as Geri turned the key in the front door. She crossed Highbury Green where the lush grass was in need of a cut and noticed for the first time this year that the sun was yet to set — the clocks had gone forward last week. Spring was her favourite season, the promise of so much. Despite her sarcastic and dour demeanour, Geri was a hopeless romantic who always believed this was going to be her year.

This year, for sure.

She waited an eternity at the traffic lights as always, so texted Laura to make sure she was still on for picking her up. Eventually, the green crossing man illuminated and the crowd of pedestrians walked across the road to the tube, the drivers glaring at them as they went.

Once inside the tube Geri got swept along with rush-hour commuters, so she concentrated on getting the correct train and on what to do once she got to Paddington. After careful thought she decided to make a stop at Marks & Spencer for some food and wine for the journey, perhaps some fancy chocolate too. Or even a cake. She was on holiday after all, so calorie count be damned.

Chapter Three

Nearly two hours later, Vic & Stevie's Fiesta finally pulled up outside The Flowerpot pub, the rendezvous point for picking up the keys to their rented Devon house. The A-roads had been a doddle, it was the B-roads where they'd struggled. Still, they'd made it.

"Looks good," said Stevie. She unclicked her seatbelt and rubbed her eyes — they felt gritty. "Let's just hope the house is as nice as the pictures and they didn't use those wide-angled lenses. Remember that place we stayed in Rome?"

Stevie recalled the tiny apartment that had appeared so enormous on the website, a trick of angles and mirrors. She also recalled the romance of that trip, which seemed a long way from where they were now. Long-haul flight far.

"It'll be fine," Vic said, but Stevie didn't hear as she was already out of the car and stretching madly after nearly seven hours on the road.

Vic slammed the car door shut and it flashed then beeped as Stevie locked it and walked towards the pub, Vic falling in beside her. Vic was a couple of inches shorter than Stevie and her short, brown hair was in need of a cut, her blue shirt creased from hours in the car.

"You remember who we have to ask for?" Vic pushed the heavy, black pub door open.

Stevie rolled her eyes — Vic's memory was shocking.

The Flowerpot turned out to be a solid local pub and fairly large by London standards. In the Big Smoke it'd be called a gastro pub, but in Devon the pubs were just where you ate and didn't need to be dressed up with a fancy name. The wooden bar was directly ahead as they walked in but the pub spread out in all directions, with tables tucked into nooks and corners everywhere they looked.

Vic and Stevie stood at the bar, waiting to be served by a tall brunette with hair beyond her shoulders and a winning smile. She gave her previous customer their change and then turned the same smile on them.

"What can I get you?"

"We're looking for Grace or Tom?" Stevie rested her elbow on the impressively polished brass that ran around the edge of the bar.

"That's easy, that's me," said the barmaid, grinning wider if that was possible. "Well, the Grace bit at least." She paused. "Tom's not back from one of our suppliers yet, was meant to be but got stuck in traffic." Grace gave Stevie a 'whatchagonnado?' shrug. "So I was hanging on for you guys. You must be Stevie?" she continued, her voice rising at the end of her sentence.

Stevie picked her accent as Australian. "That's me," she

said, shaking Grace's offered hand across the bar. "And this is Vic." Stevie indicated her wife, who gave Grace a shy wave.

"Stevie like Stevie Nicks?" Grace enthused.

Stevie smiled like she'd never heard that one before and gave Grace a nod.

"Way cool!" Grace said. "Let me just go and find Pete to man the bar and I'll get the keys. Do you have a car?"

"Outside," Stevie said, flicking her head in its direction.

"Great — gimme two ticks."

Grace dutifully reappeared in a couple of minutes, keys dangling from her well-manicured fingers.

"Okay, ready," she said. It was a statement, not a question.

Vic and Stevie followed her out the pub door which was no mean feat — Grace moved at some speed. It was probably why she stayed so slim — nervous energy. Stevie knew, she suffered with the same issue.

"Now don't worry, I'm not going to come with you and show you round the house — it's all in the welcome pack and it's pretty self-explanatory. Besides, I hate it when owners are too overbearing," Grace said, handing Stevie two sets of keys.

Up close and out from behind the bar, Grace was an imposing presence, standing a few inches taller than Stevie with an attractive figure to match her face. She was dressed simply in jeans and a green top, sunglasses atop her head. Stevie would lay bets the shades were a permanent feature, whatever the weather.

"Front and back doors are marked on the keys," Grace said, pointing at them in Stevie's palm. "I hope two sets is enough? It usually is..."

"Should be fine," Stevie said.

"That's it, really. Have a great time and any problems, call me on my mobile. The number's in the pack or pop into the pub. We run it so one of us should be here."

"Sounds great," Vic said. "We're probably just going to dump our stuff and come back for some food anyway."

"Great!" Grace's positivity was infectious. "Our chef Evan is awesome. He's Aussie too, so I trust him 100%. Just drive straight out of here," Grace continued, directing them with her hands. "First left and then right at the top of the hill and there's the house. It's Tom's family house — we love it, so hope you do too. I'll be round Monday lunchtime so just leave the keys inside. Have fun!"

Grace waved as she rounded the corner of the pub, fishing her phone from her handbag as she did. They heard the beep of a car lock as they unlocked their own and got back in.

"Well she was super-friendly." Stevie put the key in the ignition. "Do you think everyone in Devon is going to be the same?"

"Nah, we're sure to meet the odd psychopath too." Vic clicked her seatbelt into place. "Law of averages, isn't it?"

Chapter Four

"For God's sake, Simon, can you stop acting like a moron for one minute and listen to me?"

Laura looked out the window to her right, as if doing so meant she couldn't hear the conversation her girlfriend was having with her ex. It didn't work. They were still in the same car and Tash's words reverberated off every surface, making her wish she'd got out to go to the loo at these services. It wasn't like she hadn't heard it before.

However, on this particular Thursday she could have done without it. Last night had been their annual awards dinner at work — a back-slapping jamboree where Laura was guaranteed never to win anything. On top of that, her line manager *did* win an award — on an account Laura had put most of the work into, so she'd had to sit and fume quietly.

Her response to such casual acclaim-stealing had been to bitch about her boss to her colleagues and drink as much of the company's free booze as she possibly could. Hence, today Laura wasn't at her best, her eyeballs dry in their sockets and her brain yet to reset itself to normal. So Simon being Simon wasn't helping.

To her right a blue Astra pulled up with harassed-looking parents in the front and wide-eyed kids in the back. The little boy stared at Laura as the car drew level. She stared right back. Just over from that, a dark-haired man in jogging bottoms and trainers walked back to his car with a tray of Burger King meals, replete with extra-large drinks.

"No, I told you Monday — Monday morning..." Tash moved her foot from the dashboard where she'd been resting it. It'd left a mark.

Laura risked a look left and met her girlfriend's gaze.

Tash rolled her eyes back as far as she could manage.

"Simon. It was always Monday. We were never coming back on Sunday and you've known this since we arranged it two months ago. So whatever it is you were planning on doing Sunday night will have to wait. We're having a whole four days on our own with no kids. You're their father, so deal with it." Tash paused.

Laura could hear Simon getting wound up on the other end.

Tash sighed again. "The uniforms are in the bag. They're washed and ironed. All you have to do is drive them to school." Another pause, more aggravation. "I don't know Simon — look it up on the internet. Or maybe talk to them and ask them what they fancy doing. They're real people with real thoughts, you know. Look, we have to get going — tell the kids I'll text goodnight later."

Tash clicked the red button on her phone and threw it into her handbag, which was resting in the passenger footwell. She had good aim. She leant forward and smacked the dashboard with both hands, palms down to reveal a shock of freckles that resembled a Magic Eye puzzle from the 1990s. She let out a scream of frustration.

Laura kept an eye on the steady stream of service-station dwellers and allowed the scene to play out before turning in her seat and giving her partner a sympathetic smile.

"All go okay, then? No problems as usual?" Laura's sides began to shake with laughter. She knew this wasn't the reaction Tash would want right now, but sometimes it was the only one that sprung to mind.

With her head in her hands and fingers poking through her short red hair, Tash glanced sideways and shot Laura a look. "I'm glad this is all so very amusing to you."

"Laugh or cry babe — you can't change it."

"Tell me this, though..." Tash said as she turned in her seat to face Laura, her face flushed fire-engine red, her eyes teary from exertion. "What on earth was my 27-year-old self thinking when I married that idiot? I mean really, what was I thinking?" She threw her hands in the air and twisted to face front.

"Babe, you were young." Laura leant over to kiss Tash's cheek, her long dark hair falling over the gearstick as she did. "If I'd married the girlfriend I'd had at 27, believe me I'd be in trouble too." Laura let out a low whistle. "Loadsa trouble."

"But you wouldn't have to stay in touch with that person forever would you?"

Laura shook her head slowly, knowing this argument well.

Tash let out a long breath. "I love my kids, but I wish they didn't have to involve him."

Laura squeezed Tash's leg lightly. "Well there's nothing you can do about that — he's their dad and I'm sure he'll take care of them this weekend."

Tash grumbled at this.

"But for now, we have a reunion to go to and we need to make a move. Do you need the loo before we head off?"

Tash shook her head and grabbed the bottle of Diet Coke that was resting in her drinks holder. She took a swig and offered it to Laura, who took a swig too.

"Sure? Because I'm not stopping again till we pick up Gimpy..."

"How far is that?"

"About an hour."

Tash shook her head. "I can wait."

"Okay then, let's get this show on the road. And remember, this weekend is a chance for us to have some time — together and with friends. Let's not let Simon spoil that."

Tash exhaled. "I know, I know." She paused. "Just give me ten minutes to get this out of my system and then I promise, no more Simon talk. Deal?"

"Deal. Now why don't you put on some loud music and we'll gun it all the way to Taunton."

"Whatever you say."

Chapter Five

"How you feeling?" Abby looked at Kat, her brow furrowed.

Kat's mouth twitched in response.

They were standing in Abby's kitchen — Kat had just turned up on Thursday afternoon and demanded tea, her tan suitcase standing ready in the hall.

"Okay I think." Kat shrugged as she looked around the kitchen and fixed her stare on the mug tree. "Honestly, I won't know how I'll deal with it till we're there. But I'm sure it'll be fine — I'm a big girl and I can look after myself." Kat put her hand on her hip. "Besides, these are my oldest and bestest friends, so if I can't be honest with them, who can I be honest with?"

Kat smiled her winning smile to back up her words, but Abby didn't look like she bought it. Just like all the other times Kat had tried to convince her.

Abby went to say something, then clearly thought better of it.

Kat was pleased — right now, they needed to hit the road as they were already running behind schedule.

"Are you finished packing?" Kat leant against Abby's granite counter and sipped her cup of tea. She made a face: Abby had forgotten the sugar.

"Sorry." Abby turned to grab it.

"You'd think you'd remember after six months."

Abby smiled. "You'd think you'd be sugar-free after all my nagging."

Kat took the bowl from Abby's outstretched hand. "I am down to one."

"Yeah, yeah. Anyway, I'm nearly finished — just need to bung in a hairdryer."

"I think they have them there." Kat stirred her tea, took a sip and smiled this time.

"Yeah, but it's probably from the 1980s," Abby said over her shoulder as she disappeared into the hallway and then the bedroom. Abby said something else but it got muffled as she was too far away.

Kat picked up her tea and followed her.

Kat had always particularly liked Abby's cool, minimalist bedroom and remembered being impressed with its decor and vibe as much as its owner the first time she'd come back here. She leant on the white glossy doorframe and watched Abby zip up her suitcase, her cool, ultra-styled Afro bouncing as she did.

"What'd you say?" Kat asked.

"Huh?"

"Just then, you shouted something through."

Abby screwed up her face and paused, before shaking

her head. “Dunno, can’t remember.”

She got out her iPhone and checked it, as was her habit. Abby got her work email directed to her phone so she had no escape. Beyond that, she was also a technology junkie who got shifty if she was away from a viable internet connection for more than five minutes. How she was going to cope this weekend in the Devon countryside — not known for its robust phone reception — was anyone’s guess.

Abby walked over to Kat and slid her arms around her waist, rubbing her back as she did. Abby and Kat were around the same height although Abby’s hair could sometimes make her appear almost a foot taller.

“Oooh, I remember now.” Abby leant in for a quick kiss — her lips were dry. “I was asking whether you’d seen where we’re going — did you have a look at the email?”

Kat shook her head. “Nah, didn’t get a chance. But I trust Stevie — she’s a genius at this sort of stuff.”

“The place looks absolutely amazing — the lounge especially looks out onto the sea. Can’t wait to see it in the flesh.”

Kat ran her hand down the side of Abby’s face, amazed as she always was at the contrasting colour of her white skin to Abby’s deep Ghanaian black.

“We’re going to have an amazing Easter weekend and you’ll love all my friends — promise, they’re ace.” She kissed her girlfriend slowly, gently.

Abby deepened the kiss and ran a hand over Kat’s curved buttock — it was her favourite part of her body.

They both pulled back a few minutes later, Abby's eyes full of desire.

"So do you think there's time?" Abby lifted an eyebrow.

Kat smiled, but already knew the answer. Since she'd started on the pills her libido had been flatlining and she was scared at her lack of interest in sex, it having always been a favourite pastime of hers.

The beep of Abby's phone broke the moment and Kat knew she'd been saved. Abby had been extremely patient, but their fledging relationship was being tested. After just six months you were still meant to be jumping each other's bones at every chance you got.

Abby fished her phone out of her back pocket, broke their hold and stepped back. She pressed her screen a few times, frowned, then cursed. Getting these two days off had been a bone of contention between the two of them, what with Abby's work having a new appraisal system installed and her being head of HR. Abby was the queen of telling her staff to take their holiday within their entitlement time, but not so great at taking her own advice.

"Sorry, I gotta respond to this. Can you give me five minutes?" Abby ushered Kat out the door and closed it gently.

Kat waited outside, sipping her tea as she heard Abby get through to her colleague Nick who she could picture sat at his desk in one of his trademark stripy shirts. Kat remembered when she used to be glued to her work Blackberry too, replying to emails at midnight, checking incoming mail from Japan at 4am. Not anymore.

No, Kat wasn't sure how this weekend was going to pan out, but she was going to use it to reconnect with some old friends who she'd been pushing away of late while she tried to sort herself out. Only Abby knew the truth of the last six months; only her old friends knew the truth of her life. Kat was taking a leap of faith merging the two together — would they embrace or repel each other?

Chapter Six

Advertised as a seaside retreat, their home for the weekend had nothing but fantastic reviews online. Vic and Stevie were hoping it lived up to its cracking credentials and first impressions didn't disappoint. Vic whistled through her teeth as they swept down the horseshoe drive and pulled up outside the black garage door.

"How much would this cost in London?" Vic assessed the double-fronted house ahead that possessed both style and grandeur. "Looks absolutely enormous."

"I bet it costs a pretty penny down here, too." Stevie wasted no time getting out of the car and stretching again. After a few seconds, she popped her head back inside. "But just for this weekend, let's pretend it's all ours."

"You're on."

Vic's feet crunched on the gravel as she rounded the car and unlocked the boot, hauling their grey suitcases out of their confinement. She still held the view they'd packed too much for a long weekend but Stevie had told her if it could fit in the car, it was coming with them.

These days, Vic didn't make arguments where they weren't strictly necessary, so she'd said nothing.

"Come on you, let's get this stuff inside." Vic handed a case to her wife.

Stevie tried to wheel it to the front door but the gravel wouldn't allow it, so instead she picked it up with a grunt, her face flushing pink with the effort.

Stevie turned the key in the door and Vic followed her in, scanning the extensive wood-panelled hallway hung with modern artwork. Someone was clearly a Jackson Pollock fan. Light flooded in through massive windows, with added colour waltzing around via stained glass windows overhead. It made a great first impression and Vic's shoulders slumped with relief as she realised they'd picked a winner. With most other odds stacked against her this weekend, it was good to know their accommodation wouldn't be one of them.

Vic dropped her suitcase at the bottom of the grand staircase to her right, before heading across the hallway and through a door to the left. She drew a breath. This house just got better.

"Fuck me — they weren't lying. Babe, you gotta see this!"

Stevie dumped her suitcase and walked to the lounge. She too stopped almost as soon as she entered the room.

"Holy shit!"

They were standing in the living room, the feature room, the one that made them stop on the holiday cottage website and click. It was grand — in scale, in opulence, in views. The whole of the main wall which they were currently staring out of was a mass of polished glass overlooking the garden and the sea. The cliff fell away in front of them to reveal masses of oak-coloured sand and water as far as the eye could see. It was spellbinding.

Stevie broke into a spontaneous round of applause as she surveyed the rest of the room. Modern neutral-toned sofas, fancy coffee table, sumptuous stone-coloured rugs and the biggest flatscreen she'd ever seen on the opposite wall. Massive nature screen one side, enormous TV on the other.

"This is amazing — I mean, look at it!" Stevie swept her hand expansively. She dropped the welcome envelope in her excitement, then bent to retrieve it.

Vic blinked and grinned. "Wait till the others see it, they're going to be blown away. And they so owe us for finding this."

"Too right. Shall we take first pick of the bedrooms as our reward?" Stevie shifted next to Vic who instinctively put her arm around her and kissed her brow, now perked up with colour.

"Let's do it."

They sprang up the stripy carpeted stairs and chose the bigger of the sea-view rooms. It had an en-suite (as did all the double rooms), a king-size bed and a pair of welcoming red felt armchairs that looked plushly expensive.

Stevie bounced on the bed and nodded as she sprang back up without much reluctance.

Vic poked her head in the en-suite, then came back

into the bedroom. "This is incredible. It's like a fucking show home..."

Vic watched Stevie: it'd been a while since she'd jumped up and down on a bed with such glee in her presence. Before all of this, Vic would have jumped on top of her there and then, wrestled her into submission and kissed her long and hard. But these days, lines were blurred and their relationship was misshapen, wonky. Vic continually checked her actions, stopped, reassessed.

Stevie was staring at her and was probably thinking similar thoughts. When did kissing your wife become such a difficult decision?

Vic forced a smile and Stevie returned it, just as sad and ill-formed. If she were going to go with her gut it was too late; the moment had gone and there were too many thoughts clogging the air in the bedroom now. Vic bit her top lip and took off her glasses, running a hand through her hair before replacing them.

"Shall we get going? The Flowerpot awaits." Vic offered Stevie her hand.

Stevie made a slight grunting noise as she got up, something she'd added to her repertoire since turning 40 earlier in the year.

"Yep — I'm famished."

* * *

The Flowerpot was busier when they returned, despite the fact it was little more than an hour later.

A new bartender had appeared in Vic and Stevie's absence and she greeted them with a welcoming smile as they approached the bar. She had a pleasing Devonian accent that curled at the edges, along with short, dark hair and piercing brown eyes.

As they sat down with their wine, burgers ordered, Stevie checked her phone but reception was poor. She was in the country now.

"Just going to check this," she said to Vic, indicating her mobile. Stevie's bones creaked as she walked out of the car park until she eventually got three bars of signal, a couple of texts popping up on-screen.

When she returned, Vic had poured the Cabernet Sauvignon and already taken a large gulp.

Stevie's phone skittered across the shiny wooden table as she put it down and took her own slug of wine. She sighed with contentment as she felt the warming alcohol seep into her system.

"So?" Vic leant back in her chair.

"Well, they've all left at least."

"All of them?"

"Yep — even Gimpy got off work early, so she's on a train."

"I'm impressed," Vic said.

"I'm amazed." Stevie paused. "Kat and Abby reckon they'll make it by 9-ish. Stu's at his mum's and she'll bring him in the morning."

"And the other two?"

Stevie crinkled her forehead. "They left late, obviously..."

"Obviously..."

"...But they've dropped the kids off and they've got to pick up Gimpy — so who knows. Around 10pm?"

"Optimistic," Vic grinned.

"Give or take," Stevie said. "The upshot is, most of the merry band will be here soon — barring calamitous natural disasters."

"And dodgy sat navs."

"I'm going to treat that comment with the contempt it deserves, drink some more wine and hope our food comes soon before I eat this beermat." Stevie smiled at Vic, a knowing smile, a smile to a lover she'd known for half of her life. "By the way — did you get a vibe from the barmaid?"

"A vibe?"

"You know — an 'on our team' vibe." Stevie narrowed her eyes conspiratorially as she said this.

Vic flicked her gaze up to the bar and studied the barmaid for a minute, then shook her head. "Nah, I don't think they allow lesbians this far west, do they?"

"Ha ha," said Stevie. "Bet you a fiver she is."

Vic arched an eyebrow. "You going to ask her?"

"Not tonight, but maybe tomorrow." Stevie yawned. "Anyway, here's to a fab reunion." She held up her glass for Vic to chink.

"Let's hope it's not as eventful as the last one..."

"I'm kinda hoping it might be."

Chapter Seven

"You ate what?" Tash turned in the passenger seat as Laura guided the car back onto the A38.

In the back, Geri folded her leather jacket on the seat beside her.

"Nice jacket by the way — very lady-killer."

"That's the idea." Geri smiled, smoothing out her jeans with both palms. "It was salmon with pea shoots, crème fraîche and mint, pureed till it tasted odd and piped into posh bread. At least they're trying."

"Got to be better than my sandwich, which just tasted of fridge. I know it comes chilled, but I want it to taste of something other than chilled."

"Does chilled have a taste?" Geri asked.

"Yes, motorway services sandwiches." Tash turned back to face front.

"I told her to make her own before we left, because this happens every time." Laura flicked her eyes up to the mirror as she gave Geri a grin.

"We should so open a sandwich shop in motorway services that actually sells tasty stuff. We'd make a mint."

It was a comment Tash made on practically every journey. "Besides, I wasn't making sandwiches today. We're on holiday and we're childless."

Geri leant forward and put one hand on the shoulder of the driver's seat, the other on the shoulder of the passenger's seat.

"Well, I only had one person to buy for and it was shit — they always are. The wine, however — that was tasty. As was the Double Decker I got to go with it." Geri grinned, showing a wonky front tooth.

"You've had wine!" Tash pouted. "I want wine."

Laura patted her leg then checked her lights were on low as she turned left onto a smaller country road.

"We'll get you some — not long now," Laura said.

Tash squeezed her leg back.

"So what's going on with you two anyway? How are the kiddies?" Geri was still hanging in the space between the two.

"Shouldn't we be asking you that question?" Laura smirked at Geri via her mirror.

"Yes, very droll." Geri's look could best be described as withering.

"They're good — with Simon this weekend," Tash said. "And nothing's going on with us, we live in Essex, remember?" She turned her head to Gimpy, who made a face and slumped into the back seat.

"Don't think London's one long party." Geri said. "It's just more expensive."

"You not still seeing that girl?" Laura asked.

"Which one?"

"Which one?" Tash laughed.

"Well I was kinda seeing a blonde at one point, but that didn't work out. Then there was the Aussie too."

"The Aussie — Kelly?" Laura said.

"Yep, Kelly," Geri nodded. "Nope, it kinda fizzled out after a few dates. She was a bit young...."

"I rest my case," Laura said.

"How old?" Tash asked.

Geri licked her lips. "Twenty-seven."

"Oh my God, 27! I remember 27. I got engaged at 27." Tash shuddered before twisting to face Geri. "What do 27 year olds talk about?"

Geri rubbed her eyes. "I wasn't worried about the talking." A yawn. "But she did keep talking about music I'd never heard of. I mean, I'm not even out of touch. Plus, being Aussie, there was a big cultural gap. She'd never seen half the shows I talked about and she just kept wanting to go out. It got wearing."

"27 year olds will do that," Tash said.

"Yeah well, I kept up for a bit, then..." Geri puffed out her cheeks, grinning. "Still, who knows what awaits in Devon? Maybe I'll meet a hot surfer chick and move here. I've always quite fancied living in the country."

"I'm sure they have criminals here too," Tash said. "You could be like the village bobby. Or the village Gimp." She laughed heartily at her joke, as Laura joined in too.

Geri ran her fingers through her hair and rolled her eyes silently in the back.

"Ha ha, you two. You know, we're going to have words about my nickname this weekend."

Tash turned again, wide-eyed. "You want it changed to something like Gimpy The Great?"

"Or just plain Geri would be fine."

"You'd miss it when it was gone." Laura pulled up at a junction. The red arrow of the sat nav was telling her to go right but the sign ahead of her said Exmouth was left. "Should we be going right?" she asked Tash, who sat up and peered at the sign ahead.

"The sign says left."

"I know, but the sat nav says right," Laura said.

Geri leant forward again. "I'd go with the sign," she said, looking at Laura, then Tash. "And if I'm right, you have to back me up when I talk to everyone this weekend about calling me Geri from now on and not Gimpy. Deal?"

Tash turned to Geri as Laura clicked the left-hand indicator and pulled out.

"What if you're wrong, though — do we get to call you Gimpy The Great for ever more?"

Geri shook her head and sat back. "Sometimes it worries me that you're in charge of the upbringing of two impressionable children, you know."

Tash smiled in the front seat and glanced at the sat nav, which had recalibrated itself. Tash didn't have a lot of time for sat navs.

"Have you been in touch with Kat, by the way?" Laura glanced at Geri in her rear-view mirror.

Geri shook her head. "Nah, she's been a bit off the radar of late — you know Kat and her work schedule." She paused. "It'll be good to catch up with her this weekend."

Tash couldn't help rolling her eyes. "Will it?"

Laura glanced sideways and shot her a warning glance.

"What?" Tash said, her tone rising with every millisecond. "I'm just saying what everyone else is thinking. Kat's party trick of drinking as much as she can and falling over wore thin on me the third time I saw it. I just wonder when everyone else will get bored with it, too."

"Babe..." Laura said.

Tash held up her hands in defence. "And yes, I know I know, she's your old friend and we shouldn't think these things, but really, she's nearly 40 now, not 20. She needs to grow the fuck up."

Geri chuckled and moved to hanging between Tash and Laura again, a smile etched on her face. "No, tell us what you really think, Tash..."

Chapter Eight

By the time Kat and Abby got to the pub it was gone nine o'clock and Stevie and Vic were drinking the local cider which was called Rattler, rust red in colour.

The pair hugged Vic and Stevie, the new arrivals turning heads in the pub. Kat was wearing a white shirt that was only on its first or second outing, judging by its stiffness. Abby was dressed in her standard retro gear, flowery dress circling around her slim calves.

"Look at you!" Stevie held Kat at arm's length and swept her eyes up and down her body. "Damn, girl, you've lost some weight! When did that happen?"

Kat smiled as her cheeks reddened. "You know, just trying to eat right and exercise as I approach old age."

"Old age my arse — you look amazing."

As Vic and Stevie introduced themselves to Abby, the dark-haired barmaid with the twinkly eyes rounded the bar brandishing menus. She wore jeans and a matching shirt but, despite the double denim, still managed to exude allure.

"Hi — just to let you know if you want food, you'll have to be quick as the kitchen closes soon."

She looked down at Abby expectantly then flicked her eyes to Kat.

Abby smiled up at her and shook her head. "Thanks, but we already ate."

The barmaid nodded and started collecting up the rest of the menus from the tables around the pub.

Abby followed her rear until Kat slapped her leg and gave her a look. Abby grinned at being caught out.

"I could have had some chips," Kat moaned, staring after the barmaid.

"I'm just looking after your health," Abby replied.

"As well as checking out her butt."

"She passed my buoyancy test."

"You have a buoyancy test?" Stevie said. She leant forward, interest piqued.

"She's arse-obsessed," Kat stated.

"Correction — arse-inquisitive. Only obsessed with yours." Abby leaned over and rubbed Kat's knee.

"Sure," Kat smiled. "Plus, I'd like to point out the double-denim horror — no excuse for that."

"Very 80s, though, and 80s is all back in now," Stevie said.

"Back in again?" Kat made a face, before pushing herself upwards. She turned to the bar then twisted back to the group. "I'm going to get a drink — spritzer?" she asked Abby.

"The Rattler's good — want to taste?" Vic offered her pint but Abby had already screwed up her face in disgust.

"My cider-drinking days are long gone."

"When in Rome," Vic shrugged. She took a sip.

Abby turned her attention back to Kat. "Yes please — but make sure it's soda not lemonade..."

"...I know," Kat said. She turned to walk to the bar.

Stevie sat back and smiled warmly at Abby. "So you found it okay?"

"No problems at all. Is the house far?"

"Nope — five minutes away. You want to go dump the car and walk back?"

Abby considered this, then nodded. "Yeah — you mind?"

Stevie shook her head while she stood up. "No problem." She turned to Vic. "Don't drink my cider, okay?"

Vic smiled. "Only if I run out of mine."

The pair disappeared and Kat came back with drinks, looking puzzled. "What happened?"

"They've gone to dump the car," Vic said.

"Right."

"So things going well with you and Abby?" Vic asked as Kat put the drinks on the table. "Not drinking?" She nodded towards Kat's coke.

Kat shook her head. "Not tonight," she said, glossing over the fact. "And yeah, things are going well with Abby. She's exactly what I need right now."

"Right now?" Vic raised an eyebrow.

Kat shrugged. "Live in the moment." She took a sip of her coke. "What about you guys?"

Vic tried to be nonchalant, but failed. "You know, getting there. Slowly. We have good days and bad days, but

I fucked up so I have to put up with it. She's not divorcing me, so that's good."

Kat let out a strangled laugh. "Look on the bright side. But man, you really did fuck up."

"Yeah, thanks for the reminder."

Vic gave Kat a hard stare and Kat dropped it. Vic knew the topic would come up this weekend but she clearly wanted to get through the first evening at least without having to bare her soul. Kat smiled — getting deep and meaningful wasn't a pastime Vic rated highly.

"So why only good for now?" Vic asked.

"Huh?"

"Abby — she seems lovely..."

Kat considered the question for a minute. "A mix of things," she said. "I'm just... in a funny place right now. I'm working things out, making some changes. I don't know yet whether Abby's part of those long-term or not — but of course, she has a say in that too." Kat smiled and spread her hands out, palms up. "But right now..."

Vic nodded, before indicating Kat's drink. "I take it that's part of your changes?"

Kat nodded slowly, her cheeks flushing redder despite herself. There was plenty of time this weekend to reveal the rest, no point in doing it on the first night to an audience of one.

"Well this is a side of you I've never seen before..." Vic said. "What about work — that going well?"

"Great," Kat said, before looking away.

FRIDAY

Chapter Nine

The front door slamming woke Stevie from her slumber and she blinked a few times while looking around the room before she remembered where she was. Stylish bedroom. Warm sheets. In Devon. For their 20th university reunion. Twenty years. It didn't feel that long since they'd left university and yet it also seemed like it had happened to a whole different group of people from another planet. Did she really used to queue at the bar for 50p pints of cider in flimsy plastic cups? She felt beyond old and pondered briefly what it felt like to be dead. Probably not much older than this.

Stevie rubbed her eyes and exhaled, knowing she could chalk up last night as another night of interrupted sleep. It was a well-trodden path ever since the incident and was now such a part of who she was, she didn't even question it. Stevie Wright, 40, teacher, insomniac.

Sometimes though, she didn't think she even qualified for the title of insomniac. Stevie's sleeping had become a tasting menu of sleep — small portions, brought to her as and when the sleep chef desired. She knew from stark experience the sleep chef was of the Lean Cuisine variety. Even her dreams had been selected from the value range lately, distinctly lacking in flavour.

She rolled over and looked at Vic's sleeping form — she felt comforted and disappointed, again a familiar pattern. After a few seconds' tussle, she leant over and kissed Vic's shoulder. It felt 63% normal this morning.

"You awake?" Stevie whispered. Vic smelled sweet and musky. Despite everything, her smell was still one of Stevie's favourites — especially freshly baked Vic.

"Hmmmm," Vic replied.

Stevie's smile was audible. "People are getting up — either that or Stu's just arrived."

"What time is it?"

"Just after ten."

Vic turned her body to face Stevie, keeping a safe distance as had been non-verbally agreed. "Stu won't be here yet — too early."

"Well someone's up," Stevie said. She pulled the duvet up further.

"My head hurts." Vic's short brown hair was matted with sleep, the left side of her face creased with pillow marks.

"Could that be because you insisted on having another pint of Rattler last night when we all kept telling you to pace yourself?"

Vic harrumphed.

Stevie continued. "You know how it is with these things — don't get too excited on the first night, there's still three nights to go."

"I blame Gimpy."

"She put a gun to your head?"

"No, but I think she was trying to chat up the barmaid or something, so she kept wanting to go up to the bar," Vic mumbled into her pillow.

"And were you trying to impress her too by showing off your drinking prowess?"

Vic closed her eyes and frowned.

"I'm going to see who's up." Stevie swung herself left and out of bed, leaving Vic pouting as she wrapped the duvet around herself, forming a cocoon. Stevie found her slippers in the case and put on a maroon sweatshirt over her grey vest top — it had the letter 'H' stitched in large grey type covering her left breast. Her blond hair was sticking up at angles hipsters might pay hairdressers large sums of money to achieve.

"See you in a bit," she said.

Vic peeked out of the duvet and watched her wife go, feeling the familiar distance settle on her like morning dew.

* * *

"I wondered who it was," Stevie said. She smiled as she walked over to the feature window where Geri was sitting on the wooden window seat staring out to sea, a mug of tea in hand.

Geri jumped when she heard Stevie's voice. Hot tea spilt onto her purple pyjamas.

"Fuck." Geri got up, holding her mug away from her body, standing on tiptoes in the manner of a tightrope walker.

"Sorry!" Stevie tried to mop Geri's pyjamas with her hand for a few seconds, but then gave it up as a bad job, giving her a hug instead.

"S'alright, they were dirty anyway," Geri grinned. "Great view though. I was miles away."

"At sea with the pirates?"

"Sexy lady pirates."

"Are there any other kind?"

Stevie settled beside Geri and felt her warmth through the close proximity of their bodies.

Geri's lips were still glistening with tea, her hair still wavy in its pre-straightened form.

"How come you're up?" Geri asked. "I can't sleep in these days, but I thought all the couples would be busy having noisy sex. I decided not to listen in and come downstairs instead."

Stevie smiled sadly at her assumption. "You have high expectations of married life, my friend. Besides, my darling wife has a Rattler-sized hangover, so she's busy feeling sorry for herself upstairs. I think sex might make her head explode."

Geri laughed heartily and Stevie stared out the window with her old friend and old flame, hearing the huge laugh that first drew her to Geri in the university bar over 20 years ago.

The contours of Geri's body, what it felt like to kiss her and to make love to her, Stevie couldn't remember, for which she was thankful. Old lovers fade after a while, their touch, their taste — but some things remained — Geri's laugh, Geri's humour, Geri's killer green eyes. Stevie could well understand why women still wanted to sleep with Geri now. She was trim and gorgeous with a sexy police badge to boot.

Stevie also remembered that Geri cheated on her and that was why they split up. However, it was so long ago now, it was like it had happened in a book she had once read. Stevie remembered the face and the hurt of the young lover and she could empathise, but the flavour of hurt now seemed vanilla, eminently palatable, available to order online for calm, reassured heartbreak. Stevie knew they'd been young and she didn't hold grudges.

She'd seen seismic changes in herself over the intervening two decades and she'd witnessed similar changes in Geri. But what Stevie knew now that she clearly didn't know then was that Geri had difficulties with relationships. Sure, Geri had embarked on a few lengthy liaisons, but never anything over two years — as soon as she got to that stage she seemed to press the eject button, not knowing how to get over the ridge.

But that was then, and Geri's infidelity seemed like child's play compared to now. In her low moments Stevie wondered if she was just the kind of woman who got cheated on and that was her lot in life. But she knew in her heart that wasn't true. Stevie was way too much of a romantic to believe that.

She wasn't one to keep in touch with her exes, but being bound up in her close university group, Geri was one she never wanted to shake: Geri was like family. She was proud of the way they'd navigated their way out of their sexual relationship and back to friendship — where they'd first met and where they should have always stayed.

Now it felt to Stevie like it was where they'd always been and she was more than comfortable with that. After everything that'd happened in the last six months, it was good to feel the connection of old friends with such rich, shared history.

"I need coffee — come with me to the kitchen?"

Geri nodded and padded behind Stevie in socked feet through the hallway and into the kitchen, which was classic white with hints of red, an island and breakfast bar at one end.

"I could seriously get used to a kitchen like this — it's bigger than my flat." Geri took a seat at the breakfast bar on the left while Stevie filled the kettle.

"No need for that you know," Geri told her, nodding to the kitchen counter.

Stevie followed her gaze to the Nespresso machine and bowl of coffee pods sitting beside it, reassuring in their metallic colourings.

"Too much for my brain this morning." Stevie grabbed a mug and flicked on the kettle.

"It's what all the movers and shakers have these days. Cafetières are so last century." Geri scratched her head. "Who'd have thought Devon was so hip?"

"Who indeed." Stevie yawned and stretched her hands up over her head — her muscles wheezed as she arched backwards. "You sleep okay?"

"Yeah — that Rattler knocked me out. That and the gin when we got back."

"That'll do it — especially the measures Tash was pouring." Stevie paused. "Wish I could get the hang of sleeping again."

They stared at each other silently for a few seconds before Stevie began again.

"You think Kat's alright? She shot off to bed when we got back from the pub and she looked a bit on edge there, too."

Geri shrugged. "Probably just tired — it was a long drive."

"Not like Kat, though — she's party-girl central normally. Did you notice she wasn't drinking, either?"

"Maybe Abby's tamed her," Geri said. "And after last time, it wouldn't be the worst thing in the world."

"Maybe." Stevie paused, reassessed, changed the subject. Something wasn't right with Kat but she'd get it out of her over the next three days. "So how's the world of crime-fighting going? Is London a safer place to walk because of you?"

Geri snorted. "Crime never goes out of fashion, so it's all good." She paused. "And our drug squad just did a big drugs bust in East London, so if you want to get some cocaine for your Saturday night out, you might be out of luck."

"Ha!" Stevie said. "Did you sneak some for yourself?"

Geri smiled. "Not my department or the done thing."

"Shame — we could have truly relived our university days." As the kettle boiled, Stevie grabbed the cafetière from the shelf and leant her hip against the counter. "God, I haven't done drugs for ages. Have you?"

"Negative." Geri shook her head. "Could that be something to do with the fact we're not 21 anymore and have responsible jobs?"

"It makes no sense though, does it? I mean, we've got the cash to buy them now, haven't we?" Stevie looked puzzled.

"That's true. But if push came to shove, you'd probably spend it on new homeware than weed or speed, wouldn't you? Some lovely new pasta bowls or a bone-china mug would give you far more pleasure." Geri grinned at her summation.

"How did you know we need new pasta bowls?" Stevie added coffee to the pot and filled it to the top.

"I'll have one of those please." Laura yawned as she walked across to hug the two women good morning. She was dressed in red pyjamas and her long dark hair was flyaway this morning.

"Another couple not having sex — what's going on?" Geri said.

Stevie flinched but Laura laughed.

"We had a drunken shag last night if you're keeping tabs. Besides, Tash is not a morning person. Believe me, I've tried," she said. "What were you two gassing about, anyhow?"

"Drugs and where to get them," Geri said.

"Isn't that bad in your line of work?" Laura yawned again.

"It's not me," Geri replied. "Stevie's decided she truly wants to relive our youth."

Laura didn't look convinced. "Really? I haven't even had a cup of coffee yet."

Laura sat at the large white table in the dining room, just off the kitchen. She watched as Stevie plunged the cafetière then filled the mugs, bringing her one.

"Your head alright this morning?" Stevie asked.

"Yep," Laura said. "I paced a bit. We eating in tonight?"

"That's the plan," Stevie said. "Vic can work her magic later, then we can go to the pub tomorrow."

"FlowerPot?"

"Yep."

"Perfect — then Gimps can try to charm the barmaid and settle our bet." Laura grinned.

Geri looked put out. "I'm not just here for your amusement, you know."

"Yes you are — you're youngish, free and single, you are completely here for our entertainment," Laura said. "None of us are going to pull anyone else, are we? We're all married!"

As soon as the words were out of her mouth Laura

looked at Stevie and pulled a face. The sentence vibrated in the air as if the music had stalled.

"Sorry, Stevie, I didn't mean... shit," Laura began.

Stevie waved her right hand through the air, batting the statement away. "It's fine. We're getting over it, so don't worry." She almost meant it, too. "Besides, I don't want everyone walking around on eggshells this weekend because of it."

"I know, but still..." Laura's face had flushed burlesque red.

"How are things, though? I didn't like to ask with Vic there too last night," Geri said.

"We're getting there, slowly," Stevie said with a not-quite-as-indifferent-as-she'd-hoped shrug.

"She seems genuinely sorry — I mean, she was so upset when it happened," Laura said.

Laura and Vic had always been close and, truth be told, Laura knew about the fling before Stevie. However, these were facts that shouldn't be disclosed right now — or, in fact, ever.

"Not as upset as me," Stevie said. *Defensive.*

"You know what I mean." Laura risked a glance at Stevie before bouncing her focus around the room.

Stevie shook her head and pursed her lips. "I don't want to talk about this really — I'm bored with it, I've talked about nothing else for six months. This is a weekend off to have some time together. Like the old days when we didn't have adult problems. Remember them?"

Stevie smiled wistfully but Geri laughed as she swung round on her stool.

"Nah, that's just your memory clouding things," Geri said. "We had bigger problems back then. Like how to carry ten pints of cider and black back from the bar when the tray will only fit six?"

Stevie threw her head back, a laugh catching in her throat. "Those were the days. And I know the answer to that problem — drink the other four at the bar." Stevie laughed some more at her own joke.

"Don't know about you but I'm starving — shall we make a start on breakfast?" Laura got up and headed for the fridge. "If I put the bacon on, I bet the others will come down. It works with Taylor and Alex at any rate." Laura located the bacon and put it on the countertop, closely followed by the eggs.

"How are the kids?" Stevie asked. She'd already decided to forgive Laura, which she thought was rather magnanimous of her.

Laura turned, considering the question. "You know... kids."

Stevie nodded. Being a teacher, she'd dealt with enough parents to know how you were meant to react — conspiratorially.

Laura grinned, telling her she'd passed the test. "Nah, they're good. With their father for a whole four days. I'm not sure who's more scared of the possible outcomes — them or us. Still, he does have his parents just down the road, which I think is what finally persuaded Tash to leave them that long."

"Is he really that bad?" Stevie asked, as Laura sliced open the packet of bacon with a small black-handled knife and began arranging them in a bacon jigsaw on the grill. Stevie heard Laura snort.

"He's okay, just a bit clueless at times. Tash did most things before she left, but now she's gone he's still trying to figure out how to cope and be a dad. Even after all this time. But he's never been anything but nice to me, to be fair to him." Laura reached to turn on the grill, still with her back to Geri and Stevie. "I can't help it if his wife threw herself at me, can I?"

Geri laughed. "She's only human after all. I mean, remember Steph at uni — and Kat last time?"

Laura spun at such dramatic speed that both Geri and Stevie snapped to attention. Laura clicked together the kitchen tongs in her fingers and stood frozen to the spot, shaking her head rapidly. The tongs snapped together in the resulting silence.

"*She doesn't know.*" Laura was using such an exaggerated whisper it was almost a hushed shout.

"Who doesn't know?" Stevie asked in the same tone of voice, as if she were a Hollywood diva saving her voice for the concert of her life.

"Tash — she doesn't know about Kat. You know, *last time.*" Laura had the decency to look embarrassed at least.

"And you don't want her to know, I take it?" Grim amusement coated Geri's words.

Laura rolled her eyes. "I'm not whispering for no reason," she hissed, nearly loud enough for the whole house to hear. "She's just... funny about Kat, that's all."

Stevie walked to the counter, removed the tongs from her hands and put an arm around her. "Sweetheart, Kat was five years before you two got together, so why would it be a big deal?" The question was rhetorical. "But we won't utter a word, will we Gimps?"

Geri scowled. "It's already forgotten. Unlike the casual use of my nickname."

* * *

Half an hour later the whole crew were sitting down tucking into bacon, eggs, beans and tomatoes. Hot toast made steamy patterns on a plate in the centre of the table and a pot of tea was waiting to be poured.

Vic smiled shyly at Stevie as their hands clashed going for the scrambled eggs.

Tash's hair was still bedhead, ginger and wiry.

Geri was ploughing through her plate of food at rapid pace.

Kat and Abby were the only two already showered and dressed. Stevie noted that Abby's hair was already perfect at 11am and didn't know whether to be impressed or appalled — nobody's hair should be that perfect at this time of the morning on holiday.

"So are we going to do some coastal path today?" Tash asked between mouthfuls of breakfast. Being a mother, she tended to do the organising in the group along with teacher Stevie — taking charge was second nature to both of them. The group nodded as one.

"I was having a look at the map yesterday and I reckon there's a good eight-mile loop we can do, take in a beach, have lunch then come back for dinner."

"Sounds good," said Geri. "Stu's not coming till this evening now as Darren's running late — he texted me earlier to say go ahead with plans and he'd meet us later."

"Shame, I want to give our boy a hug," Laura said.

"Not Darren?" Geri asked, smirking.

"Let's hope his train's delayed, shall we?" Laura replied.

Chapter Ten

Tash was on the phone when Laura got out of the shower. From her smile and relaxed tone, Laura guessed she was talking to her younger daughter, Taylor.

Laura's calves and buttocks ached from the walk today and she knew she'd be sore tomorrow. She didn't mind, though — aching from physical exertion was a pleasure she enjoyed, climbing out of her mind and into her body.

Laura had surprised everyone in the group when she'd got together with Tash, a single mother with two young girls in tow. But as she always said, she hadn't planned it: the children simply came as part of the package, an unexpected bonus prize.

It was five years ago when Laura had decided to move out of her house-share in Benfleet, Essex, and so she'd arranged to view a prospective flat to buy. When the ginger-haired estate agent got out of her red Golf wearing heels and a certain swagger, Laura knew instantly the day wouldn't be a total write-off.

The flat itself had been a disaster, smelling of damp and looking like a place where you'd come to die a grizzly death. However, Laura had still nodded and made encouraging noises, her interest piqued. She had picked up a certain vibe from this estate agent and had admired the way she stood with her hands jammed into the side pockets of her mint green trousers.

Laura had looked at a few more flats she wasn't really interested in just to get into Tash's red Golf again before she'd plucked up the courage to ask her out for a drink. Tash's eyes had widened but she'd accepted. That was then.

Now, Laura walked over to Tash, who stroked her leg as she dropped her towel. Laura walked naked around the room trying to locate the body lotion — she mimed squirting the bottle to Tash, who pointed her back to the bathroom. Laura heard Tash say her goodbyes into her mobile phone, then within seconds she was standing in the bathroom doorway watching her moisturise.

Tash leant in and gave Laura a kiss full on the lips, then simply leant.

"All good?" Laura said.

Tash nodded. "Yep, they sound happy. Simon's taking them to his parents today and they're sleeping over. I wonder if that means he's got a new woman on the go or whether he's just being lazy." Tash looked thoughtful.

"Well, they love going there so I'm sure they're happy whatever. Did he remember Taylor's medicine?" Laura put her leg up onto the closed toilet seat and rubbed cream into her left calf with some vigour.

"Yep, he seems to be doing okay in daddy duties so far. Maybe he's growing up at last."

"Let's not go too far," Laura said.

Tash smiled. "Maybe we should get an en-suite built in our house — then the kids won't steal our expensive creams and I could stand in the doorway watching you naked all the time."

"You'd soon get bored."

"I doubt it," Tash said, winking.

Chapter Eleven

Laura eventually made it down to the lounge, hair still bouncy from hairdryer heat.

"Check out that view." Laura walked right up to the window to breathe it in. It truly was a spectacular panorama, the sea a sparkling carpet of diamonds stretching as far as the eye could see.

"Trumps my arrival, clearly," Stu said. He got up with a creak before walking over to the window. "And check out your hair — it's like you've just stepped out of a salon."

Laura turned to smile up at him warmly. "Or maybe I was born with it." Laura let herself be embraced by her old friend who, at over 6ft, easily towered over all the women.

When Stu let go, he pushed Laura out to arm's length and took her in. "You were born with something," he said. "But I gotta say, you're looking glowing Ms Turner. Motherhood clearly suits you."

"Or a weekend away from motherhood." Laura hugged him back.

"Pish and pash, I've met those children — they're

adorable." Stu took her hand and led her towards the group — Geri on one sofa, Kat and Abby on the other.

"No Darren?" Laura said.

"Not yet." Stu waved his phone in the air as if it was a physical representation of his boyfriend. "He got held up at work. Gives me a chance to catch up with my girls anyway, so I don't mind."

Stu pulled down his green T-shirt as he sat and Laura caught a glimpse of his hairy stomach and back. She remembered going on holiday with Stu back in their uni days and how odd it was to be rubbing sun cream onto someone so hairy.

"Where's your better half?" Stu asked as Laura sat next to Gimpy, the sofa wheezing slightly as she did so.

"She won't be long. Did I hear Vic in the kitchen already?"

Kat nodded from across the room, licking her lips. "Yep — concocting dinner for us all, the saint."

"She's a keeper, that one," Laura said.

Everyone felt the weight of the comment as it toppled out of Laura's mouth and spun on the floor, taking an age to finally stop. Laura wondered when she'd stop saying the wrong thing when it came to Vic and Stevie this weekend. She squeezed the bridge of her nose with her thumb and index finger and grimaced slightly.

"Let's hope Stevie thinks so, too," Stu said, confirming what was on everyone else's mind.

"What should I be thinking?" The whole group jumped as Stevie entered the room.

Stu sprang up and hugged her warmly. "We were just saying how fab a cook your wife is and is it beer o'clock yet?"

Geri smiled up at Stu's quick thinking, while Stevie glanced down at her watch.

"It's 7pm so I'd say it's definitely beer o'clock. And since when am I the beer-keeper?"

"Since now," Stu said. "Hands up for beer," he said, holding both his hands high in the air — he nearly touched the ceiling.

Geri put up her hand as did Stevie and Laura. First to react were Kat and Abby who jumped up from the sofa.

"We'll get them." The pair brushed past Stu at some speed.

* * *

In the kitchen, Abby and Kat stood over the steaming pan of lamb tagine. Kat removed the lid, sucked in the resultant steam and made suitably enthusiastic noises as Vic shooed them away.

Kat already knew Vic was not a fan of kitchen crawlers while she was in the middle of creating and this invasion fell squarely into that category — but it was still an act they played out every time.

"Put the lid back on so it can cook — go on, skit!" Vic replaced the lid on the pot. She had a can of chickpeas in one hand, a tin opener in the other.

"Smells fab — I'm getting hungry now." Abby grinned at her.

"Well, that's for dinner — I'm just putting some canapés together for starters, too. So bugger off while I do." She clapped her hands in front of her stomach.

"All hail Delia," Kat said, bowing.

"You haven't tasted it yet." There wasn't an ounce of conviction in Vic's statement. She put the tin and opener down on the side.

"Don't be modest, sweetheart, it doesn't suit you," Kat replied, giving her old friend a hug.

Vic accepted without a murmur.

"We're getting beers — you want one?" Abby poked her head around the fridge door.

"Please."

Abby scowled into her phone before pocketing it, then unloaded the bottles of Peroni onto the counter-top.

"Still being good?" Vic asked, eyeing six bottles.

"For now," Kat smiled. "Going to make us some tea, would you believe." She walked around Vic and filled the kettle.

"Good for you," Vic replied.

Abby gave Kat a kiss on the cheek as she left the kitchen, beers in hand.

Vic stirred the tagine, opened the tin of chickpeas and drained them before adding them to the pan. Then she went back to making her tapas starters — garlic prawns, croquettes, ham, olives, chorizo, cheese.

"I'm not sure when you turned into a gourmet chef, but it wasn't until after uni, was it?" Kat furrowed her brow. "You couldn't even boil an egg when I first met you."

"All true." Vic grinned.

Kat remembered showing Vic how to make scrambled eggs and the amazed look on her face when she realised it was simply a case of whisking, adding to a pan and then moving it about a bit. It was amazing the difference 20 years could make.

As Kat made the tea, she took in Vic's strong arms and hands as she worked.

Vic felt the stare and looked up, shifting her glasses back up her face with the back of her hand. "Great day today — beautiful walk."

Kat nodded. "It was amazing. Makes you wonder why we live in London, doesn't it?"

"Totally. But then, that's what makes it special, I suppose. When we come here it's something different. Maybe we'd say that about London if we visited from here."

"I guess."

Vic looked up again. "I'm still impressed with your restraint," she said, indicating the two mugs of tea Kat had just picked up.

Kat shrugged. "Maybe I'm finally growing up."

"I hope not too much because, take it from me, it's a trap and it sucks."

Kat grinned and gave Vic a peck on the cheek as she walked past. She stopped in the doorway and looked back.

"You want some help with any of this?"

Vic thought for a moment, then shook her head. "Nah — you can wash up."

* * *

Vic stood at the lounge doorway and clapped her hands to attract the group's attention. "Right, you lot — you want to come through? Dinner is nearly served."

There were cheers as they got up and wandered through to the dining room clutching remaining canapés and drinks.

Laura and Tash had set the table and it looked inviting, with candles burning in the middle and eight settings ready to be filled, silver place mats complimenting the shiny cutlery.

"Who wants to be mum and dad?" Stu asked.

"Well I think you should definitely be dad for obvious reasons and Gimps can be mum," Stevie said. "Vic and I will sit this side so we can get to the kitchen easier."

"Oh no, I'm not being dad, I'm not nearly old enough, I'm only 37!" Stu pouted his best pout. "Besides, Vic's way more butch than me. I'll sit next to Gimps at this end and do as I'm told."

Vic brought over the tagine in an orange Le Creuset dish while Stevie grabbed the couscous then returned for the flatbreads. When the wine was poured, Stevie tapped her wine glass with her fork and everybody turned towards her.

"Attention please," she said in her best teacher voice, her soft Scouse roots evident. "Before we start our first meal, a toast. To 20 years since we all met at Bristol — the original seven anyway. A big shout-out to Michelle in New York — she said hi, by the way. Here's to lasting friendships and laughter always."

The group cheered and drank their wine, Kat sipping her first glass of the night.

"And thanks to Vic for doing the honours as usual," Tash said.

More cheers, then it was down to the food.

After a few mouthfuls, Geri piped up. "Actually everyone, I have something I'd like to say."

The group stopped mid-forkful and all heads turned to Geri who tucked her hair behind her ear and pinned her features into a taut smile.

"You're not pregnant are you, Gimps?" Laura said.

"Yes, with triplets." Geri gave Laura a deadpan stare. "No I'm not pregnant but I am turning 40 next year..."

"...Don't remind me," Laura said.

Another Geri stare.

Laura shut up.

"I'm also a police sergeant and both of those facts mean there are some things that are no longer quite as amusing as they were when we were 20. Like, say, for instance..." Geri clicked her fingers in the air and looked skywards. "Oh I don't know, my nickname perhaps?" Geri paused to assess the reaction.

Stevie frowned. "Huh?"

"My nickname. Gimpy — you remember, what you've called me for the past 20 years."

"Nineteen," Stevie corrected her. "We didn't start till the second year."

Another stare.

"Now I know it's because my initials are GMP..." Geri continued.

"Geraldine Marie Paterson — the original Gimp!" Kat crowed, as if the intervening 20 years had never happened.

"...But now that I'm nearly 40, getting 'Gimp' shouted at you in a bar isn't quite so cute. Imagine what it's going to be like when I'm 50. Or 70." Geri's face got more appalled as she upped the age. "What I'm saying is, can we please try to call me Geri a bit more. I know old habits die hard but I think it's more age-appropriate, don't you?"

She waited for the group's reaction.

Stu was first. He burst out laughing. "Age-appropriate? Have you been reading the Daily Mail online again?"

Now the whole table was laughing.

"Thanks guys, really supportive." Geri blew out her cheeks, trying to stifle a grin at the same time. "I'm serious — can you make an effort to call me Geri from now on, please?"

Laura looked puzzled. "Is this because you don't want us calling you Gimpy in front of that barmaid tomorrow?"

Geri's patience ebbed away. "No, this is because you

try being called Gimpy all your life and see how you like it."

Vic held up her hands and intervened. "Gimp..." She clamped her hand over her mouth. "I mean Geri. I think we will all absolutely try to call you Geri if that's what you really want. But I can't promise it won't slip out in moments of weakness. Or extreme drunkenness. Will that do?"

Geri smiled at Vic while the table murmured agreement.

"It's the most I can expect, I know," Geri said. "But just try. *For me.*"

Kat raised her wine glass. "A toast. To Gimpy. Rest in peace, old friend. I'll miss you."

Everyone looked suitably solemn.

Geri shot Kat a look. "Yes, thank you Ms Drama Queen. I'm not dead yet."

Geri loved having a nickname — it was a term of endearment after all — but she just wished it was something cool or fun, not the name of a masked sex slave.

The group settled back into conversation and Geri went back to her dinner, watching Laura to her right, who was concentrating hard on her food; she favoured the bolting method, which involved not so much eating the food but more inhaling it. Geri watched Laura pour the tagine into her mouth, her teeth patting it on the way as though cheering on a marathon runner. If eating were a sport, Laura could be a world-beater. To her left, Stu wasn't far behind.

"Have you tasted any of that or are you just inhaling it?" Geri smirked.

Laura looked up from her food trance, lips still glistening with tagine jus. "I'm starving and this is fucking amazing. If Vic wasn't married already, I'd marry her." She slapped her lips around the edge of her mouth to reign in any stray tagine.

"I'm sure you could have had her for free a few months back, no questions asked," Geri said.

Stu almost spat his food out. "Harsh," he spluttered, before wiping his mouth with a serviette. "Anyway, don't you start about quick eaters — you sound like Darren."

"Maybe he has a point?" Having said that, Geri knew this was the way Laura and Stu had always eaten and they weren't likely to change anytime soon.

"Apparently health gurus say you should eat slowly and think about what you're eating. But I bet they've never had Vic's tagine and I was thinking the whole time — I was thinking 'Please sir, can I have some more'?" Stu mopped up the juice on his plate with some flatbread before continuing. "By the way, my mum calls you Geri — maybe you can add her to your friend list?"

Geri pursed her lips. "Knock you off and put her on it instead, you mean?"

"Touchy. Is it your time of the month dear?"

"Slap him, Gimps," Laura said, before clamping her hand over her mouth. "Sorry, it just slipped out." Laura's face spelt apology.

"I give up — attacked from both sides," Geri said, smiling. She turned to Stu. "No news from Romeo yet?"

Stu shook his head.

"And what would he say about this dinner — fatty lamb, carby couscous and bread the enemy, too?" Geri leant her elbows on the table and looked Stu in the eye. "How much not to send him a picture of this forbidden banquet right now?"

"Ha ha," said Stu, reaching into his jeans pocket and pulling out his phone. He pressed a few buttons, raised an eyebrow and started to type something. Then he looked up and saw Geri and Laura watching him, so put the phone back in his pocket.

"Not coming until tomorrow now — got a work thing to go to later. Plus, I think he was hoping to miss out on the walk tomorrow. You know Darren — he thinks walking's a bit low-key. He'd rather spend the morning pumping iron in the gym and then arrive for the evening later, all buffed and ready."

Stu nudged Abby beside him to pass the tagine down the table for seconds. He spotted the glare of her iPhone from under the table and smiled — he knew a fellow phone junkie when he saw one, but even Stu might draw the line at being on Facebook at the dinner table as Abby seemed to be.

Stu ladled some more tagine onto his plate and offered it to Laura, who took it eagerly.

As Laura spooned seconds on to her plate, Tash put her arm around her.

"You trying to fatten my girl up, Morgan?" Tash asked Stu.

Stu smiled and shook his head. "Just reinforcing our age-old university alliance — survival of the fittest where food's concerned."

Tash kissed Laura on the cheek. "I've no idea where she puts it, but she's a hot slab of gorgeousness."

Laura stopped eating and frowned. "A slab?"

Tash nodded. "Yep. Sturdy. Reliable. Good for paving."

Tash, Stu and Geri all laughed loudly.

Laura rolled her eyes.

* * *

Across the table, Stevie watched Kat glance at Abby before refilling her glass of red wine and taking a healthy slug.

Abby wasn't paying attention, scrolling through something on her phone with her right hand, eating dinner slowly with a lone fork in her left.

Kat deftly refilled her glass again and sat back, triumphant.

Was this how their relationship was most nights, a game of cat and mouse?

"Still having issues at work, Abby?" Stevie asked across the table.

Abby didn't hear, so Kat nudged her.

Abby looked up. "Sorry?" she said to Stevie, her face showing a smile, her eyes showing annoyance.

"I said are you still having issues at work, being on your phone." Stevie almost managed to keep the tone out of her voice. *Almost.*

Abby waved her phone slightly, too late realising that everyone could see the tell-tale Facebook branding. She styled it out with aplomb.

"Yeah — something to do with our social media campaigns so I was just checking something and amazingly I got a signal. Sorry, rude of me." Abby smiled smoothly which made Stevie feel slightly guilty.

"Amazing tagine, by the way — the lamb is melt in your mouth," Abby told Vic.

Kat rubbed Abby's shoulder as Stu sat back and rubbed his full stomach.

"So what is it you do, Abby?" Stu asked, even though he knew. His shaved head was glistening with sweat, as tended to happen after food.

"HR — big corporate firm. Very boring." Abby dismissed her job with a wave of the hand.

"HR director, honey," Kat said.

Abby simply gave a shrug.

Kat continued. "She's in charge of over a thousand employees worldwide, very important."

The group slid on their impressed faces.

"Bit of a struggle getting time off this week, so sorry if I'm a nuisance checking mails and all of that. America's just hitting their stride."

"Well, Kat knows all about that with her job, don't

you?" Stevie smiled across the table at her friend, the banking exec. "Always on your Blackberry — have you had it surgically removed this weekend? Or are you now so important you have a PA in your suitcase upstairs answering all your mails for you?"

Abby's body froze, then after a few seconds she glanced at Kat.

Stevie clocked it all and narrowed her eyes.

Kat, meanwhile, was still holding her grin in place and laughing at Stevie's joke, but her calmly panicked features told Stevie something wasn't quite right. But Kat was a consummate pro.

"The latter. My new PA's called Helga and she's very accommodating," Kat said. "If there was any tagine left, I said I'd take it up for her."

Abby shifted in her seat and frowned.

Stevie tried to work the puzzle out, but failed.

Geri simply grinned at Kat. "So this Helga — she cute?" Geri took a sip of her wine.

"It was the only criterion for the job," Kat said.

"Remember when you kept getting emails from America when we were in Wales on the ten-year anniversary?" Laura said. "Didn't we answer a couple through a drunken haze?"

"I think we went to but luckily we saved them as draft by mistake," Kat smiled.

"That's right," Laura mumbled, looking down at her empty plate.

Stevie saw her nodding, then blushing. What Stevie remembered about last time was Kat and Laura getting very drunk and ending up in bed together, something they'd been trying to erase from their memories ever since. But Stevie knew from experience that reality was difficult to erase, painted onto your life in permanent ink just like a tattoo.

Chapter Twelve

"You want to go first?" Stevie switched on the bathroom light in their en-suite and ran her hand over her short blonde hair.

Vic had seen flickers of the old Stevie breaking through tonight, spurred on by shared memories.

"Nah, you go — I want to see if I can get reception."

Stevie nodded and closed the bathroom door.

Vic swiped her phone from the bedside table where she'd left it with her hangover this morning and headed for the stairs. Midway, she nearly toppled over a canoodling Tash and Laura. Vic apologised and carried on, raising her eyebrows at their teenage need to begin before they were in their room — they'd been together long enough now.

It was pure jealousy of course, but she couldn't help it.

In the lounge, Vic heard Stu still up with Geri, Kat and Abby, putting the world to rights.

Vic filled two glasses with water, drank one and refilled. The cold water slid down her throat with ease and splashed into her stomach. She wanted to check her email, but reception was sporadic all over the house. Vic padded to the far corner of the kitchen and held her phone up as high as she could. She squinted at the screen. Nothing.

Vic then moved to the hallway, opening the front door and hanging out of it. Even if she *got* reception, she wouldn't be able to see a damn thing. She didn't fancy a late-night trip outside.

Instead, she abandoned hope of gaining internet access and walked quietly back up the stairs and into their bedroom. Stevie was just pulling on a white T-shirt.

"Everything okay?"

"Yep, just getting these," Vic said, placing Stevie's water on her bedside table. It echoed in the glassy silence.

When Vic came out of the bathroom five minutes later, Stevie was reading her Kindle in bed.

Vic gave her wife a wary smile as she took her glasses off and joined her.

"It's so damn quiet here, isn't it?" Stevie whispered.

Vic looked over and nodded slowly. In London, the world never stood still. Even when Vic was doing yoga in the studio down the road, she could still hear the whoosh of traffic as it rumbled past, even over the whale music favoured by her instructor.

But here, if Vic lay still and tuned out the laughter coming from downstairs, she could hear nothing apart from her own breathing. That, and the sound of the wind and of the waves crashing against the wooden sand below, the beach being carved up from its flat surface to reveal welts and scars from previous tussles.

The calm was soon broken as Vic heard a crash from the next-door bedroom, then a flurry of giggles.

She and Stevie locked eyes as they realised with a slight sense of horror that the walls between the bedrooms weren't as thick as they'd like.

Vic knew next door were Tash and Laura, who'd been pawing each other all night. She gulped — it didn't take a genius to know what was coming next.

"Shit, I really don't want to hear this." Stevie pulled a face.

"And I do?"

Vic felt Stevie's body tense up: if tonight was to be the start of something, that ship may have just sailed.

Stevie rolled over and buried her head under her freshly laundered pillow and Vic followed suit. It smelt of sunshine, the irony of which Vic grasped with both hands.

A few minutes passed. Under the pillow, the sound of Vic's breathing was amplified. Eventually she peered under Stevie's pillow, whose face was set to grimace mode.

"Have they stopped yet?" Vic asked, even though she knew the answer.

"They could be a while, they were pretty drunk." Stevie pulled the pillow back down on her head.

Vic wriggled out, propped her head on her elbow and ran her left hand up and down Stevie's slim body, feeling under her T-shirt and stroking her back. Stevie had lost weight since everything happened. Not for the first time, guilt washed over Vic. Even tonight, while everyone else had been helping themselves to seconds of dinner and cheese, Stevie had held back, her appetite not what it once was.

Stevie removed the pillow from the top of her head and twisted to look up at her wife.

Vic saw a flash of desire behind Stevie's eyes. Vic's body flooded with relief — it was still there. And even though Stevie's body tensed at first, after a few seconds she began to relax.

Vic took a chance and leant in for a kiss. It was slow and gentle at first. Vic's blood charged through her veins and her heartbeat revved. Encouraged by Stevie's response, the parting of her lips, the taste of her tongue, Vic escalated the level of their kissing.

Unfortunately for her, it coincided with the moment Tash and Laura chose to reach their crescendo, with both now groaning loudly.

Stevie pulled back and shook her head. "I can't, not with this." She rolled into Vic and buried her head into her shoulder.

Vic stilled, sighed, then took Stevie fully into her arms.

Tash and Laura were still going.

Vic thought about banging on the wall in a comedy 1980s farce fashion, but shook her head at the notion and smiled sadly, wondering when she'd become such a curmudgeon. Then she remembered she could pinpoint the exact day.

Stevie rolled back slightly and looked up at her wife, looked like she was going to say something.

Vic could see the words spinning round her brain, coating her vocal chords, ready to spring. She hoped she was giving Stevie an open expression, one which would let her know that whatever it was she wanted to say or do, she could tell her.

Stevie's eyes flickered and her cheek twitched, but then her features clouded over with sadness and the distance returned, so familiar it'd almost become a third member of their relationship. Stevie searched Vic's eyes and couldn't locate what she'd been looking for, so she simply gave her a peck on the cheek instead.

"You'd think they'd build some proper fucking walls, wouldn't you?" Vic said quietly.

In response, Stevie got out of bed.

Vic's eyes widened.

"Earplugs," Stevie said, bending down to rummage in her case. Stevie settled back into bed, kissed Vic goodnight and turned onto her side, her back to her wife.

Vic felt Stevie still, felt her breathing steady. Vic lay in the semi-darkness as the stillness enveloped her, not hearing anything apart from her heartbeat thumping in her ears, keeping pace with a kick drum.

When they'd tied the knot three years ago she never thought they'd end up as one of those couples with an invisible line between them, but that's exactly where they were. In the next room she heard giggling and low murmurs. Vic knew just how that felt. It was what she wanted back so desperately.

Maybe tomorrow? Vic turned to gulp some water. Tomorrow would be different.

She rolled onto her side, trying to still her mind and her emotions. It didn't work. Her emotions would not be stilled. Instead, they jangled like a rail of empty wire coat hangers.

Chapter Thirteen

"Is there any more wine left?" Stu got up from the sofa to a cacophony of crackling, which caused Geri to peer up at him.

"Was that your knees?"

"Fraid so." Stu ran his hand over his shaved head. "Blame Darren. Ever since he got me down the gym they've never been the same. Don't believe the hype on exercise — it's actually one big con. I've never been such a wreck as I am now. Should have stuck to eating pies."

"You do still eat pies, just not when Darren's watching," Geri laughed. "You need to get some WD40 on your knees," she added as Stu left the room. Geri stretched out her legs and yawned, knitting her fingers together in front of her face, palms facing out.

"You still running?" Kat asked from the other sofa. She had stains on her lips and teeth from the red wine, her cheeks Merlot splotched. Her focus had also narrowed somewhat, although she seemed to be doing her best to focus by alternately squinting one eye, then the other. Abby was asleep next to her, her bouncy hair bunching up on the side of the stone-coloured faux suede sofa.

Kat went to drink more wine from her glass, but it was empty. She frowned.

"Stu just went to get some more," Geri told her.

Kat smiled. "So are you?"

"What?"

"Still running?"

"Course — got to for the job. This ain't LA, we can't sit around eating doughnuts in the West End, it's not the done thing." Geri rearranged herself on the couch as Stu returned brandishing three bottles of Stella.

"All we got left I'm afraid, girls." Stu handed one to Geri, one to Kat.

Kat took a deep gulp and polished off nearly a third of the bottle in one go.

"What about you? You must be doing something, you've lost a bunch of weight."

Kat shook her head, opened her mouth but then clearly thought better of it. "Not running — just cutting down on the drinking, going to the gym, eating better. I've got a lot more time on my hands these days so..." As she said the last bit, Kat took another swig of her beer, leaving the bottle nearly empty. She winked at her friends on the opposite sofa.

"That's Helga's doing, right?" Stu said.

Kat frowned. "Helga?" She looked puzzled.

"Your PA?"

It took a couple of seconds for the penny to drop, then Kat laughed. "Oh yeah… absolute godsend."

"Well, I'd rather run than cut down on drinking. Does that say something about me?" Geri said.

"That you like beer?" Kat drained her bottle as she got up off the sofa with a sudden spring in her step. "I'm going to get some more," she told them.

They heard her clatter into the kitchen doorframe with some empties, followed by a distinct "Fuck!"

This woke up Abby who squinted at Geri and Stu, then sat upright, yawning and looking around for Kat.

Geri nodded towards the kitchen. "She's gone to get more beer."

Abby checked her watch and frowned. "Fucking hell." She gave Geri and Stu a look, before hauling herself to the kitchen, fishing out her iPhone from her pocket as she went.

"D'you feel like you've just been told off by the headmistress?" Stu asked.

Geri didn't answer. Instead, there were raised voices in the kitchen, the clanking of bottles, voices quietened, mumbling.

A few minutes later Kat appeared in the doorway.

"Abby says it's gone 1am and we should go to bed. She's probably right so I'm taking my leave. Night you two." She gave them a little wave and they heard her follow Abby up to bed.

"Bloody hell, pussy-whipped or what?" Geri said.

Stu smiled and stroked his goatee. "I don't think it's such a bad thing where Kat's concerned — Abby's nothing short of a miracle-worker. I mean, she was still standing at 1am, still conscious *and* she hasn't hit on any of us."

"Yet."

The pair pondered their friend's apparent new leaf, listening to the waves outside the house as they did. The wind had picked up and the sea was stormy tonight, making them glad they were high above it.

"I take it Kelly's out of the picture completely now?" Stu's question brought Geri back to the present.

She nodded slowly, resting her beer in her lap. "Yeah — never going to work was it? Still, she was gorgeous while she lasted."

"Perhaps you could try going for someone your own age next time?" It was more of a statement than a question.

"That's what Tash and Laura said, too." Geri rolled her shoulders. "It's easier said than done though, isn't it? I mean, I'm 39 now, I'm damaged goods." She sucked on her bottom lip when she said this, studying her fingernails. They needed a trim.

"You're in the reduced pile?" Stu said. "God I hope not, I'm only a year and a half behind you. And I have the added bonus of HIV."

"Yes but you have a boyfriend, remember?"

"Well, yes," Stu replied, looking less than impressed with his lot.

Geri batted his comment away with her hand.

"Oh Darren's Darren. You know how he is — he hasn't changed. He's always been a bit flighty. I think maybe you've changed is more to the point. Have you tried talking to him?"

Stu shrugged like he didn't care.

Geri wasn't buying it. "Talk to him. He loves you. He wants to be with you. So you like different things sometimes — that's good! You don't want to turn into Ken and Ken, do you?"

Stu shot her his best look of derision, at which Geri laughed.

"Talking of HIV, how are your counts doing?"

Stu looked nonplussed. "Fine. I mean, I take my pills every morning, I try not to catch a cold and my body is the same as ever. I don't feel like a weapon of mass destruction. Even my mum doesn't worry I'm going to die anymore, so things must have turned a corner, mustn't they?"

SATURDAY

Chapter Fourteen

Kat let her hand flop out of the covers and trailed it through thin air, rippling imaginary water. Next to her, Abby was flat on her back. She was breathing so loudly, it sounded like a recording of breathing, like there was no way it could be real, but it was. Asleep, she looked angelic, almost too perfect for words, her dark skin smooth and soft, her hair splayed artfully across the white pillow.

Kat frowned as she tried to bring to mind the complete memory of last night but she had a nagging feeling there was something she'd missed. Abby hadn't been amused when she'd tried to get more beer at 1am, but she shrugged internally, writing that one off to holiday excitement. She hadn't drunk a drop on the first night, after all.

Kat sighed the sigh of a woman who felt trapped — by what she didn't do as well as what she did. She was grateful in some ways to Abby for coming into her life, but she seemed to have turned up at just the moment that Kat's world had imploded.

Kat lifted the covers and got out of bed, tousling her short dark hair as she did. She tiptoed across the room as wince-inducing pain shot through her skull, opened the en-suite door and closed it in the manner of a cartoon burglar.

This morning her brain was a toxic tangle of emotions that she didn't really want to think about, and she didn't want a Friday night analysis session, either. Abby would want to try to untangle the emotions, tidy up the mess, whereas Kat could happily carry on and simply walk around it, pretending it wasn't there. It was a skill she'd been born with.

This morning, what she most wanted was to pee, get in the shower and let the hot jets wash away her ills, followed by a coffee. Then and only then could she usher the rest of the day into her grey hangover fug, slap on a smile and start all over again. Life was monotonous like that.

* * *

As the bathroom door closed, Abby opened her left eye and imagined Kat on the other side, sat on the loo and massaging her temples — typical Kat morning-after pose. She knew she'd been right when she'd told Kat to bail on this weekend — her girlfriend simply didn't have the tools to deal with it right now.

Abby smiled ruefully as she thought about the night they'd met at a networking event for lesbian professionals

— really just an excuse to get a group of hot, powerful gay women into one room to drink cocktails and check each other out. Still, it worked for her and the hundred or so other women there.

Abby had spotted Kat about midway through the evening, leaning against the marble bar and checking out the talent. She'd been wearing black trousers with ruby red brogues, a smart shirt and a well-cut black jacket, which on closer inspection turned out to be Ralph Lauren. She'd also been adopting the well-worn lesbian stance of one hand in pocket, one eyebrow raised, exuding an air of nonchalance to all around her.

Abby hadn't been fooled.

Kat's short dark hair was longer at the front and kept falling into her eyes — she spent an inordinate amount of time pushing it back off her face. Their eyes had met across a crowded room in the manner of a million Hollywood movies, only this was on a wet Wednesday in the City.

In a matter of moments Abby had gravitated towards Kat's side, introduced herself and bought Kat a second vodka martini — Abby favoured bubbles. They'd chatted all night and Kat had impressed Abby with her sense of humour, her pert rear and her confidence. She was clearly a woman used to these surroundings and supremely at home within them.

That was then.

Six months later and here they were, with Kat having lost interest in most things, including food, sex and life.

The only thing she seemed to maintain a passion for was drinking.

Abby heard the toilet flush and closed both eyes, pretending to be asleep. She wasn't sure why. Abby pictured Kat staring at her reflection in the mirror, sticking out her tongue to gauge her health. The door to the bathroom opened and Kat got back into the bed as silently as she could manage. Abby responded by rolling over and gathering up her girlfriend, feeling her bones through her grey pyjama top.

"Sorry, did I wake you?" Kat whispered, not turning around to look at Abby.

Her girlfriend kissed the back of her neck. "Probably time I was awake anyhow." Abby's voice was croaky, not lubricated sufficiently yet. "How you feeling?"

Kat arched her back and stretched.

Abby could sense her turning over the question in her mind, trying to work out what answer to offer up.

"Bit of a headache but okay," was the outcome. "My tongue looks a bit manky, though."

Abby smiled, despite herself.

"What you smiling about?" Kat asked, rolling over to view her lover's grin.

"How'd you know I was smiling?" Abby's smile widened.

"I just know." Kat narrowed her eyes.

Abby leant forward and kissed Kat once, twice, three times. Kat's skin was hot beneath her and Abby's blood rushed down her body to her very core. She ignored it, knowing it would go nowhere today.

Surprisingly, Kat ran a hand absentmindedly up and down Abby's side, caressing her body lightly.

"So." Abby sensed Kat was in a relaxed, receptive mood. "Are we going to talk about *It*?"

Kat looked her directly in the eye — she could hear the capital letter at the start of the last word.

"It?" Kat was stalling for time and they both knew it.

Abby curled her lip. "You know damn well."

Kat lowered her gaze and sighed. "I know," she said quietly. "I'll tell them today."

"But why didn't you just do it last night?"

The question hung in the air.

Kat waited for the thud as it landed but it never happened. There was only silence and the sound of their breathing.

Abby went for the slam dunk. "You had the perfect opportunity and you just took the funny joke. I don't get it. You were made redundant, it's not something shameful. You weren't caught fucking the office intern like some people I could mention."

"I know, I know."

Abby threw her head back on the pillow in exasperation and stared at the ceiling. "I know this is difficult, but you have to at least tell them you're unemployed. Then you can lead on to the fact you're not feeling that great. But you have to tell them the first bit to begin with."

Kat's face had turned the colour of concrete.

Abby took her hand and kissed it. She then kissed the top of Kat's head and felt her draw in breath, then her body shook slightly and she knew the tears had arrived, the ones that arrived most days now. Abby hugged Kat towards her and kissed her head again.

"This will get better, but you have to want it to," Abby said as she stroked her girlfriend's back. "And you might want to can the tears unless you want to go down to breakfast looking like you've just gone six rounds with me. For one thing, your mates might beat me up..."

Kat made a sound like a wounded animal underneath her, then shifted her body away. She lay still on her back and stared upwards before rubbing both eyes with balled fists.

"I know you're right and I will tell them today," she whispered, peeking out from under her knuckles. "Promise."

Abby smiled her winning smile. "Good enough. Now go and freshen up and don't forget to take your pills."

Chapter Fifteen

Stevie opened her eyes just after 9am. She'd managed just five hours of unbroken sleep. Not even the wine had been enough to knock her out — she bet Kat hadn't had any issues after the amount she'd drunk. Stevie knew they all worried about Kat, but maybe she had it right and *they* all had it wrong. Maybe the world was just that bit easier to deal with if you were sedated enough.

Beside her, Vic slept on. Stevie knew change had to come. She'd truly willed it yesterday, but she'd been waiting for it to come naturally — and the Tash and Laura sideshow hadn't helped.

Stevie realised now that just waiting for something to change was wishful thinking. She was living in real life, not some marshmallow land where fairytales came true. If Stevie wanted this one to have a happy ending, she knew she had to make the first step. After all, the power was with her and had been ever since Vic threw such a curveball into their lives.

Stevie winced again as she thought about it — time was dulling the hurt and betrayal, as was Vic's relentless congeniality. But what never seemed to change was the utter futility of her actions. A college intern and as Vic was just approaching 40? Vic had sleepwalked into being such a cliché it made Stevie gasp at times. But something had to give in order for sanity to prevail and Stevie knew she held the trump card. Plus, Vic's constant graciousness and apologetic gestures were frankly getting on her tits.

Stevie decided on a run to shake herself into the right frame of mind for the day. She eased herself out of the bed, being careful not to wake Vic, and pulled her running gear from the case. Then she slipped quietly down to the kitchen which was still home to the debris from the night before, the port glasses and cheese plates perched on the counter top. Vic and Kat had been putting the world to rights last night over some Stilton and Tawny port, leaving no subject unturned.

After a glass of water, Stevie headed back out into the hallway where their coat collection was hanging like a still-life painting, shoes neatly lined up underneath along the skirting board. She pulled on her trainers, clicked the front door shut and strode up the drive, turning towards the sea, glistening and infinite.

Her shoelaces weren't quite tight enough, so Stevie squatted and retied, then rolled her neck from one side to the other, flexing her hips into the bargain, then stretching her arms. She arched her back, looking into the sun until its glare made her squint. Should she go back for her sunglasses? She could squint it out this once. She set her training watch to 00:00 and slowly began to run.

Stevie never thought she'd become one of those running types, but that's exactly what had happened. She had a best time for a 5k and a 10k but was yet to go for more than that — she worried her knees might cave in if she did. For her, running wasn't about doing a marathon or competing with others — she just loved having the time to herself, thinking about her life, running through her day.

Throughout this whole sorry mess, running had been her constant companion, even more so than before. It cleared her head and had stopped her from strangling Vic on more than one occasion.

This morning, as she ran round the back of the house and towards the coastal path, she stopped to take in its majesty. As far as the eye could see, cool blue water shimmered in the morning sun, its surface dimpled by the wind. But although it was sunny it was still April, and the wind needled at her legs, wrists, neck.

Stevie took a deep breath and set off to her right, the dusty path kicking up as her feet connected. The air was incredibly cleansing here, so removed from London. What was it she breathed in at home? In Devon, the air was packaged with an extra shot of freshness, the faint hint of manure coating it.

As she ran on, daffodils lined her route and blossom spilled itself in the heady breeze. She grinned as she felt her stride click in, her body begin to settle and her mind was finally released. Today, she recalled the day after Vic's infidelity, the hurt she'd felt. Not even three years married, but nearly ten years together and this was what they'd become.

When she'd found out, Stevie had fled back to her native Liverpool, back to the family home, and had lain in her mum's spare room, wondering why her, why now? She'd have stayed there too if her mum hadn't made her get up and face the problem head-on. Mrs Wright was not one to pussyfoot around.

First, Stevie's cousin Dave had appeared and dragged her out for a night on the town, trying to get her to snog random women in a bid for revenge — but Stevie was not one to play games.

Then, while she suffered through her hangover the next morning, her mum reminded her she'd taken an oath. For better or for worse, she was now committed to Vic, come what may. Had her mother brought her up to throw in the towel so easily? She had not.

So, after letting Stevie wallow for a few days, her mum had given her a stern talking to and packed her bags for home, with instructions to talk and sort the sorry mess out. But it hadn't been quite that easy.

Stevie's body glided as her thoughts spun. Today, her trainers were coated in magic dust and she was flying. She felt gracious, unbeatable. Perhaps it was a sign. Perhaps today was the day to take the plunge, to fully reconnect with Vic. Yes, she'd found it hard to forgive. But the bottom line was she didn't want to be with anyone else, so perhaps it was time to get back to being with the woman she loved.

Stevie raced on in her body, letting her thoughts settle this time. If there was one thing she was sure of, it was that she wanted to sleep with Vic — she missed her so badly. She grinned at the prospect and ran on, feeling invincible.

Yes, today she could tackle anything. Stevie picked up her speed and angled her face into the sun. Today, she'd decided to run home.

Chapter Sixteen

Laura woke with a sore head and sore thigh muscles. *How much had Vic and Stevie heard last night?* She pulled the duvet up over her head and closed her eyes.

On the light blue pillow next to her, Tash screwed up her face and wiped some dribble from her mouth, before grunting and turning the other way.

Outside, the sea was grinding against the shore, the sun trying to peer in through the gaps in the curtains. It looked like another sunny day with another walk on the agenda. From the sounds drifting up the stairs, someone was already up and getting ready.

Laura stuck her tongue out of her mouth. *Furry.*

Laura turned her head to the right. Had she had the forethought to bring a glass of water upstairs? She had not. She stared at the empty space on the bedside table. Her chest felt claggy too, like she'd smoked 20 Benson & Hedges.

"Why are you awake?" Tash asked without opening her eyes.

Laura turned her head, smiling. "I thought I was being quiet."

"You don't even blink quietly."

In response, Laura moved a foot to her right until it connected her to Tash's body. She rubbed it up and down her leg and felt the press of her lover's lips on her head in return.

Whenever Laura was awake and in bed with Tash, she liked some part of their bodies to be connected. In winter, she wrapped herself around Tash like bindweed, clinging to her very own human radiator for warmth. In the summer it was just a foot, a hand or a hip, before sleep took her and she rolled away. But whenever they were both awake, her first thought was always to touch Tash.

Laura hoped their relationship never ended because she knew she could never just be friends. The compulsion to touch Tash and kiss her had been ever-present since the moment they met inside that dank, depressing flat. Laura didn't imagine it was something that would change anytime soon.

Laura moved closer to Tash and shifted her arm to just above her head, the cue for her girlfriend to lift her head and settle into her arm nook.

Tash duly obliged.

"So how much do you think the house heard last night?" Laura said, kissing Tash's fiery ginger hair.

"Enough to make them jealous as hell?"

Laura broke into a wide grin, looking pretty pleased with herself.

Tash shifted her face back onto Laura's shoulder and

breathed in her lover's morning smell, kissing her bare neck. "And I don't know what you did to me last night, but my calves are really tight." Tash reached down to rub them.

"I don't recall any complaints last night."

"None here, no ma'am," Tash said. "If anyone asks, I'll recommend you without hesitation."

"Good to know."

"Beautiful, sexy, great line in multiple orgasms. Almost illegal tongue skills. How's that for a personal ad?" Tash flicked her eyes up towards Laura, who tilted her head to consider the question. "Also, wicked spot forming on chin," Tash added.

Laura frowned. "I was just adjusting to my stud status and then you had to go and spoil it, didn't you?"

Tash reached up and kissed her girlfriend. "I love you and I love your spot." She placed her lips against Laura's and pressed with passion.

"Aren't I the lucky one?" Laura replied, once Tash had moved away.

"Well, yes, since you ask." Tash paused, propping herself up on her elbow.

Laura lowered her gaze to Tash's naked, pale breasts, now on view as the duvet dropped. She reached out a hand to caress them — she couldn't help it, it was an automatic response.

"So what about me, then?" Tash grazed Laura's wandering hands with her lips.

"Huh?"

Tash batted Laura's hand away, bringing her back into the room. "Focus, sweetheart." Tash grasped her girlfriend's chin in her hand. "What about me? What's my personal ad?"

Laura's mouth twitched and she looked thoughtful. "MILF wants thrill-seeker for lasting passion. GSOH, great tits." Laura reached down to kiss Tash's breasts, first the left, then the right.

"I'm not sure that sets the right tone." Tash clipped Laura lightly round the head, then ran her fingers through Laura's long hair in contrition.

Laura lifted her head so that Tash felt her breath on her face. She shifted her body right, causing Tash to topple backwards and within seconds she was on top of her, an eyebrow arched in anticipation.

"On the contrary, I think it sends out exactly the right message." Laura grinned down at her, before closing the space between them, kissing Tash with undisguised passion.

Tash had no response apart from to succumb to the moment.

Laura pressed her thigh between Tash's legs, causing her girlfriend to take a sharp intake of breath. She followed up by running her right hand up and down Tash's inner thigh, then began to tease her lover with caresses around her groin, her soft thatch of hair, her sex.

"I know you're not a morning person," Laura whispered throatily in Tash's ear. "But like the ad said, you're definitely a mum I'd like to fuck."

Chapter Seventeen

Geri was in the kitchen with the kettle burbling when Stevie got back from her run 40 minutes later. She'd cleared up last night's debris, so the kitchen was now refreshed and ready to get dirty all over again, highlighting — if ever it were necessary to do so — the futility of housework.

Stevie's face was flushed beetroot with exertion, making Geri laugh. "I hope that's just effort and not sunburn."

Stevie padded her way to the sink and gulped down a glass of water, swiftly followed by another. Her hot-socked feet left pristine sweat patches on the grey slate flooring but then disappeared almost as quickly, as if some invisible monster were roaming the kitchen.

Geri watched Stevie's throat pulse as she drank, then grabbed some kitchen towel and mopped her brow.

"Too early for sunburn, isn't it?" Concern stained Stevie's voice.

"I think you'll be okay," Geri said. "Although I can't believe you went for a run without me."

"Sorry — didn't want to wake you."

"I didn't bring my stuff anyway — thought I'd give myself the weekend off."

Stevie was still panting slightly. "Why would you want to give yourself time off when you can run in an environment like this?"

"True enough. Didn't think that through did I?" Geri paused. "You want a cuppa?"

"Nah, I'm going to go jump in the shower before everyone else gets up." Stevie banged her glass down on the counter before exiting the kitchen.

Geri made her tea then grabbed Tash's sweatshirt which she'd left on the back of a chair, retrieved her trainers from the hallway and opened the patio doors, stepping out into the back garden.

This was what she missed living in London — being able to step outside your house and straight into the sun. Geri had a Juliet balcony in her Highbury flat which she considered pointless: a two-fingered salute from the builders who couldn't be arsed to build a proper one.

However, while it was sunny, as soon as Geri stepped outside she realised it was still April. Simultaneously the wind cut her and the sun bathed her — pleasure and pain in equal measure. The sky was ever-changing, a mass of aqua blue, flickering sun and a variety of clouds — some stringy, some cotton wool. She drank in the sea, sky and cliffs, a riot of primary colours all bending and stretching, limbering up for the day ahead.

When Geri had first considered coming on this

weekend, she hadn't been sure about the couples dynamic — even her drinking buddy Kat had met someone. But, having spent two days with them, Geri had concluded that while she might sometimes be lonely, she was sure she didn't want *any* of these relationships. Not for the first time, she wished she'd brought her video camera — this would have made a great documentary.

Kat and Abby seemed weird; Darren hadn't turned up; Vic and Stevie were walking a tightrope; and while Tash and Laura seemed happy, she wouldn't want the baggage that came with having two kids and an ex-husband. So yes, she might be standing out here on her own drinking tea in the sunshine, but there were worse things.

Geri walked to the edge of the grass and sucked in the sea air. It felt crisp and salty, coating her nostril hair as it jogged into her airwaves. To her right she could see other houses dotted along the top of the cliffs in all manner of shapes and sizes. There was so much space and greenery around each plot that it truly was a world removed from her London building-block reality.

To her left the houses were strewn equally haphazardly along the cliffs, as if some drunk had thrown them there after a night on the Rattler. Their assorted bricks and mortar held the dreams of owners past and present, some of them succeeding in their clamour for beach life, others failing dismally and having to put up For Sale and For Rent signs.

* * *

Vic leant on the frame of the patio doors and watched Gimpy — aka Geri — her neck craned towards the odd-looking orb in the sky which had been casting an unfamiliar glow through their bedroom window since early that morning. Geri seemed lost in the moment and, for a brief second, Vic was jealous — jealous of Geri's independence, of her refusal to settle down, of her commitment to life on full throttle.

To Vic, Geri seemed to have life sussed — cool flat, cool job, never-ending conga line of younger women. Plus, the leather jacket she'd brought on this trip made Vic want to weep. Vic needed to update her wardrobe desperately, but it hadn't been top of her list of late.

Geri turned as if sensing she was being watched and clocked Vic in the doorway.

"Morning!" Geri walked over to stand in front of Vic, hopping from foot to foot. Geri stood a good four inches taller than Vic.

"Morning. Doing a little dance?" Vic's face gave little away.

"It's not as warm as it looks in the shade."

"Which is why I'm staying put here." Vic looked down at her feet, still firmly placed on the wooden floor inside.

"Lovely in the sun, though — feels like it's your secret." Geri leaned out to try to catch some more rays.

They both stood in silence, staring out at the beautiful vista as the clouds silently shifted eastwards, the wind whistling past their faces.

After a few seconds Geri eased past Vic, patting her arm on the way. "I need another drink — you want one?"

"Yeah — I was gonna try this coffee machine, see what it's like. You had one yet?"

Geri shook her head as she filled the shiny kettle. "I'm more a tea girl."

Vic stepped up to the machine, ready for the challenge. She did, after all, market herself in the modern school of butch dyke — she cooked, she cleaned, she could work machinery — and this fell squarely into that bracket. Particularly with Geri there, pretending not to judge when that was *exactly* what she was doing. There was no question — Vic *had* to succeed.

Beside the Nespresso machine was a round flume of capsules in various colours, each one sliding down their section and ending up in a joint pool at the bottom — a coffee-capsule fairground. Vic studied the coffee card as if choosing a race horse, before gingerly picking up a capsule, inserting it into the machine and closing the lid. She remembered her childhood, when making a coffee was as simple as unscrewing a jar and adding hot water. Those days were gone.

Vic was wearing plain blue pyjama bottoms and a grey T-shirt that rode up as she stretched and yawned, revealing a toned, flat stomach. Her arms were toned too, the result of a recent punishing gym regime.

At university, Vic had shied away from playing sport and been a library dweller, determined to get the best law degree she possibly could. However, the gym had been a great place to take out her recent frustrations, and as a result she'd shed a stone and become a mass of firmer, angular shapes. She turned to see Geri's eyes appraising her. The machine finished its whirring and Vic was left with an espresso. She'd passed the test.

"So, how are things?" Geri shifted her eyes upwards quickly.

Vic retrieved her coffee cup from the machine's slatted shelf. "Okay." She nodded briskly. "Life goes on, you know."

Geri nodded back.

"How about you, still saving the world?" Vic asked.

"In between drinking tea and filling out forms."

Vic nodded. Silence fell over the room.

Geri stepped back in. "And you — work's good?"

"Can't complain. People get divorced, have accidents and need to move house in all climates — recession doesn't stop that."

Vic was aware these conversations she had with Geri were always a bit strained, a little awkward. At university, their difference was masked by lager, exuberance and loud noise. But now they were in their late thirties and the noise was dimming, Vic was aware that as a pair, they grated slightly.

Vic would love nothing more than to break down the walls and laugh with Geri the way Stevie did, the way Stu did, the way everyone else seemed to. But, for some reason, whenever the two of them were left together the conversation felt thorny and exposed, leaving just the deathly sound of small talk contaminating the air.

* * *

The sound of footsteps in the hall saved the day. Stevie walked through the door and Vic's face flushed with relief. If it had been Abby, she might have been a little overwhelmed.

"Morning, my two favourite people!" Stevie's blonde hair was still wet from the shower. She gave Geri a hug which she returned, then kissed Vic on the lips and stood beside her, still three inches taller.

Vic slipped a hand under Stevie's sweatshirt.

"Je-sus! Your hands are fucking freezing!"

Vic laughed at this standard reaction because it was true — her extremities often never reached room temperature, even in hot weather. Stevie insisted on an electric blanket in winter these days just so her wife's fingers and toes didn't send her into a frosty shock. It worked a treat.

"Cup of tea, m'lady?" Geri asked, already getting a mug from the cupboard.

"Yes please," Stevie nodded, but then raised an eyebrow. "Or maybe a coffee?" she asked, putting her nose in Vic's cup to sniff it. "Did you use the machine?"

"I did."

"Make me one then."

Vic did as she was told.

"So what were you two talking about down here?" Stevie knew the dynamics between them.

"Oh, you know, this and that," Geri said as the coffee machine began to whir. That told Stevie all she needed to know. "Work, life…" Geri added, before running out of nouns.

"Well, enough about work — I want to talk about how much we're going to party later, seeing as it's Saturday night." Stevie grinned, dancing around on the balls of her feet.

Geri leaned back against the counter and yawned. "You're a bit perky this morning."

"Been for a run already. I'm ready for the day!" Stevie nudged Geri on the arm. "So come on, who's going to do the most embarrassing thing this time?"

"Bagsy not me," Geri said, raising her hand.

"And we're not 30 anymore." Vic handed Stevie her the coffee. "I think we all might have grown up a bit since last time." Vic's tone was finite, almost acidic. She should have known better.

"Doesn't mean we don't all do stupid things that we regret now and again though, does it?" Stevie connected with a cultured right hook.

Vic's face contorted and she looked winded.

Geri wished she could vanish from the kitchen and have the good sense not to be on her own with a warring couple. Still, even she had to concede that Vic had walked into that one.

"Oh come on, nobody can beat Kat's efforts from

last time," Geri said. "At least I hope they can't. Vomiting up the stairs one night and sleeping with Laura the next. I mean, in staking a claim for best story, it's difficult to beat." Geri smiled at the memory, as did Stevie and Vic.

"Unless you're planning to vomit up this plush carpet and attempt to shag Kat yourself?" Geri asked Stevie.

"Er, no!" Stevie visibly shuddered. "God, no!"

"I hope not," Vic added softly, pulling her close.

At first Stevie resisted, but then something seemed to shift and she allowed Vic to manoeuvre her, allowed her body to melt into her.

Vic took advantage by placing both arms firmly around Stevie's waist.

"I'm going to stick to kissing my wife if it's all the same to you," Stevie said. "But if Kat does vomit up the stairs again, she's got a girlfriend here to clean it up this time, thankfully."

"Remember trying to clean the carpet?" Geri wrinkled her nose.

"Don't." Stevie held up her right palm, her face going green.

"I'm all for making new memories this time around, but preferably vomit-free," Vic said. "I certainly remember better ones from ten years ago too. Like, for instance, me and Stevie getting together."

Stevie could sense Vic's smile and she placed her hands on top of Vic's hands, drawing them up to her mouth for a kiss.

"God, last time around was a shagfest, wasn't it?" Geri shook her head wistfully.

"I think this time around, age has caught up with us. It's called growing up," Stevie replied.

"Well I hope we haven't all grown up too much," Geri said. "Otherwise I might get a late train back to London and go out in Soho with Darren instead."

Chapter Eighteen

An hour later, Geri wrapped her knuckles three times on Stu's door but didn't bother waiting for an answer. Instead, she burst into his room to find him sat on his bed, mobile in hand, thumb poised over the keypad.

"You ready, husband? I've been told to round up the troops."

Stu turned to look up at her, frowning. "Are you trying to re-enact university life completely by barging in like this? What if I'd been naked?" He put his phone back on the bedside table and got up, putting his wallet into his back pocket.

"Nothing I haven't seen before from you, Morgan." Geri paused. "So are you nearly ready?"

"Be down in a minute — just gotta send Darren a reply and brush my teeth."

"Okay — send him my love." Geri pushed herself off his doorframe, steadying the sunglasses on top of her head. "You walking or villaging by the way?"

"Walking — I need the exercise."

"Sure you do." Geri saluted him and took the stairs two at a time.

Abby was standing at the bottom frowning at her phone. She was wearing a 1950s inspired red-and-white skirt, a lightweight white top and a red, white and black scarf knotted loosely around her neck. She looked like an advert for a wholesome post-war lifestyle campaign. Where had Kat found her — on special in some retro shop?

Geri saw her late and managed steer right, not flattening Abby completely. However, her lessened impact still knocked Abby's iPhone from her grasp and it sailed into the air before crashing against the front door, the case coming off and the rest skittering horribly across the wooden floor.

Geri stood frozen on the stairs, wincing as she awaited the news.

Abby bent to retrieve her phone and didn't get back up quickly.

"Sorry — is it okay?" Geri already knew the answer.

Abby shook her head but didn't look up. "It's buggered," she said, easing herself upwards and holding out the phone to Geri. The screen was shattered and deathly black, making this now officially a day of mourning.

"I'm so sorry, I should slow down." Geri furrowed her brow. "It might still work though, it might just be the screen. Are you insured?"

"Yes, but that's not going to help me today is it?"

Abby was not seeing the funny side yet. "I wanted to download some stuff in the village, reply to some emails."

"You're coming with me?" Geri said.

"We were," Abby sulked.

"You still can," Geri enthused, clicking her fingers. "Look, we'll do a bit of shopping, have a bit of lunch and you can use my iPhone to do all your mailing. Can't you get a colleague to forward the important emails to my address?" Geri was smiling a bit too much.

Abby pursed her lips but didn't look convinced. "Maybe. Let me take this upstairs and see if I can get it working. If not, that could be a workaround." Sorrow stained her face as she assessed the phone's remains, cradling it gently.

"See what you can do. I'll wait in the kitchen." If Geri had intended to rip out part of Abby's soul, it was job well done.

* * *

In the kitchen, Geri sat down and thumped her head onto the kitchen table.

At the counter, Laura and Tash were making cheese and pickle sandwiches for lunch, wrapping them in cling film.

Laura spun round at the sound. "What's happened?"

Geri lifted her head slowly. "I just killed Abby's phone."

Tash put her hand to her chest. "I thought you were

going to say you just killed Abby." She held up her hand. "Just her phone… I can cope with that."

"I'm not sure Abby can." Geri gave Tash a thin-lipped grimace.

"I bet," Laura smirked, turning towards Geri. "That phone is like a child to her." She paused. "Deary me, you just killed Abby's child." Laura wagged her finger and laughed. "Bad Geri. Bad, baaaaad Geri."

"I think you might be right. Quick, let's keep talking to block out the sound of wailing from upstairs." Geri stood up and went to assess the couple's efforts.

"You guys are too much — you've even got a multi-pack of crisps. It's a good job you did the shopping, I wouldn't have thought of that." Geri leant against the kitchen island, leaning over to steal a slice of cheese and getting a slapped hand from Tash.

"Did you buy some Club biscuits, too? I'm almost sad I'm not coming with you now I've seen what you're having for lunch."

"Want me to make you one, too?" Tash asked.

Geri waved her hand. "You're okay. Besides, I'm sure we'll be headed somewhere fabulous for lunch, being that I'm going out with the cosmopolitan power couple." Geri paused. "That is, if they're still talking to me and not sticking pins in a tiny version of me upstairs right now."

Geri sat back in her chair and assessed the couple in front of her. Tash and Laura were dressed in jeans, T-shirts and hoodies, ready to take on the coastal winds.

Minus the kids, these two were definitely the pair she'd like to emulate because they seemed to have it all — love, sex, friendship, trust, the works.

As if to prove it further, Tash ran a hand down Laura's back as she leant across her for the cling film and Laura returned the favour by pecking Tash on the cheek.

The door opened and Stu walked in with a small rucksack on his back, phone in hand, wraparound shades already in place. He looked tall and lithe and the logo on his zip-up top read 'Hollister'. The room filled with the unmistakable scent of men's grooming products.

"I'm just going up the drive to see if I can catch Darren again. Shall I see you up there?" Stu waved his phone in his left hand.

"Pick you up at the end of the drive." Laura passed him a bag with his lunch in it.

Stu held it up to inspect it before nodding his approval. "Thanks mum — see you up there."

Chapter Nineteen

Geri read the welcome pack for the house while she waited in the kitchen for Kat and Abby to appear. That was another thing about couples: they seemed to take far longer than single people to get ready. The pack rated a pub called The Feathers in the local village and Geri made a mental note to check it out for lunch.

The walkers had departed with their lunches on their backs and sturdy shoes on their feet, so the house felt strangely quiet after a rowdy mid-morning filled with eggs, toast and coffee. Geri had managed to persuade Stevie to run her up to the village and the group lauded her introduction of toasted slices of white Bloomer — the simple things in life were always the crowd-pleasers.

She flicked her eyes up at the clock and saw it was just past midday — it'd been nearly half an hour since Abby disappeared to do emergency phone surgery. Geri tutted.

To kill time, she headed into the lounge to take in the cinematic view — it was still there and still just as impressive in the early afternoon sun. She switched on the TV and Football Focus flickered into view, hosted by a trio of men in stiff shirts, one of them sporting flicked hair and a moustache that were straight out of central casting, circa 1976. One of the presenters made a sexist joke and the other two laughed for far longer than they should have. She sighed.

Geri still followed the fortunes of her native Bournemouth FC and went with her dad whenever she was home to eat lukewarm pies and drink cooking lager. However, the racism, sexism and homophobia inherent in football made her blood hot with rage if she was exposed to the game for too long, so she preferred to keep it at arm's length.

She channel-surfed, ending up as she often did on a cooking show where a chirpy-looking young chef was tasking three teams to come up with the best meal from a limited set of ingredients in just one hour.

It always amused Geri's friends and family that she was so hooked on cooking shows, seeing as her kitchen was generally used for making tea and toast. Her sister had christened her the modern-day Carrie Bradshaw, and Geri often wished it was that nickname that had stuck. She was sure some of the knowledge she'd gleaned from these shows was bound to trickle down to her fingers one day though, then she'd amaze her guests with a show-stopping menu. It just hadn't happened yet.

Geri fiddled with her phone for a while, adopting what the group were now referring to as the 'Abby frown'.

After a few more minutes, the lounge door opened

and Kat appeared, looking as sheepish and red-eyed as she had over breakfast.

"About time — thought you'd died up there. I was just going to send a search party."

"Sorry — time ran away." Kat looked apologetic. "Anyhow, we're ready now — shall we?" She idly picked something in her ear as she said this.

Geri flicked off the TV as she stood, slipping her small bag over her head. "Phone, wallet, ready."

She followed Kat out into the hall where Abby was standing, looking like she was about to do a photoshoot rather than go for lunch and a spot of shopping.

"How's your phone?" Geri asked.

Abby gave her a tight-lipped smile. "It's still kinda working but the screen's buggered. I'll have to get a new one, but I can borrow Kat's for today."

"Great," Geri said. "And I'm sorry again."

Abby said nothing. She clearly wanted to punch her.

"Do you know where we're going Gimps?" Kat asked over her shoulder, before covering her mouth. "I mean Geri."

Geri rolled her eyes. "Yeah, where we went for bread this morning. It's not far."

The heavy front door closed with a satisfying thud and the gravel churned underfoot as the trio headed towards Kat's green Beetle.

Geri was looking forward to the day she could justify having a car — maybe when she met the right woman and moved to the suburbs with two cats. She planned to blow a large chunk of her monthly budget on one just like this. She and Kat had taken many day trips in it when they were both single, windows down, music blaring.

"I love this car, have I mentioned that before?" Geri clambered into the back, banging her head as she did.

"Once or twice," Kat said. She clicked the seat back into place, got in and started the engine. "Is it left at the end?"

"Yep — then just keep going. I found a pub that looks good for lunch, by the way." Geri leant forward between their two front seats as Kat steered the car out of the drive. It was where Geri seemed to spend most of her life these days, the single friend in the back seat.

"Good work." Kat looked left and right as they came to a junction.

Abby already had both her and Kat's phones in her lap expectantly and kept glancing downwards to see if the reception had got any better.

Geri couldn't quite detect the mood of her host couple this lunchtime but they seemed civil enough for now. She hoped it stayed that way.

As Kat steered the car down the narrow country lanes, Geri marvelled again that this was England — an England she never saw usually, only ever on TV. But once you escaped the M25 she knew that most of the country was exactly like this — green and pleasant. Fields spilled out before her on either side, hedges and fences guiding their path with grazing animals dotted throughout as if staged.

Just as Geri was beginning to entertain thoughts about moving to the country and starting a fudge business with a herd of dairy cows and a sexy milkmaid, Kat swerved to avoid a dead animal, swearing loudly.

"Was that a badger?" Abby asked, her voice rising. She twisted in her seat to get a better look, as did Geri.

"Think so," Geri said over her shoulder. "There were a few on the drive here, too." Geri dropped back into her seat and swallowed — her saliva tasted of fudge. She might have to buy some later.

"And there was me thinking the country was a safe place for animals." Abby patted the top of her hair, checking it was still there.

"Fewer cars than the city, put it that way," Geri replied.

"I guess," Abby mumbled, not really registering the reply. She held up her phone and Geri saw Kat glancing over at her.

"Anything yet?" Kat asked.

Abby nodded briskly. "I think I'm getting that file I needed yesterday — *finally*. I might have to call Nick when we stop — so long as we still have a signal. Honestly, how do people survive here?"

Geri had a few answers, but thought it best to keep them to herself.

The trio pulled into the picturesque village five minutes later and Abby was thrilled to have reception — it was the happiest Geri had seen her since they'd arrived. The sun was still shining so Kat and Geri agreed to leave Abby in the car and text her where to meet them for lunch.

Abby looked like someone had just granted her favourite wish.

* * *

The village was probably considered more of a town in these parts, but was definitely more village to these two Londoners as they strolled up the High Street. There were a sprinkling of what Geri would class as 'hippy shops' selling joss sticks, candles and precious stones, along with moon charts and over-priced jewellery. A book shop, a butcher, a bakery, a few more gift stores and three Chinese takeaways were also visible on a first glance up the main road.

What's more, the foodie and home decor revolution hadn't missed this part of Devon. Right in front of them was a kitchen store with a window display of cool breadbins — since when did breadbins get funky? Next to that was a bathroom store showcasing a selection of wet rooms that nobody had space for, along with some tiles that probably retailed for around £50 each. On the other side of the kitchen shop was a small garden centre with a healthy array of gargoyles littering the pavement in front of it.

"Tempted?" Geri asked Kat as they stopped in front of a statue of two grinning frogs hugging each other.

"Shame I don't have a garden, isn't it?" Kat replied.

The other thing that struck Geri as they strolled back up the road was that every store had a small Union Jack flying on a miniature pole above the door. Had they stumbled into the most patriotic village in the UK? Or perhaps they were all like this.

As they approached the middle of the High Street, Geri saw the pub from the welcome pack. She and Kat stopped to peer through the window. There were a smattering of blokes at the bar but, significantly, it looked modern and was flooded with natural light, thanks to its massive wraparound windows.

"Looks like a pub," Kat said.

"Got chairs and tables," Geri added, still looking in the window.

"Serves beer. Shall we lunch here?" Kat stood back and shielded her eyes from the sun.

Geri nodded and a look passed between the two, followed by a cheesy grin.

Kat looked at her watch. "Too early for a beer?"

"Gone midday," Geri said, walking past Kat and into the pub. "You can text Abby and tell her to meet us here."

Kat raised one eyebrow. "You're a genius, you know?" she said to Geri's back, slapping it as they walked into The Feathers.

Chapter Twenty

Vic wasn't sure if she'd ever seen such vivid colours in the UK — if she had, she certainly didn't remember. The sky was crisp, baby blue, the sea a bath of inviting aqua. What's more, the clifftops and fields surrounding them were such a rich shade of green that Vic might as well have been living in a Famous Five story. With every step the group strode along the coastal path, with each bend, descent and ascent, the route ahead was gradually, beautifully revealed.

Today, instead of turning right on the coastal path at the bottom of the garden, they'd gone left. Vic had already driven a car out to the finish point, 11 miles down the track, with Kat following to drive her back. Ahead of her were Stevie, Tash and Stu, all three of them with their hoodies tied around their waists already, exposing their pale arms to the lunchtime sun.

Stu said something and all three laughed.

Vic smiled — her wife seemed in good spirits this morning.

Laura nudged Vic. "Penny for them. Five pence if they're really juicy."

They were walking a good five paces behind the leading group.

"Very dull. I'd save your money."

"I'll be the judge of that. You looked deep in thought whatever it was." Laura brushed her long dark hair off her face and hopped on one foot. She dislodged some gravel from her trainer before falling back into step with Vic.

"Not really — you give me too much credit." A rueful grin spread across Vic's features and she readjusted her glasses. "I was just thinking how great nature is. And then how old my thoughts are. Do you think it's only a matter of time before I start to rush home for Countdown?"

"I already do that — don't you?" Laura grinned. "But well done on choosing this place — it's an amazing location."

"Don't thank me, thank Stevie. You know what she's like with stuff like this — ruthlessly efficient."

"I know." Laura bumped Vic's hip with her own. "But I'm being nice and giving you some credit for choosing such a great wife."

Vic smiled. "Thanks, I think."

The pair walked on for a few seconds in amicable silence, the only sound the scraping of their shoes on the dry, sandy path, dust flicking up every few seconds and rising up unseen into their airways.

"It's all a bit more civilised than ten years ago isn't it?" Laura broke the silence. "I think we only left the house to go to the pub then, didn't we?"

Up ahead, the other three were singing a hiking song and performing exaggerated skipping as they linked arms and screeched 'Vol-der-eeeee, vol-der-raaaah, my knapsack on my back!'

Tash turned and waved an arm at them to join in.

Laura and Vic smiled obediently, but ignored the call to action.

Vic remembered the way Stevie looked ten years ago and the moment when her blonde hair suddenly shimmered for her. She remembered wondering why she was feeling jittery and tongue-tied around her old friend and then realised with shuddering clarity what those feelings meant.

Vic recalled being terrified of saying or acting on it, for fear Stevie would just laugh at her. But when Vic had approached Stevie, fuelled with a healthy slug of Dutch courage, Stevie hadn't rebuffed her. In fact, more than that, Stevie had been more than open to the idea, and within hours they'd been naked in Vic's king-size bed, laughing at the improbability of the situation — friends of ten years suddenly getting jiggy.

"We're like Monica and Chandler!" Stevie had espoused in her lilting Scouse accent — and indeed they were.

They'd slept together on the final night of a tumultuous weekend, then sat silently opposite each other through the following morning's strained breakfast in their hired Welsh holiday cottage, rain drumming on the roof. Slinging glances and trading winks across the toast and marmalade, they had managed to remain under the radar, which is exactly where they wanted to be until they'd worked out whether or not this was *something*. Vic had been sure this definitely *was* something, even at such an early stage.

"Seems such a long time ago," Laura said, breaking into Vic's thoughts. "I can't imagine my life without Tash and the kids, like it was back then — I've got a family now, it's who I am. And if you'd asked me to predict that ten years ago, I wouldn't have been able to. I was only just getting over sleeping with Kat."

Vic noticed she mumbled the last bit.

"I was just thinking about that — thinking how I was grateful to you for taking the spotlight off me and Stevie last time." Vic patted Laura on the back. "So thanks again," she said, laughing.

Laura shook her head and shuddered. "I don't think about it for years — I mean *years*, sometimes not even when I see Kat. But then I come on this weekend and it's like it happened yesterday." Laura looked down and kicked the gravel. "Just got to get through the next 48 hours and then I can forget about it till another ten years' time."

"It'll be a breeze," Vic said, wondering again why Laura hadn't just told Tash. But then, she was hardly one to be dishing out relationship advice.

* * *

Up ahead, Stu and Stevie were discussing the various merits of running-shoe brands — Stu was a vociferous Nike ambassador while Stevie favoured New Balance. Tash, meanwhile, had only just started running regularly, so tuned out of the conversation when it got too technical. She spun around and saw Laura and Vic deep in conversation, so left them to it.

Tash gulped down the sunshine, loving the way it felt on her skin, how it tasted, the way it smelt. Her skin tingled as her body loosened, spurred on by the fact she was here with no kids and no responsibilities — just her, Laura and good friends. Tash allowed herself a grin — she'd come a long way since the days of her marriage to Simon and the despair that had left her in. She'd managed to turn her life around and that was all thanks to Laura. *Her Laura.*

She still remembered the first time they'd made love in her bed, three dates in. On their first date, they had gone for coffee. On the second, they'd ventured out for dinner. However, for the third date, Tash had shipped her two young daughters off to their grandparents for the weekend and invited Laura over for dinner, fully understanding what the dessert would be.

Tash had served up lamb shanks and chocolate mousse before inviting Laura into her bed. When Laura's dark hair slid down her pale, naked body, Tash had shaken like she'd never shaken before. When Laura's fingers had filled her and circled her clitoris, Tash had thought she might die. She hadn't, though. Instead, she came harder than she'd ever come in her life before, clinging to Laura. And she hadn't stopped since.

Suddenly, the world made sense and she'd realised where she'd been going wrong all her life. Sex before had been adequate, sometimes pleasurable, but often lacking any form of climax. But this — this blew her mind. And when she'd returned the favour to Laura, it affected her almost as much — she could feel her juices flowing as Laura's smooth, sensuous body writhed and exploded beneath her.

That she'd managed to snag herself such a woman filled Tash with pride. Sometimes, it still amazed Tash she could have got it so wrong for the first 35 years of her life. Although, as she did remind herself, it wasn't all wrong — she did come out of her marriage with two beautiful daughters.

She drank in more of the sea view, watching the waves crash against the rocks below as she peered over the edge. Hearing footsteps, she turned to see Laura next to her, a massive grin on her face.

"What's a gorgeous woman like you doing on a clifftop like this?" Laura's smile was wider than the Humber Bridge.

"Waiting for you, clearly," Tash replied. She leaned in and gave Laura a kiss on the lips, stopping only when Vic cleared her throat next to them.

"Sorry!" Tash took Laura's hand and they fell into

step beside Vic. "Sometimes she's just too gorgeous not to act there and then."

Vic held up both palms in front of her. "Far be it from me to stand in the way of love. Carry on, carry on..."

Chapter Twenty-One

Geri and Kat sat in the main bar with their pints of Peroni, feeling smug to be doing so on a Saturday lunchtime.

"Now I really feel like I'm on holiday." Geri took a sip of her pint and wiped the condensation from the vase-like glass as she sat it on her Peroni beermat. Order made her happy.

"Me too — drinking on a Saturday lunchtime, how terribly naughty." Kat took her first sip and grinned from ear to ear.

Geri ran her hand through her hair. "I wonder what the others are up to right now."

"Not sitting in a pub drinking beer," Kat said.

"No, they're probably singing that annoying camping song — vol-der-ree, vol-der-rah?"

"I like that one."

"Loser." Geri looked around the bar.

At the table opposite a young couple had just arrived, him with a pint and her with a white wine. They were looking at the food menu which made Geri's stomach growl with hunger. She picked up their menu and ran her finger down a list of pub classics. On the stereo, Kylie was singing about having someone stuck in her head.

"So what do you reckon about Vic and Stevie?" Kat glanced across at Geri who'd just decided on the fish and chips even though it listed the calorie count on the menu — a whopping 1,125. She blocked that fact out, then shook her head at Kat's question.

"Jeez, I dunno — isn't this what we all dreaded happening when they first got together? But I think they'll get through it. They have to. They're my rock. They're who I measure everybody else's relationship against."

"There's still Ellen and Portia." Kat took another sip of her beer. "Flying the lezza flag."

"Yeah but they're celebrities, they're *bound* to split up at some point — isn't that inevitable in Hollywood? I wasn't *waiting* for Vic and Stevie to split up. *At all...*" Geri frowned as she said this. "But I might be more upset than when my mum and dad split up. They always seemed so right together, whereas my mum and dad..."

"...Apart from the initial weirdness," Kat countered.

"My mum and dad have always been weird..." Geri said, which received an eye roll from Kat.

Geri took a moment to chuckle at her own joke. "Yes, there was initial weirdness but we all got over that soon enough. Now they just... are." Geri sat back in her seat. "But then, don't ask me, I'm not exactly the expert on long-term relationships, am I?"

Kat snorted. "You got over six months once, didn't you?"

"Ha bloody ha," Geri said. "If they do split up, there's clearly no hope. But I still have faith. It's whether Stevie can forgive Vic for putting her hands in someone else's pants, isn't it?"

Kat choked on her beer at Geri's no-nonsense assessment.

"Anyway, enough of other people — what's going on with you? And quick while you can be honest with me before Abby gets here." Geri twisted in her seat and invaded Kat's space so she had nowhere to hide.

Predictably, Kat went on the defensive. "I could be honest if Abby was here." Kat gulped more lager.

"Slow down there, cowgirl." Geri nodded at her pint.

"Oh, don't you bloody start," Kat bit back, her mood souring by the second.

Geri was perplexed. "What the fuck is going on with you?" Geri frowned. "You're drinking, you're not drinking, you disappear off the face of the planet and now you're a fucking basket case when I ask you a simple question." Geri gave Kat a puzzled look. "Please explain..."

And so, Kat decided she would. "I lost my job." Kat cast her gaze downwards and ran her index finger along the wooden table in front of her.

"When?"

Kat focused on her finger. "Three months ago. Three and a half now, actually." She stared straight ahead.

Geri exhaled loudly. "Three months? *Three months?!*" Geri repeated. "But I've... we've spoken in the last three months. I've tried to get you to come out in the last three months and I thought it was because you were busy *at work*..."

Kat shrugged. "Yeah, well... I *was* busy. And then I got made redundant and marched out of the building that afternoon with a cardboard box. And that was it."

"Wow," Geri said, taking it all in. "I'm sorry." She knew what Kat's job meant to her — like hers, it was a defining part of her character, of who she was.

"Did you get a payout?"

Kat nodded. "Yeah, I did okay. I'm not destitute or anything..."

"I didn't mean that..."

"...I know..."

"...And anyway, you know I'm the last one to come to for a loan."

"I know." Kat licked her lips. "Yeah I got money and three months' gardening leave. Only I don't have a garden and, well, it seems I'm now depressed. At least, that's what my therapist said."

"Therapist?" Geri wasn't a big fan.

"Yes, therapist — and before you say it, I know what you're thinking, so please don't."

Geri stayed silent, which said enough.

Kat crossed her legs and smoothed down her jeans on her slim thighs.

"Anyway, yes, I'm in therapy, I'm depressed, I'm on antidepressants. And I'm jobless. All in all, I'm a real catch." Kat smiled ruefully. "And if I drink too much it might interfere with the pills but if I don't drink, what else am I going to do?" A shrug. "You see my problem?"

Geri leant over and gave Kat a hug — it wasn't their usual pattern, but this wasn't usual news. Geri smelt Kat's familiar Ralph Lauren perfume as she leant in and held on to her friend for far longer than normal rules allowed. Normal had long since left the building.

"Why didn't you say anything?" Geri settled back into her place.

Kat gave her a look that said 'Would you?'

Geri took the point. "It certainly explains why Abby's been so jumpy with your drinking. I thought you'd told her about last time and she was trying to save you the same embarrassment again."

"Well, that too," Kat said. "She's been brilliant actually — holding me together, getting me off the couch and back into the world."

"And let me guess — she wasn't too keen on coming here after your stories."

"Not really." Kat shook her head. "But I wanted to come to see everyone. It wouldn't have been the same otherwise." She paused, put both elbows on the table and rested her chin on top of her clasped hands. "So there you go, soul bared. Feel free to spread the good news — that way I don't have to."

Geri smiled sadly and rubbed Kat's back. "Well now I know, there's no escaping me. I'm going to come round to get you off the sofa too. And of course I'll tell everyone else if you want me to..."

"...If it comes up — don't make a big deal of it."

"Sure." Geri paused. "Only it kind of is a big deal, don't you think?"

Kat looked over to the door where she saw Abby striding in: saved by the bell. Kat gave Geri a look that told her this conversation was over and slipped on a smile.

Behind Abby, two nut-brown cyclists followed her into the bar, removing their helmets as they walked, their small black shoes click-clacking on the bare wooden floorboards.

"Hey, babe — all done?" Kat got up and gave Abby a kiss on the lips.

"Not really. I need to do some other bits and a buggered phone isn't helping." Abby tried but failed to hide her scowl — she clearly wasn't a woman who forgave in a hurry.

"Sorry," Geri said, thinking unkind thoughts.

Abby waved her hand. "It's happened, now it's time for wine," she said. "Am I driving back?"

Kat shook her head. "No — I'll save myself for later, you have a wine with your lunch." She indicated the menu. "Choose what you want and I'll get the drinks. Spritzer?"

"Yeah — but with soda..." Abby said, pulling out a chair.

"I *know*..." Kat replied.

* * *

After lunch in The Feathers, Geri, Kat and Abby took a tour of the village, which, if they'd walked at London pace, would probably have been completed in 20 minutes. On this lazy Easter Saturday though, they managed to spin it out for nearly two hours. Abby bought a silver necklace in a jewellery store, Kat made jokes about having no money, and Geri picked up eight Smarties Easter eggs for the group.

The crowd in the village had picked up mid-afternoon and they found they could no longer walk three abreast on the pavement to chat, with a steady stream of Saturday shoppers and buggies cruising the area at a relaxed pace. This tactic suited Abby, however, who left Geri and Kat to catch up while she drifted behind them, an iPhone in each hand answering emails and making calls while she could.

Kat seemed to be used to this sort of behaviour, but Geri made a mental note to never get together with a captain of industry.

* * *

Once back at the house, Abby disappeared to their room for a power nap, claiming the two glasses of wine had gone straight to her head.

Meanwhile, Geri and Kat unloaded the supplies they'd picked up in the village before retreating to the lounge to soak up the relative calm with a coffee.

Geri settled into one end of the large sofa facing the panoramic view, wiggling her toes and flexing her shoulders as she got comfortable.

Kat took the other end but both women could still kick their legs out without touching the other, such was its size.

"So how you feeling today — is it lifting the depression being here?" Geri asked.

"Well, I'm not thinking about it so much so I guess it is — change of scene and all that. But it's not real life, not what happens to me on a daily basis, is it?"

Geri looked thoughtful as she sucked her top lip. "You need a massive sofa and a new view, clearly."

"I think I might need more than that."

"Have you been applying for jobs?"

Kat shook her head, her short dark hair not moving with the motion. "I just don't feel up to it. I feel like... I don't know really. Numb. My shrink said it's not to do with just losing the job, that there must be some other part to it. She wants to go into my childhood but that shit's never appealed to me. Too much to uncover."

"She might have a point, then."

"That's what Abby said."

From not knowing Abby, Geri's opinion of her was going up by the hour (if you discounted the phone addiction). It sounded to Geri like she'd had a gutful of Kat to cope with and she'd done so admirably.

"Anyway, enough about me. I've been doing way too

much talking lately," Kat said, leaning down to retrieve her coffee from her feet. "Tell me more about you and women far too young to be your girlfriend."

Now it was Geri's turn to shake her head. "You know, all you couples, I'm sure you're living vicariously through me. I can't promise to check their age before sleeping with the next lucky punter, either. I can't help it if young women find me attractive — it's just the way of the world."

"Do you flash your badge at them first or your cleavage?" Kat put one leg underneath her.

"No need," Geri said, framing her face with both hands. "With these chiselled good looks I'm onto a winner in the first place. Then the badge usually seals the deal. Unless they're on the run."

"Or they see your hair all frizzy in the morning and run of their own accord." Kat smiled as she sipped her coffee. She heard Abby shouting her name from upstairs, so put her cup on the side table and swung her feet onto the carpet.

"That's not until at least date four." Geri paused. "Something I said?"

Kat pointed towards the ceiling. "Abs just shouted me — better go and see what she wants." Kat disappeared through the lounge door.

Geri finished her coffee and stared out into the view, getting lost in thoughts of moving here and opening up her dairy fudge factory. How hard could it be?

Her thoughts were interrupted a few minutes later

by the doorbell — so much for enjoying some peace and quiet. She padded out to the hall and saw a short-haired figure through the wobbly glass on the other side that she recognised instantly. She opened the oak door to find Darren grinning back at her, Louis Vuitton bag in hand.

Where Stu was tall, solid and bald, Darren was slightly shorter and bronzed. Geri would lay bets that any hair on his body he considered superfluous had been waxed off, as Darren was no stranger to pain in the name of beauty. He also had a thick head of brown hair which was styled to perfection, and today was clad in blue jeans, black scuffed boots, a black top and black leather jacket.

In fact, Geri and Darren's style was not so far off each other and they could often be found comparing notes on clothing and beauty products. Darren was often told he looked like the lead singer of an art-college band, which did nothing for his modesty.

"Hello, trouble." Geri hugged Darren on the doorstep.

"And it's lovely to see you too," he said over her shoulder.

"Just telling it like it is." Geri stepped back as he put his bag down. "I'm pleased to see you and I'm sure Stu will be too once he's forgiven you for turning up late."

She leant up, grabbed Darren's right cheek between her thumb and index finger and gave him a squeeze. "How could he fail to love this face," Geri said in a see-saw voice that made Darren slap her hand away.

"Judging from his messages, fairly easily." Darren looked around. "You home alone?"

"Almost — Kat's upstairs with Abby, but the rest are still out walking."

"Sounds like I timed it just right, then," he said. "How did you get out of it?"

Geri shrugged. "Kat, Abby and I slunk out to the local village pub and fuelled the local economy instead by lunching and shopping. There's only so much walking a girl can take. Anyhow, enough chat — cup of tea and I'll show you the house?" Geri took Darren by the hand and led him towards the kitchen. "Your hands are baby soft," she added.

"Gay hands, darling," Darren said, doing jazz hands either side of his head. "In the fine print." He paused. "And, excuse me, a cup of tea? You got anything stronger?"

Geri opened the fridge door and pulled out a bottle of Peroni.

Darren's eyes widened as he shook his head in alarm. "Er, hello, have we met?" He gave her a quizzical look.

"Oh yeah — I forgot for a moment. Been in a houseful of lesbians too long."

"I bet Stu's forgotten, too." Darren disappeared and Geri heard him rummaging in his bag, before reappearing a minute later with some Prosecco and a bottle of vodka. "I brought less carb-laden drinks for me but you go ahead, I know what your tribe's like." Darren walked over and put his swag in the fridge.

Geri raised an eyebrow. She hoped they were going to see happy Darren later and not bitchy-queen Darren who had a tendency to piss off all those around him. She turned to see him grinning at her and holding up his right hand, currently clenched into a fist.

"Guess what else I brought to the party, as well as my style, charm and charisma?" Darren looked terribly pleased with himself.

"Tell me," Geri said. She wasn't one for guessing games.

"You're not even going to try to guess?" Darren pouted at her.

"A wild guess," Geri said, scratching her cheek. "But could it be cocaine?"

Darren winked and opened his fist to reveal some neatly folded tiny paper packages.

"Ta da!" he gestured camply, before putting the drugs back in his jacket pocket, hanging it on a dining chair and crossing the kitchen. Darren picked up the kettle and flipped open its lid.

"Maybe I will kick off with a cup of tea first after all." His voice was somewhat drowned out as the water hit the kettle.

"Stevie is going to *love* you." Geri bent over and grabbed two mugs from the dishwasher. "She was just saying yesterday morning that she hasn't had drugs in ages and now here you are like a prince charming. It's a fairytale ending."

"Fairytales are my speciality," Darren said. "Wouldn't have thought it was up Stevie's alley, though. Kat, yes — but Stevie?"

Geri waved her hand. "Oh, she won't do any. We both decided we'd rather spend our money on pasta bowls."

Darren smiled. "I'm sure that makes sense on planet lesbian." He swiftly turned his attention to doing some squats while the kettle boiled.

Geri had seen such behaviour many times before so she didn't even comment. As Darren often pointed out, in the battle for thighs of steel, there wasn't a moment to waste.

Once tea was made, Geri took him on a tour of the house which received the required oohs and aahs from the main room as well as from his bedroom, with its king-size bed and en-suite bathroom. Darren tested the bed and gave Geri a thumbs up.

"It'll get a good workout later," he told her.

Geri grimaced. "I'm sure it can't wait."

The sound of the door slamming and raised voices alerted them to the fact the walkers had returned.

Geri started towards the door, turning in the doorway. "You coming?" She was greeted by Darren's arse as he bent over to get something from his bag.

He turned to face her, smoothing his black top down over his flat, toned stomach as he did. "Can you send Stu up first?" Darren looked bashful. "I'd rather he was mad at me alone and not in front of everyone."

Geri nodded and pushed herself off the doorframe. She trotted towards the top of the stairs before taking them two at a time and nearly bowling over an advancing Stu in the process. She made a mental note to herself again to slow down.

"Jesus!" Stu muttered when he recovered his balance. "Where's the fucking fire?"

"Sorry! Sorry!" Geri said again, giving him a hug before recoiling. "Eugh, you're all sweaty! But you'll like me in a minute — go have a look in your room."

Stu narrowed his eyes and gave her a look. "Have you put bananas in my bed again?"

"That was a one-time only special, never to be repeated. In contrast, I think you might like what's in your bed this time..." Geri skipped past him before he could ask more questions.

Stu took the stairs two at a time and padded along the carpeted hallway in his socked feet. When he reached his room, the door was open and Darren was lying on the bed with his top off, his hands clasped behind his head, his face cracked with a smile.

"Took you long enough. I've been waiting all day," Darren said, grinning.

Chapter Twenty-Two

The group arrived at The Flowerpot at 6.30pm, Tash having rung ahead to book a table. They were all determined to enjoy their penultimate night together — Saturday night, the big night out.

"So, is it too early for shots?" Darren's voice boomed over the music in the pub — somebody working the jukebox was a fan of Elton John. "Who's in?" he asked excitedly, fishing his wallet out of his pocket.

Vic was the first disdaining voice, just as Kat's hand shot up in the air.

"How about we eat first? Let's start off sedate and try not to get chucked out till at least after 9pm," Vic said.

Darren rolled his eyes only half-mockingly. "Okay, mum," he said. "Food first. But I hope they serve salad in this part of the world as no chips are passing this gay's lips."

"I'd forgotten what a delight you are to eat out with," Geri told him, pursing her lips. "We'll get you a salad, rabbit boy. But I'm going to waft my chips right under your nose."

"Waft away!" Darren blew on his fingernails. "My body is a temple."

"A temple of doom," Stu added.

Geri took the food order up to the bar where she encountered the cute barmaid from Thursday. Her cuteness was still intact: short dark hair, black polo shirt, tight-fitting jeans, sexy smile. Geri licked her lips and within a couple of minutes she'd discovered the bartender's name was TJ, she was local, and that she had an endearing dimple and piercing brown eyes.

Geri gave the order and added a drink on for TJ, who gave her a coy look in return. What were the chances of finding a lesbian barmaid in a tiny village in Devon? Geri was unsure, but her gaydar didn't often fail. Geri gave TJ a wink as she left the bar and returned to the table with cutlery in hand.

"Having a nice chat?" Kat said.

"Yes, thanks." Geri sat down on her dark wooden chair. "See what you reckon next time you're at the bar, but I think Stevie might be right."

"Interesting." Kat drummed her fingers on the table in an agitated manner.

* * *

When it arrived, the food exceeded expectations, the burgers juicy, the fish fresh and herb-loaded. Wine arrived to accompany it — a chewy Malbec for the meat-eaters, a crisp Chablis to go with the fish.

"Have you spoken to your kids today?" Stevie asked Tash midway through the meal, who nodded mutely while chewing a mouthful of food.

"Yep, called them when we got in. They seemed happy enough — Simon had taken them shopping and bought them whatever they wanted to eat for the evening. I think the man's actually learning, miracle of miracles." Tash was wearing a green top that brought out the colour of her eyes and complemented her red hair perfectly.

"I think it's great to have kids," Darren piped up.

Stu, who had already finished his burger and chips, choked on his wine. "Something you want to tell me, dear?"

Darren smiled at the waves his comment had caused. "I'm just saying — look around the table, who's going to look after all of us when we're old and grey? Our cats and dogs?"

"We're happy to pimp ours out if you like — our kids, not our cat. But they've got to look after us before they look after you." Laura had finished her fish too and was watching Tash eat hers with hungry eyes.

"I thought you were serious there for a minute," Stu told Darren, looking flustered. He paused. "We have been thinking about this though — not the child-slavery bit — but the whole getting old and being gay. I mean, what happens to older gays? There's got to be a market for gay retirement homes. Me and Darren are going to run one when we're older." He sat back in his seat then gestured round the group. "Discount rates for mates, obviously."

"Think about it," Darren said, looking skywards as if looking at an invisible departure board, painting the picture with his hand. He was still eating his fish and salad but had rested his cutlery on his plate. "State of the art TVs, on-site gym, huge cinema, pool, swim-up bar, boys in tiny shorts..."

"They already have that — it's called Mykonos or Sitges." Kat made a face.

"Yeah, it sounds more like a holiday resort than an OAP home. Have you been to one lately?" Abby added.

"Plus, I think we might want some things done differently. I'm all for the swim-up bar and the on-site gym and cinema, but I want my drinks served to me by scantily clad lovelies like a Carry On film," Tash added, laughing.

"Wow — you guys are certainly projecting your old age well. If my eyes are well enough to see these ladies and my hips agile enough to swim up to the bar, I'll be happy," Abby said.

Nods of approval all round.

"True," Geri said. "But this is fantasy retirement. Plus, Stu's paying for it so I'm 100% in." She turned to Tash as she chewed her food, and swallowed before continuing. "Much as I love your kids, I'm not sure I can rely on them wholly. So it's off to Stu's nursing home we go."

"So where's it going to be?" Vic asked, dipping one of her chips in ketchup and popping it in her mouth. She'd thought about going for something other than the burger but remembered how good it had tasted on Thursday and so abandoned that idea. Vic was a creature of habit.

"We were thinking somewhere posh and by the river so we can go for waterside strolls with our bespoke ivory walking sticks. Greenwich maybe?" Darren said. "Or perhaps Highgate."

"That's not near the river," Geri pointed out.

"...And it might be cheaper to widen your search to somewhere out of London. Cheaper, more space," Tash said. The whole group were swept up in the idea now.

"What about Southend?" Laura said in a moment of clarity. "Fuck the river — you can have the sea! Fish and chips, candyfloss and honeycomb in bags all year round."

"And a million Essex queens glinting in gold going up and down the pier on the little train. I love it!" Stu guzzled more wine as Darren raised an eyebrow beside him.

"So let me get this straight..."

"...Or not," Geri quipped.

"...Or not," Darren smiled. "While everyone else is planning their retirement to Cornwall or a new life down under, we're all getting hot under the collar about a nursing home in Southend?" He stretched the final word out like an elastic band, his gaze roaming around the table daring anyone to speak. Nobody did. Darren clapped his hands together.

"People people people!" he grinned. "We can do better than that, can't we?"

"Not if my pension pot is anything to go by," Kat said. "A room with a view might be the best I can hope for."

Stu and Geri exchanged glances.

"I'm still gunning for Southend," Stu added. "But no florals. Strict rule. And none of those terrible chairs with the wooden armrests that look like they were made for you to die in."

"Deal," said Tash, scraping the last mouthful of sea bass onto her fork. "And who knows, if it's in Southend, maybe we *can* employ my lovely daughters. Although don't come running to me when they don't show up for work on time."

With their retirement plans sorted, Stu focused his attention on Kat while the rest of the group chatted and finished their food. She seemed fragile, on edge, as if anything could tip her over the edge. He leant over to Geri.

"Did you speak to Kat today, by the way?"

Geri nodded.

"And?"

Geri swallowed and leant in closer. "She lost her job three months ago and she's on antidepressants."

Stu's face dropped. "What the fuck?" he whispered. "Shit, no wonder she looks out of sorts. She okay?"

Geri gave him a look. "What do you think?"

Stu licked his lips and wondered what he could do for his friend. Suddenly it came to him.

"Too early for shots now?" he asked, checking his watch. "Just after 8pm and we've eaten. Who's in?"

Kat's face shone once more; Abby's was the opposite.

"Babe..." Abby began.

Kat barely glanced at her. "Woo hoo, shots!" She paused. "Could do with another pint to chase it, too."

Stu dipped into the booze kitty, took the drinks orders and disappeared to the bar just as Geri's favourite barmaid arrived to clear the plates.

"Everything okay for you?" she directed to Geri, her broad local slur softening every syllable. In response, Geri turned on a smile that had its own crew, lighting and stage production — hell, it should have had its own show on the Reality channel. The object of its attention looked suitably dazzled.

"More than okay — perfect. Compliments to the chef — and to the server, of course." Geri cranked up her charm offensive, fixing her gaze on TJ and ignoring the amused glances around the table.

From the wide smile on TJ's face, it was working.

"We're ordering shots — you want to take a break and join us?" Geri continued.

TJ let the offer roll across her brain but rejected it just as quickly. "No time right now." She began stacking plates expertly on her toned forearm. "But ask me later and you might get a different answer." TJ flicked her long lashes Geri's way.

Now it was Geri's turn to be dazzled. "I may well just do that."

As TJ walked away, Laura nudged her old friend. "I may well just do that," she mimicked, clutching her sides. "I'd forgotten the Gimpy charm offensive — top marks, mate, top marks."

Geri turned and glared at Laura, pinning Laura by the chest with her right index finger.

"One mention of the word Gimpy in her presence and I won't be accountable for my actions. *Capiche*?" she asked, the last word in Italian brogue.

"Sorry Gimps — promise."

* * *

By 9pm the group's night was in full swing, desserts eaten and a second round of shots lined up at the bar. At the table, Abby was proving to her receptive audience that she'd ingested far too much management speak into her vocabulary, talking about how to leverage off the failing relationship of one of her friends.

Stevie put another cross in her Abby con pile. Abby struck Stevie as calculating and ambitious — and she meant that in a positive way. Stevie had always known she wanted to be a teacher, always known she wanted to work with kids. Similarly, she could see Abby had always wanted to be in management, to have people listen when she spoke, to hold a position of power. Even though their career fields were totally different, perhaps the two of them were not so dissimilar after all.

Stevie turned now to her wife of three years, her partner of ten, and felt a wave of love for her. Maybe that was because she'd shared her profiteroles with her after

Stevie had finished her dessert of tarte tatin. Maybe it was because, even though she was a solicitor, she didn't use the words 'leverage' or 'bifurcate' in everyday conversation. Or maybe it was because she could see things from a slightly altered angle and, right now, staring into the all-too-evident cracks in other people's lives, Stevie reckoned it was time to start plastering over the one crack in hers. She leant over and kissed Vic on the cheek.

"What was that for?" Vic asked.

"Just because," Stevie said.

Vic's caution failed to lift.

* * *

Kat might not call the shots but she could certainly drink them as she proved now, arriving back at the table with a tray of tiny drinks. Obediently, they all picked up their tequilas and sambucas, applied salt and lemon where necessary, licked, slammed, sucked, winced. Before Stevie even knew what was happening, another glass of wine had appeared in front of her, another shot and the night flipped to fast-forward, taking on a life of its own.

What did the locals think of their pub being infiltrated by tourists? Or was it something they saw every weekend? The place was stacked high with young men sporting tousled blond hair and faded jeans, looking like they'd surfed in direct from the beach. A few young couples were dotted around sharing a romantic Saturday night dinner and, by the door, a foursome of 60-somethings were enjoying their steaks with red wine, faces flushed, cheeks pinned into grins. This was how life should be — fine wine, fine food, fine friends.

Behind them, sitting at the only other larger table in the pub were a group of what Stevie assumed were tourists, too — either that or they were local royalty. Three men and three women who all exemplified the term 'power-couple'. It'd been applied to Stevie and Vic before now, but they'd have to bow down to this altar of prestige.

The men wore pristine shirts, litres of expensive cologne, shimmering gold watches; the women had miles of shiny hair, yards of red lips, hundreds of white teeth, a blur of cleavage. Stevie caught one of the brunettes casting a glance their way and couldn't help but smile. For a moment she imagined trading places with her and playing the dutiful wife and mother, doing the dinner parties, wearing the sparkly dresses. Then she frowned, shuddered and kissed Vic once again. The brunette raised a single eyebrow and smiled.

When Stevie tuned back into her table's conversation, the talk had turned to who had the sexiest job.

"Got to be Gimp... Geri," said Stu, winning points with the group's lone singleton for the nomination as well as for correcting her name. "I mean, CID sergeant — what's not to love? The badge, the power, the handcuffs..." This last comment brought whistles from the crowd.

"Brought them with you for later?" Tash asked Geri, laughing.

"Keep it down!" Geri cast an apologetic eye towards the bar. "Anyway, you're way off the mark. Stu and Darren work in PR and that means free drinks and parties, so they get my vote. Plus, being gay is part of the job description — who doesn't love that?"

"Works for me most days." Darren raised his wine glass in approval.

Stevie pulled her 'disagree' face and held up one hand.

"Permission to speak granted," Geri said.

Stevie smiled graciously. "I know her job isn't the best paid or the most powerful, but if I had to swap jobs for a day with someone, I'd go for Tash."

At this, Tash perked up visibly: she'd been squinting out of one eye for the past ten minutes.

"Me?" she said softly.

"Absolutely!" Stevie said. "You get to nose round other people's houses all day. You change people's lives by getting them their dream home. Plus, you clearly get to meet some hot clients while you do it, too. If I had to have a career change, I'd be an estate agent."

"I hope she doesn't meet too many other hot clients," Laura said, sipping her bottle of Heineken.

"None that match up to you, gorgeous," Tash replied, kissing her girlfriend on the cheek before turning to address Stevie. "Thanks for the vote of confidence but I can tell you it's not all glamour. But I do love seeing inside people's houses. It's the perfect job for a nosey-beak."

"No votes for HR director, then?" Abby grinned at her own joke. "Don't all rush at once..."

Geri cleared her throat. "I agree that my job has a certain sex appeal," she said, leaning on her elbows. "But if I could choose my ideal job for a partner, it'd be a chef. Someone who could make me pancakes for breakfast and it not seem like a big deal. Someone who could just whip up a plate of something delicious at the drop of a hat. That would be awesome. Someone like Nigella perhaps..." Geri stared off into the distance.

"We're talking about jobs around the table, not who you'd like to shag." Stevie rolled her eyes.

* * *

All this job talk made Kat twitchy, so she headed to the bar and ordered another pint of Rattler. She didn't ask for the drinks kitty — paying out of her own pocket would mean fewer pairs of concerned eyes draped on her. She was served by an older woman with curly brown hair that bounced as she bent to retrieve a glass from a shelf below the bar.

"Looks like a fun night," the woman told Kat, indicating the jocularity at the table.

Kat nodded, watching the pint glass fill with the rust-coloured liquid and feeling the saliva flood her mouth in anticipation. "Yeah — weekend away."

The woman smiled as she flicked the cider tap the other way to give the top a final fizz. "You over from London?" Her accent was surprisingly West Country-free.

"Most of us — renting a house on the cliff."

"Tom and Grace's house probably? I love that place, great views." The woman set the pint down on a beer mat on the bar.

Kat paid her the money and reached out for the pint. She was already drunk but she also knew this wouldn't be her final drink. Tonight's path was already becoming clear and it ended in oblivion. It was just a question of when Kat would reach it.

At the table, Vic was speaking to the rest of the group and all, bar Stu and Darren, were listening intently. The lighting in the pub was too bright, making Tash squint as she focused. The jukebox, meanwhile, had taken a slightly more modern turn, now churning out a selection of hits from the 90s.

It was currently playing a track that made Kat frown as she tried to remember it — who had a secret smile again? She plucked her phone from her pocket and hit the Shazam app. It whirred for less than a minute, then told her it was Semisonic in 1999. She wondered again how pub quizzes worked anymore now everyone had smartphones.

Her attention shifted back to Darren and Stu who were having a mutely animated conversation and looking down into their laps. She fixed her focus, then saw Darren get up and go to the loo while giving Stu a conspiratorial wink. He returned, sat down next to Stu and like a professional tag-team, Stu seamlessly made his trip to the bathroom look routine and anything but a cocaine-run.

Stu motioned to Kat as he passed her and she nodded. He gave her a wink and sauntered towards the loo, his long legs encased in jeans, his blue T-shirt sitting just-so on his torso. Within a minute Stu was out and approached Kat at the bar.

"Not coming to sit back down with us?" Stu's eyes never left Kat's face as their hands grazed each other's and Kat took the tiny package.

Kat's heart raced a little faster as it always did when she was carrying Class A drugs.

"Will do after this," she told Stu, licking her lips.

"Same again?" he asked as she walked past him, brushing his shoulder.

"Why not?"

Kat pushed open the door to the ladies which she imagined had once been a brilliant shade of white but now had peeling paint with a mass of smudged grey fingerprints. The toilets were strip-lit and all three were empty — Kat chose the cubicle on the right.

She rolled a note, shook out some powder onto the top of the cistern, flushed the toilet and with the noise of the flush in her ears, snorted her line, chasing the runaway flecks to finish. She stood, performed a final power-sniff and flushed the toilet again before stepping back into the light as if nothing ever happened. Whoever perpetuated the myth that drugs were glamorous had clearly never done them off the top of toilets like most people Kat knew.

She stepped up to the sink and washed her hands,

studying her face in the mirror. She had lines where there were none three months ago, she was sure of it.

The door opened and Stevie walked in. She was dressed in denim dungarees but, strangely, she managed to pull it off. It wasn't a trick that everyone could manage.

Stevie smiled widely but Kat's response was too slow.

"You okay, lovely?" Stevie asked, putting an arm around Kat's waist.

"Just looking at my wrinkles — this is what nearly 40 looks like."

Stevie kissed her shoulder. "All in the mind — you look gorgeous." She jigged from foot to foot. "Gotta go, I'm bursting." Stevie pushed into the middle cubicle.

Kat heard Stevie unclick her buckles, so turned on the tap to mingle the sounds. She felt the coke sinking down from her nostrils to her throat, felt her front teeth going numb, was comforted by the familiar sensation. Cocaine was what had kept her going at her former job — that and the energy drinks. To use it now as a recreational drug rather than a means to stay awake seemed almost decadent.

Kat added some more lipstick, air-kissed herself in the mirror and then, with chemical confidence beginning to thump through her veins, strode back into the pub.

Chapter Twenty-Three

Vic could tell that Kat was close to the edge when she saw her parading across the pub on her way back from the toilets. Her eyes looked wider, her stride longer, her smirk firmly in place.

Stu was getting more drinks at the bar and she chatted to him briefly as she passed. Kat sank a half pint of cider in the blink of an eye, then immediately grasped another full one. Kat turned to Abby to see if she'd registered the scene, but for the first time this weekend her girlfriend seemed to have dropped the reins and was in deep conversation with Darren.

Or rather, Darren was talking at Abby.

Kat walked back and plonked herself down next to Abby, putting her arm around her and giving her a sloppy kiss on the cheek as she did.

Darren grinned at Kat, his cheeks all Chablis splotch, his eyes alight with cocaine glitter.

"The mystery solved!" Abby told Kat, kissing her on the lips.

Kat wobbled slightly on her stool, then grinned.

"Mystery?" Kat tried to raise an eyebrow, but only succeeding in grimacing slightly.

"The mystery of the missing girlfriend."

"Just been at the bar chatting to Stu, shooting the breeze." Kat smiled through her eyes, slid one way and nearly fell off her stool.

Abby held out an arm to steady her. "You okay?" she asked, bringing her head level with Kat.

Kat nodded obediently.

It was plain to see she was anything but.

* * *

Stevie and Stu arrived back at the table together, handing out drinks to everyone and then taking up their positions. Drinks refreshed meant another round of cheers for the group and then, with everyone sitting down, conversation went retro.

"What would our university selves say about us if they could see us now?" Stevie ran her hand through her short blonde hair.

"I think they'd be impressed we were out when we're *this old*," Vic laughed, stroking her wife's back.

"They'd be impressed we could afford it, too — dinner and drinks. We forgot to drink a bottle of Martini before we left the house, though," Stevie added.

"You used to do that?" Tash asked, eyes wide. Not having been to university, she wasn't as up to speed with their previous drinking antics, although she'd heard tale of a few.

"Oh my God, I'd completely forgotten about the Martini!" Laura screwed up her face. "How on earth did our livers survive? We're all walking miracles of modern science to be here today."

"Oh, I don't know." Stevie beamed round the table. "If you'd shown me this picture 20 years ago, I'd have been ecstatic."

Tash laughed and not for the first time, she wished she'd known this group earlier in her life — not only to stop her marrying Simon, but also to understand who she was in such a supportive environment. She was glad she'd met them all eventually, though — she counted them all as her friends after five years with Laura and, she hoped, many more to come. In fact, she was even thinking about proposing to Laura now it was legal.

"Never mind 20 years ago. If the stories I've heard about ten years ago are correct, then we need to get this party started!" Darren clapped his hands together.

Tash couldn't wait to hear more stories, but clocked the look of alarm on Stu's face.

"Babe…" Stu began.

Darren talked over him. "I mean, Vic and Stevie shag for the first time, Kat and Laura shag — who's going to be the naughty one tonight? I vote for either me or perhaps Geri if they have to be single." Darren glanced at Stu, grinning.

Stu simply stared, then put his drink down on the table as quietly as he could. He was trying to stay calm but panic was seeping into his facial features.

Tash frowned. Hang on, what had Darren just said? Kat and Laura? *Her* Laura? Tash looked around the table and saw minds whirring, foreheads frowning, heads twisting, daggers flashing.

Vic was the first to speak, clearly going for the damage limitation option. "I remember ten years ago very well and yes, it was the start of something amazing for both of us. I hope this weekend is too." Vic didn't dare look to her right where Laura, Tash, Kat and Abby were sitting.

"Darren, you're a complete fuckwit." Laura's tone could cut slate.

"Yeah — that was well out of order," Kat slurred.

Tash was looking confused. "Did he just say what I think he said?" She looked from Darren, to Laura and then back to Kat. Once, twice, three times. Tash furrowed her brow and focused her attention on Laura.

"*You and Kat?*" Tash moved her index finger between the two, pendulum-like. "Since when, you and Kat?"

Laura raised her eyebrows to the ceiling. "It was a drunken mistake. *Ten* years ago. It was *nothing*."

Kat looked disgruntled at this description, but said nothing.

Darren, with exquisite timing, chose this moment to wade back in. "Oh come on, lesbians, let's not get dramatic — it was ten years ago! Ten years! You're all happily married now, so who cares?" Darren put his palms on his thighs and looked around the table. Still grinning.

Stu took the opportunity to back him up. "Exactly! Who cares what happened ten years ago? We're all adults now in happy, healthy relationships after all." His voice was sing-song. It was a long shot to style this one out, but he had to give it a try.

"I can't fucking believe this," Tash said, massaging the bridge of her nose, her brain now flooding with images she didn't want to entertain. Perhaps hearing more stories was a bad idea after all. If Tash had a headache before, it'd just quadrupled in size. A marching band was tap-dancing on her brain, a team of builders hammering behind her eyes. "*Kat? You fucked Kat?*"

Tash glared at Laura. She needed some air, to get out of this group. She needed to breathe. She scraped her chair back and her head nearly exploded with the movement. She heard Laura say her name as she left but she didn't look back. She passed the group of power couples, passed a couple having a steak and the risotto with a bottle of wine, passed the group of upmarket pensioners by the door enjoying their Saturday night.

As she reached the door she felt a presence behind her and turned around. Laura was standing not three inches from her, looking freaked. Part of Tash wanted to cup Laura's face, to tell her it would all be fine — and she really hoped it would be. But right now, Tash didn't want to look at her, didn't want to be the only one not in on the secret. She put a hand on Laura's chest and pushed firmly.

"Not now," she said. "Just... leave me. Go back, reminisce some more and work out if there are any other secrets you need to get off your chest."

Tash knew it was harsh, she knew it was in the past, but if it meant nothing, then why not tell her? That was the question playing on her mind.

* * *

Laura stood back and watched the pub door slam in her face. Were her eyes spinning in their sockets? It seemed possible right now. She was floating up and outside of her body, looking down on the wreckage of this situation, assessing the damage. She looked down to her arms, her legs, her torso, her feet — all still there. She was 50% giddy, 50% disbelief. This must be happening to someone else.

Laura focused on getting herself back into the present. Her spirit fused back into her body and then the music was turned back up and blood flowed through her system, crashing into her ears. Colours that had been on 10% now slid up to full hue, edges sharpened, as objects whizzed back into their three-dimensional realm.

Voices and laughter flooded her reality — apparently it was only her world that had just stopped. She picked up her feet which turned out to be not as leaden as she believed and twisted back to her group, who'd already lost interest and were chatting among themselves.

Pulp's Misfits was playing. Tash disliked Pulp — said that all 90s Britpop was overrated rubbish. It was an argument they'd had many times and had now agreed to disagree. But Tash wasn't here right now. She'd run off into the night TV drama-style, so Laura could enjoy Pulp in this instant without any sly looks or justification. All around her the volume got louder with laughter piercing the air, glass banging against wood, lights burning.

Stevie was first to react, seeing her approach. She got up and gave her a hug. "You okay, sweetie?"

The table looked up at Laura expectantly.

Darren couldn't quite hold Laura's gaze.

Kat couldn't either but that was because she was drunk already.

"Peachy," Laura said.

"Has she left?" Stevie asked.

"Yep. Told me not to come after her. Well done, Darren, good work." Laura spat the final few words Darren's way.

In a game display of chivalry, Stu rode to his man's rescue. "Leave it out," he said. "I know he shouldn't have said it, but he didn't know it was being kept under wraps."

Stu paused as Stevie put a consolatory arm around Laura's shoulders. "Sit down, babe, have a drink and then we can all go and find Tash. Just give her a bit of time to cool off first. Agreed?"

Laura's face ran through a gamut of emotions: punch, kick, slap, concede. She went with the last option seeing as it was the most pub- and friendship-friendly, letting Stevie guide her body to her seat and handing her a drink.

"Did she say where she was going?" Stu asked.

"She wasn't really in the mood to chat," Laura snapped. She still wanted to punch Darren but he'd slipped off somewhere, already departed the scene of the crime.

Stu was sitting with a smile on his face, jigging his knee up and down, drumming his fingers on the table top.

"Well, it's either the house or the beach. If I was feeling particularly dramatic I'd choose the beach. Did she seem dramatic?" Stu asked.

Laura ignored him for now and took another swig of her beer.

Darren returned from the toilet and touched Kat's hand.

She wobbled as she got up, drained her pint and headed to the toilet. When Kat returned, Abby chastised her for buying more cider.

However, Kat simply grinned loosely, as if the wires in her face had been cut and then restrung by a team of cowboy builders, lop-sided and off-kilter.

Kat was high and drunk, the exact combination she and Laura had managed ten years previously when they'd ended the night fucking each other at odd angles. It was the last time Laura had taken drugs. She was sure neither of them came, that they probably fell asleep before that happened. If the awkwardness of the morning after was anything to go by, Laura was sure the sex had been a disaster.

Right now, though, Kat was headed for the same

outcome she always got, performing the same circus routine they'd all come to know. Ten years ago it still seemed funny because to some extent, they were all still at it. Now, it just seemed a bit tired, faded, sepia.

Now, it made Laura want to punch her.

* * *

Geri propped herself on a stool at the bar, her trainer slipping off the foot-rail as she steadied herself, catching the side of her ankle. A hot stab of pain shot up her body and she grasped the bar's shiny golden handrail, wincing.

"Everything okay?" TJ was refilling glasses from the dishwasher.

Geri gave TJ her best Gallic shrug. "Yeah — just some lesbian dramas."

Geri froze, her brain acknowledging too late she'd just come out to the barmaid. She raised one eyebrow at TJ and wondered if this would be the last she saw of her. However, when TJ's face crinkled and her dimple shone brighter than ever, Geri realised she might just get a happy ending to this night. Her stomach flipped with the realisation and her blood hummed in her veins.

"I've seen a few of those dramas in this pub." TJ's face remained stoic and a small smile played on her lips.

"Really?" Geri intoned, leaning in conspiratorially. "Well, this is a good one tonight." She paused wondering what the next topic of conversation should be. "So what does TJ stand for?"

"Whatever you want it to stand for," TJ replied. "More to the point, why are you called Geri *and* Gimpy?"

Geri's face dropped as she realised somebody must have uttered her nickname in TJ's earshot. She was going to kill Laura when she got back from trying to find Tash.

"We'll agree to skip the name game." Geri leant over the bar. "Listen, you fancy coming back to our place? We have tons of red wine and a killer view. And crisps." She paused. "And chocolate."

Geri's knee was jigging up and down beneath the bar, her stool rocking slightly. Luckily, from the waist up which was all TJ could see, she looked a picture of unflustered cool.

"Crisps and chocolate?" TJ replied. "How could a girl refuse?"

And with that their fate for the evening was sealed, which seemed to suit both parties.

TJ leant in so their faces were just a few inches apart. "You might even get a kiss out of it," she said, before moving backwards as another customer came to stand next to Geri at the bar. The spell broken, Geri leant back, her eyes never leaving TJ.

"I hope so — I am providing crisps and chocolate." With that, Geri peacocked back to their table, her shoulders swaggering with triumph.

"Fuck me, look, it's the cat that got the cream!" Stu had seen this walk before.

Geri gave him the finger and sat down. She was still

grinning until Darren asked where the drinks were. She'd forgotten to get them. She looked suitably abashed and got back up to rectify her mistake.

Abby pushed her back to her seat with a chuckle. "Honestly, I'll go," she said. "It'll be quicker with zero flirting."

Geri grinned and sat back down, although her eyes followed Abby to the bar, and to TJ who was serving her.

TJ obviously felt the heat of Geri's stare, because after a few seconds she lifted her eyes Geri's way, smiled and shot her a wink.

Geri blushed at being caught out and turned her focus back to her friends.

She was flustered and TJ knew it.

* * *

The pub shut at midnight, an hour and a half after Laura had left to find Tash. The group were still there as TJ and her two fellow bar staff were stacking chairs, spraying tables, emptying drip trays. The pub was moving from its usual smells of lager and hot bodies, onto its night-time smell of disinfectant and polish, neither of which went very well with drinks.

Darren choked as the disinfectant got trapped in his throat and declared he was off, gathering up his coat, his face crumpled like he'd just swallowed a bluebottle.

"We have to wait for Geri." Vic put a restraining hand on his arm, which Darren immediately shook off.

"Why do we have to wait for Geri? The house is a five-minute walk and I think Geri knows the way, as, I suspect does TJ, seeing as she's local. So I think we can go without her say-so."

Vic nodded — he had a point. Besides, the smell was sticking in her throat too, even though her OCD side was glad to see the pub had a vigorous cleaning regime. She picked up her jacket from the leather bench and told the others to do the same.

Kat stood up and then promptly fell down just as quickly.

"Oh fucking hell, here's the cabaret." Darren sighed heavily.

Abby dropped to her knees, alarmed. Somehow, Kat had managed to avoid banging her head and was now attempting to stagger back upright, one hand grappling for her chair seat, head lolling. Abby's mood had gone from concern to stoic anger.

"For fuck's sake, get up," she said. She stood and surveyed her girlfriend and looked up to see everyone else focusing on her. "I've never seen her this bad before."

"We have, many times." Stu shook his head and blew his nose. "What goes up must come down."

Abby put her hands on her hips and stared around the group. "So why do you encourage it? Why give her loads of booze, drugs…"

"…keep your voice down," Darren stage-whispered.

"…If you were her *real* friends, you'd see she was in

trouble. The last thing she needs is to come to a place where the primary activity for the entire time is drinking. But no. We get here, everyone's on my back for working, Geri smashes my phone and then you all buy Kat a ton of alcohol. Perfect. No wonder she couldn't wait to come away..."

The group were stunned into silence at Abby's outburst, with Geri at the bar still unaware. Everyone stared at each other, Abby daring someone to talk and not letting her gaze drop.

Stevie was the first to pipe up. "I know you're upset and I don't blame you, but I don't think you can lay the blame with any of us," she said. "Kat's a big girl, we can't tell her what she can and can't do. Believe us, we've tried before."

Kat made a grunting sound as she tried to lever herself upwards, but her grip slipped and she slumped onto the floor again.

"Fuck," she muttered.

"I don't think now's the time for accusations — let's just get her up and get her home shall we?" Stu glared at Abby. Before she could start up again, Stu grabbed Darren and together they got Kat upright, put her arms around each of their shoulders and headed towards the door. Behind them, Stevie and Vic shrugged on their coats while Abby walked ahead in stony silence.

Once outside, Stevie shivered and Vic put an arm around her, the April air not quite warm enough for enjoying the night-time yet. The stars were blaring in the ink-black sky, no light pollution to contend with on the coast. It was a clear night, the air was still and somewhere nearby they could hear a dog barking. The only other sounds were Stu and Darren's laughter bouncing off one another, the drag of Kat's flaccid shoes and the definite crunch of their own feet on the slight incline.

Vic wagered Kat would have scuff marks on the toes of her shoes tomorrow.

"She'll be fine, you know, just needs to sleep it off," Vic told Abby as they drew level with her.

Abby nodded in response and pulled her thin jacket tighter around her torso, her breath solidifying in the spring air.

Chapter Twenty-Four

Geri sat upright at the bar and glanced at her reflection in the mirror as she watched TJ cash up — it was just the two of them now. Geri had never worked in hospitality before so this was a new experience for her. Sure, she'd taken part in her fair share of lock-ins, but she'd always left before the drip trays overflowed and the money needed counting.

Now here she was watching her date — could she call her that? — laying £10 notes in a neat pile on top of each other on the freshly cleaned bar. TJ stopped when she got to ten and started a new pile, a look of intense concentration on her face. Geri noted her muscular forearms, her strong hands, her short fingernails. She really should have noticed those before — lesbian 101.

Geri took a swig of her bottle of Peroni and thought about her friends. Had Laura found Tash and talked her out of her funk? Had Abby stopped blaming everyone else apart from Kat for Kat's behaviour? Had Stu pushed Darren off the cliff for having a big gob? Geri let out a snort of laughter.

"What's funny?" TJ looked up. She'd gathered up the small piles of notes into one big stack now and had wrapped them in flesh-coloured elastic bands.

Geri shook her head. "Nothing." She paused. "Nearly done?"

"Yep." TJ put the final clear plastic bags of coins back in their allotted slots in the till and shut it with a firm slam. "Let me put this in the safe and I'm all yours." TJ disappeared into the back.

Geri kicked one foot against the bar to create a rhythmic thud. Empty and quiet, the space looked and felt very different to how it had done all evening. Without the noise of music, people and the creak of the toilet door it felt odd, even a little eerie. This pub could definitely tell some stories. Geri shivered. Had anybody ever died here? Were there ghosts circling right now, waiting to tap her on the shoulder...

"Ready?" TJ walked up behind her.

Geri screamed, toppling off her stool and clasping her chest. "Oh my God, you scared the shit out of me!" Doubled over and breathing heavily, she struggled to regain her poise.

TJ laughed. "I did say I was going to the safe..." She put out her arms to hold Geri on either side.

"I was just... I was..." Geri started, breathing deeply. Regaining her poise was not going well. She shook her hand in front of her as she stood upright. "Never mind. I was just thinking about something else."

TJ closed the space between them. "Let me give you something else to think about altogether." She brushed her lips against Geri's and all bets were off.

Geri was caught off-guard and was helpless as she sank into the powerful warmth of TJ's kiss. Her body buzzed in a way it hadn't in years.

TJ took that as a clear sign of encouragement and moved her whole body closer so their hips locked and her arms circled Geri. Then she slid her tongue gently into Geri's mouth.

Annoyingly, Geri gasped. Her arm hair stood on end, her blood rushed, her reality swam.

TJ was better than she could have ever imagined.

In Geri's experience, one-night stands weren't usually that great, hence they stayed one-night stands. But she had to admit that this kiss, this confidence was turning her on without her even thinking, no concentration required. Her body was coming alive under TJ's touch and she kissed back with just as much passion, this time bringing a groan from TJ.

Stepping it up a level, Geri caressed TJ's arse through her jeans and they both groaned again.

Then they both started to laugh at all their groaning.

Within a minute, the kissing had stopped, replaced by a sudden attack of the giggles. They were both leaning against the bar, doubled up, almost clashing heads amid their laughter.

TJ straightened up first and stroked Geri's arm,

pulling her close again. Geri wasn't used to this swagger, she recognised it in herself. Geri had been dating so many younger women over the past few months, she'd forgotten what it felt like to have someone who knew herself and knew how to take the lead. Geri felt giddy, as if she was in some 1950s movie as the leading woman. She smiled at the thought.

"Okay, we have to stop groaning so much," TJ said. She leant in again and brushed Geri's lips lightly with her own. "Or we might spontaneously combust."

"It's just going to get worse now though, isn't it?"

"Not if it gets better straight away." TJ raised an eyebrow.

Geri sized her up. What was she suggesting?

"Unless you want to get back to your friends?"

Geri looked into TJ's eyes and clearly saw what she was suggesting now. Her Devonshire barmaid appeared to want to use her as her plaything for the night and if Geri were watching this as a play, she would have stood up and applauded. This was improv at its best.

Geri shook her head and leant in so she could feel TJ's breath on her face again.

"They can wait. What did you have in mind?" Geri's voice was throaty as she locked eyes with her paramour.

TJ grinned and kissed Geri again with just as much intent, if not more. Geri's lips clung to TJ, holding on to their skill and passion for dear life.

Geri felt her body pulse and respond. Holiday sex in a place without a banana boat and beach bars — it was a first. She was usually hustling on some gay-friendly Greek isle or the Costa Brava, but home soil — she felt a vague sense of national pride pushing at her psyche. Geri could also feel TJ pushing her backwards against the bar as her hands slid up and around her breasts, right thumb grazing her left nipple as the lace on her bra was pushed back with ease.

TJ's breath was on her neck, her tongue brushing against her ear then sliding up the side of her neck, hot and wet. Geri fell backwards slightly — her neck had always been her weak spot.

TJ slid one arm around her waist to catch her. "So do you want me to fuck you on a bar stool where there's a danger you might fall off, or would you prefer to retire to the couch?" she whispered hoarsely in Geri's ear.

A zap of desire shot down Geri's body: she was putty in this woman's hands. She followed TJ's eye line to the large brown leather couch in front of the massive fireplace at the back of the pub — the fire's embers were struggling to retain their flicker in the late of night.

While Geri pondered TJ's question, TJ kissed her again, sliding her tongue into Geri's mouth and jamming her thigh between her legs. Geri fell backwards and conceded defeat.

"For health and safety reasons, perhaps the sofa wins." Geri's gravelly tone screamed "Take me!"

TJ didn't need a second invitation. Her hand was warm as she took hold of Geri's and led her over to the sofa, ordering her to put her hands up before she sat down. Was TJ about to undress her or shoot her? Geri needn't have worried.

TJ delicately stripped off Geri's T-shirt while kissing her neck.

Geri closed her eyes and her mind reclined.

TJ unclipped Geri's bra to reveal full breasts, which were always a surprise unclothed, swaying pendulously.

"Good god," TJ muttered as she eased Geri gently backwards, pressing herself into the sofa beside her. TJ's mouth clamped down on Geri's breasts, sucking, biting, teasing.

The sensation flowed to every crevice of Geri's being.

In a matter of minutes there was a clink of a belt buckle, a zip came down, trousers off and underwear discarded. And then TJ slid her left hand to cup Geri's butt cheek and sucked her breast, while her right hand went to the heart of the matter, sliding down, circling, honing, wanting. Geri soaked up the feeling of flesh on hot flesh.

Within seconds she was inside Geri, whose mind jumped to safety as her body took over. Waves of desire washed over her and she was rocking to TJ's beat. In, out, round and round, the motion was seamless, the passion building. They locked mouths, tongues and lips desperately clashing, throats emitting guttural sounds.

"Fuck, fuck..." Geri dug in and waited, gripping TJ's arm so that she left a mark. She opened her eyes but the world was out of focus — the only reality was her, naked, being fucked by a stranger on a pub sofa. Perhaps in the morning it might seem a bit sluttish but right now it seemed heroic, like this was what she was born to do. All the blood began to rush down her body as her orgasm built. She was in full flight, she was soaring, majestic.

TJ ramped up her rhythm and brought it home with a final flourish, kissing, rubbing, fucking, licking.

Geri's head flew back as she came full throttle, arching her body as if she was the star of an orgasm commercial. There was no let up as TJ played her out, not stopping for a moment, biting down on Geri's lip as she slid deeper into her while applying just the right amount of pressure where Geri needed it.

Geri thrust against TJ, rode the second wave, the third and then grasped her lover in a full embrace, holding her tight, feeling the aftershocks, her breathing ragged. Her mind was a mess as TJ kissed her neck, her breasts, her stomach, then travelled back up to her lips, smiling down at the spent force beneath her.

"I've been wanting to do that since the moment you walked in the pub on Thursday." TJ's mouth curled up at one corner in a triumphant smile. "I could seriously fall in love with you."

Geri opened her eyes and forced herself to focus on TJ's dimple. Had TJ really just said what Geri thought she'd heard? Her heart was hammering in her chest — nobody had ever said that to her this quickly, and with that amount of intent. TJ slowly extracted herself and Geri felt the loss. She closed her eyes. Did life get much better than this moment? She doubted it.

"It's a shame we're going home on Monday because I'd let you do that all over again and say that all over again." Geri's breathing was still ragged, uneven.

TJ smiled her hundred-watt, dimple-laden smile. "Glad you approved. I wondered if a London chick like you wouldn't be used to a whole other selection of moves..."

"Just trying to fit in with the locals — and look where that got me," Geri said. "By the way, how come I'm naked and you're still fully clothed?" She pressed a hand to TJ's right breast.

"Because it's my manor, my rules," TJ said. She leant down to kiss Geri, her lips still warm and inviting. "But if you get dressed now I could be persuaded to come back to yours — where you staying?"

"You should know it, the couple that run this own it apparently — The Lodge, up on the cliff."

"Yeah," TJ said. She stood up, nodding quickly. "I've been there before. Nice place."

Geri wondered why she felt as if there was a sudden awkwardness in the air, looking up at TJ who was standing over her. She narrowed her eyes but couldn't fully concentrate, her mind still refusing to fall back into some kind of order.

TJ could fall in love with her — now that was news.

Right at this moment, Geri was totally sure she could fall in love with TJ too.

TJ picked up Geri's jeans for her, shaking them out as she did. Geri's black wallet fell out, falling open to reveal her identity. The glare of the light on the police badge caught TJ's eye and she picked it up, flipping it open.

"I wouldn't have taken you as someone who carries around a mirror," she began, but the smile faded when she saw it was a police badge. TJ swivelled quickly on the sofa, just as Geri swung her legs onto the ground and got up, groaning. Geri located her pants and hopped into them, then took the jeans from TJ's hands.

"You're a cop?" TJ said it like that was the last thing in the world she'd expected tonight.

Geri leant over and whipped the badge out of her hand, pocketing it back in her jeans.

"No need to sound so shocked — do I not look like a cop?" Geri tried to work out the tone of TJ's questioning and whether or not this was a deal-breaker. Geri hoped it wasn't, as she'd already been playing through a number of scenarios in her head and they all involved TJ naked. She leant down and kissed TJ just to make her intentions clear.

TJ kissed her back, then shook her head. "You don't look like one and you don't act like one, that's all. At least, not like the ones around here."

TJ paused and assessed Geri, who was pulling her T-shirt over her head and smoothing it down before concentrating on doing up her belt, head bowed. TJ stood and put her arms around her, kissing her exposed neck.

"But if I'd have known this was how they bred them in London, I might have ventured that way earlier and got myself arrested," TJ whispered, her breath hot in Geri's ear.

Geri felt her body tingle from head to toe, her clit's memory in particular still very fresh as it pulsed anew.

"We're not going anywhere fast if you keep doing that," Geri said, ticking off her new lover with a pointed index finger.

TJ narrowed her eyes wickedly. "I hope you brought your handcuffs for later."

Geri swallowed hard and fixed TJ with a smile of intent. "I never leave home without them."

Chapter Twenty-Five

Back at the house, Stu and Darren readied themselves to drag an inert Kat up the stairs. Stu was hot and bothered, swearing at regular intervals.

Abby, in contrast, continued the silence she'd kept up since they'd left the pub. She gave Darren and Stu a weak smile as she went up the stairs ahead of them.

"Should we have taken her shoes off first?" Darren asked on stair two.

Stu looked at him like he'd gone mad. "I'm not fucking stopping now. We'll sort it out when she's horizontal. How she's made it this far in life I'll never know."

On stair seven both men nearly dropped their load, Stu thinking about Geri and hoping she was okay. They both regained their hold before any major damage was done.

"You shouldn't have given her so much coke," Stu chided as they reached the top step. "It just means she can drink more." He frowned at Darren who shot him a look, his muscular biceps popping out of his T-shirt.

"I'm not her fucking mother."

Now they were on level ground, they shifted Kat's weight again for the final push, carrying her through the door by both turning sideways, then dropping her on the bed. There was hardly any noise, just the bounce of Kat's body and the slump of her head sideways.

Stu and Darren stood at the end of the bed looking down sadly.

Abby stood at the side, looking beaten.

"You need any more help from here?" Stu wrinkled his nose.

Abby took the hint and shook her head. "I can take it from here." She looked tired, drawn. "Thanks, guys."

Abby sat sideways on the bed looking at Kat sleeping, her breathing shallow. Her girlfriend was out for the count but for Abby, the fight was already lost. This whole situation was ridiculous.

Perhaps it was her background of addict parents that made her stay so long — Abby always wanted to fix the problem, make it better. But it hadn't worked with them and it wasn't going to work now, either. Kat's issues ran deep and it wasn't Abby's job to fix them. At least, she didn't want it to be anymore. Kat had made it this far without her and she'd have to make it the rest of the way, too.

But it didn't stop Abby grieving for what might have been. She swallowed a wave of sadness, biting her lip to stop the tears.

Action would help. Abby got up and walked around the bed, taking Kat's blue brogues off — they were scratched and dusty from the walk home. Then she grabbed Kat under both armpits, struggling to pull her up the bed — she was a dead weight. After a few tugs, Kat's head was on the pillow. Abby didn't bother getting her undressed — waking up in your clothes was never a good feeling and Abby didn't want Kat to get away with this scot-free. Instead, she simply folded the duvet around Kat and pushed her onto her side and into the recovery position, just in case.

Abby leant over and kissed Kat on the temple, then silently slid the wardrobe door open, took out her case and began to pack her stuff.

Kat didn't stir.

* * *

Laura's right ankle throbbed. She'd gone over on it this afternoon on the walk home and navigating the coastal path in the dark with just her phone to light the way had done it no favours. She'd tripped no less than three times on the journey down and once on the journey back up. She was nearly back at the top of the cliff now and there was still no sign of Tash. Her heart hammered in her chest.

Perhaps she should have searched the house thoroughly first before diving dramatically down to the sea? If Tash was at home having a cup of tea she was going to feel like a gigantic berk. But Tash hadn't been in the kitchen, the lounge or their bedroom when Laura had checked earlier.

Laura's ears tingled with the night chill, but it was eerily calm. Under normal rules, she might be spooked at her situation — on a clifftop, alone, in the pitch black. But tonight was far from normal so she didn't allow such thoughts to manifest.

She was breathing heavily after walking back up the incline and absentmindedly rubbed her belly which was protruding slightly over her jeans. After this weekend, after she sorted things out with Tash she needed to start eating better, maybe even take up running like everyone else. Still, this unexpected trip to the beach and back would have worked off some of those calories from tonight.

Laura limped up the dusty, cold path and, after a few seconds, the light from the house illuminated the way. Then, senses heightened, she smelt Tash before she saw her. Laura opened the garden gate and turned left, seeing her girlfriend sitting on one of the garden benches, this one perched at the bottom of a wooden trellis, covered in ivy. The slatted wood extended up the back and jutted out overhead, providing shade on a sunny day. Tonight, as Laura looked at Tash, it seemed to be providing solace.

Tash sat looking up to the house, chin resting on her knees, making herself as small as possible. She didn't move an inch as Laura approached.

"Mind if I join you?" Laura tugged down her hoody over the top of her jeans and flicked her hair to one side, tucking it behind her ears.

Tash didn't respond.

Laura tentatively sat down next to her girlfriend, the cold wooden bench seeping through her jeans even though it wasn't wet.

Tash still had her eyes facing forwards, although she hugged her knees closer to her, burrowing down. She only had jeans and a top on, no second layer.

"Are you cold?" Laura was already unzipping her hoody to give to Tash.

This at least drew a response as Tash shook her head and put a hand on Laura's arm.

Laura stopped and rezipped, before settling beside Tash, staring ahead towards the house. Through the widescreen windows she could see the occasional body moving and the occasional head bobbing, but she couldn't make out who it was.

"I went down to the beach looking for you. I was really worried. Nearly fell off the cliff in the process," Laura said.

Still no response.

"You must be really cold. It's freezing out here." Laura paused. "Can we do this somewhere… warmer?"

"Do what exactly?" Tash's words had more bite than the air. "Talk about your past conquests, how many of your friends you've slept with? How many more are there, Laura? How many more skeletons are going to keep jumping out of your closet?"

Laura's stomach heaved and she gulped. Yep, harder than she thought.

Chapter Twenty-Six

Geri and TJ walked out of the pub bumping hips, their laughter piercing the air.

TJ's arm landed around Geri's shoulders and happiness flooded Geri's system. She wanted to punch the air, to sing. A feeling of safety wasn't something Geri was used to, but she'd found it in TJ's embrace. It was an odd feeling and one Geri had never expected.

This had already gone way further than she'd ever expected and, what was more, Geri was stupidly happy. Perhaps TJ was the missing part of her jigsaw? Perhaps TJ secretly wanted to open a fudge shop, too? Maybe they could set one up together, making fudge all morning and making love all night.

Whoa. What the fuck? Geri shook her head to dislodge such bizarre thoughts. Her orgasms had clearly affected her mental abilities. She blinked rapidly and sucked in sharply. Fresh air, that was what she needed.

TJ placed a kiss on Geri's cheek as they fell into an easy stride, TJ's arm still wrapped around Geri's shoulder.

"So are you going to tell your mates how friendly the bar staff are in Devon?"

Geri turned her head. "You want me to advertise your services? That would make me your pimp, you realise."

"Sexiest pimp I've ever known."

"How many have there been?" Geri laughed. "I'll just leave what happened between us to their imagination. Besides, they're probably all still wrapped up in their own melodramas right now."

The pair turned up the final small incline to the house before the steep drop down the drive to the floodlit abode.

Geri was amazed at the number of stars on view in the blackness above them. Orion's Belt, Cassiopeia, The Great Bear, The Frying Pan. Or was The Great Bear also known as The Frying Pan? Astronomy had never been her strong point.

TJ had removed her arm, so instead, Geri took her hand as they strode down the drive together, looking for all the world as if they'd been doing it for years. Geri chose not to dwell on the fact TJ felt so right, but it hadn't escaped her notice. Every sinew of her body was screaming to be close to TJ, to taste her, smell her, feel her.

"I would ask if you were ready to meet my friends, but you've kind of already done that, haven't you?" Geri tripped slightly on the uneven surface — she'd drunk more than TJ, although recent events had sharpened her focus, sobered her up.

TJ reached out a hand to steady her. "Yep, but now I'm ready to meet them under different circumstances."

Another wave of happiness crashed down.

Geri was just about to reply when a car's headlights illuminated the drive from behind, slowing when it registered the duo in its headlights.

"What the fuck..." Geri said.

TJ and Geri moved to the side of the drive to let the car past, and Geri saw it was from a company called Abbeydale Cars.

The driver gave them a crooked smile as he overtook them.

Geri ran to catch him up, her knuckles banging on his window as he pulled up outside the front door. The driver rolled down his window and Geri did a double-take — she hadn't seen anybody do that for quite some time. Rolling down a window rather than pressing a button. How quaint.

"Alright mate — can I help?" Geri's curiosity was out of the bag. Was this a cab for Tash? That would be a serious over-reaction.

"Taxi for Abby?" the young man said. He had a crew cut and was wearing a Lonsdale nylon zip-up top which wasn't quite as thick as his accent.

Before Geri had a chance to respond the front door of the house opened. Abby stood in the doorway, suitcase in hand.

Abby clocked Geri and TJ and stopped in her tracks. She'd clearly been hoping to make a quick, painless exit.

"You're *going*?" Geri said, her voice rising.

Abby nodded and walked briskly to the cab, opening the door, leaning in and throwing her case onto the back seat. She went to get in, then stopped and hung on to the roof of the cab with one hand.

"I think it's best all round," she said to Geri. "Kat's passed out on the bed and I've had enough for one weekend. Tell her I'll call her tomorrow."

"Look, I said I was sorry about the phone," Geri said. Her humour was misplaced: Abby just stared at her. "Just like that — without saying goodbye?"

Abby straightened up, looked taller somehow. "I'm putting me first for once this weekend." Her words hit the air with unexpected force. "Besides, I don't think you'll miss me much — I was only ever a sideshow in your gang. Now you can all get back to being your gang and I get to go home and wake up in my own bed without having to deal with one of Kat's hangovers *again*."

Her last word was long, drawn out, exaggerated.

Geri got the point as Abby went to get in the cab again, then paused.

"One other thing — take care of Kat because she's a mess. Get her to take her meds, get her to go to therapy, get her to talk about her feelings because nothing will ever change until she does."

"Are you sure going tonight is a good idea? Can't you stay till morning and tell her all of this?" Geri walked around the car to stand next to Abby.

Abby shook her head. "I've tried. Kat has to stand on her own two feet for once."

Geri gave Abby a sad smile and moved to hug her.

Abby who held up a hand in response. "Don't," she said, shaking her head slowly. "I have to go." She paused. "Might see you around," she said as an afterthought.

Geri nodded slowly and gave her a tight-lipped smile. She desperately wanted to save the situation for Kat, but when she tried to conjure up the right words to say, her mind drew a complete blank. Perhaps there was simply nothing more to say.

Abby got into the cab and slammed the door.

Geri watched the car speed away down the drive, kicking up a cloud of dust as it did. TJ was beside her now and they both watched the red lights get smaller until they were out the drive and gone.

TJ walked over to the ajar front door and beckoned Geri towards her.

"All the way back to London — that'll be some cab fare." Geri rubbed TJ's arm as she stepped past her and into the house.

TJ shrugged. "She clearly thinks it's worth it."

"I wouldn't want to be in Kat's shoes tomorrow — hungover, on a comedown, now single." Geri rubbed her face with both her palms, then shook her head. Tonight had been some night and it wasn't even over yet.

Chapter Twenty-Seven

The garden wasn't getting any warmer when Tash looked at her watch again. 1.18am. They'd been sitting silently side by side for a few minutes with just the distant murmur of the sea and the rustle of the surrounding shrubbery for company. The only other sound to pierce the silence was a distant dog, barking incessantly.

"Sweetheart, can we talk about this inside? I need the loo and my fingers are going numb," Laura said.

Tash sighed and turned, placing both feet gingerly on the floor. She'd been sitting in one position for a while now and a pain shot up her right leg as it connected with the floor, while her left leg was numb with pins and needles. Tash stamped her feet to try to get the blood flowing once more.

"You can't even be bothered to sit out here with me for half an hour, can you?"

"You know I'm no good with the cold — and it's fucking freezing." Laura shivered again as if to prove her point.

Tash rolled her eyes. "I just... I can't get past it right now," she said. "You slept with Kat. Didn't you think this might be information you should let me know, at least give me a heads-up before coming to your next reunion where it's *bound* to come up." Tash shook her head from side to side. "Are you so dumb you didn't think it would? Frankly, I'm amazed it took so long..."

Laura shifted her gaze away guiltily.

Tash's mouth formed an 'O'. "It's come up already, hasn't it?"

Laura's silence and downcast eyes gave Tash the answer. She threw up her arms in exasperation and stood up, forgetting the pins and needles and hopped around in pain as the blood struggled back into her legs.

"When?" Tash asked, still standing on her better leg, stamping the other one on the ground as if she was trying to kill a troublesome ant. "When did you already talk about this? Was it a big group pow-wow to laugh about old times and make sure I wasn't in on the joke?" Tash paused. "I can't actually fucking believe this."

Tash walked away from Laura down the grass that was now slick with dew, turning, turning back, not quite sure where to walk or what to think. Getting together with Laura, she thought she'd left this sort of caper behind. Men played games and didn't tell you things, deceived you. Women like Kat played games. But not Laura.

* * *

Laura stood up, seeing the situation needed controlling before it gushed all over their current lives like an oil spill.

She could have cheerfully strangled Darren. Laura walked towards Tash and then stopped.

Tash was standing in combat mode, weight forward on one leg, hands on hips and ready to strike.

Laura went first before she had the chance. "Babe — you know that's not the case. Vic brought it up this morning when we were chatting, asking if I'd told you. But I hadn't and I didn't think it was necessary and frankly, I'm *embarrassed* by it. It was a long time ago and it was *Kat* — and I know what you think of her."

Tash didn't move, her stare still fixed horribly on Laura.

Laura continued. "Ten years ago I was a hot mess, not in a good place. We all met up, we got drunk and Kat and I ended up in bed. We both woke up knowing instantly it was a mistake and that was it — one night only. We put it behind us and got on with our lives. I wish I could change it but I can't. We all sleep with people we wish we hadn't in our lives, don't we?"

Laura paused, asking Tash to consider the question.

"Babe, this was five years before we met, a drunken mistake. And I know I should have told you but the truth is I didn't want you to know. Back then, I was lost. And now... now I'm not. Now I have you."

Laura stood back and let her words sink in, hoping she'd said and done enough. The air reverberated around them with aftershocks and she could feel Tash's eyes on her. Could she feel her eyes softening, the warmer wrinkles falling back and replacing the scowl lines? Laura hoped so because frankly, she'd used all her best lines. *Should she risk walking closer?* It couldn't hurt the situation.

Laura began to close the gap, but as she did, her foot hit something. There was pressure, a whirring sound and then something wooden coming towards her. She went to scream, but before she could manage it a wooden handle smacked her straight in the face and she went down with a sickening thud.

Laura clutched her face, her mouth open but no sound coming out. Her face was pulsing and when she poked out her tongue she could taste blood. Attacked by a rake. Yep, this was exactly how her night had been going so far.

Then Tash was kneeling over her: Laura smelt her, could feel Tash's breath on her face.

"Oh my God — you okay?" Tash put her hands to Laura's face, gently lifting Laura's fingers. The rake had cut her — she was going to have a black eye in the morning. There was also blood trickling out of her nose. Tash got up and went to retrieve some tissues from her handbag, stuffing one up Laura's nose.

"Ow!" Laura shrunk at the contact. Her head was now pounding too. "Is my nose broken?"

"I dunno, but just hold that there to stop the bleeding," Tash said. "I don't think so, but you really banged your head when you went down."

Laura was shaking and shivering. She closed her eyes and when she opened them again, the trees above her were spinning, the house lights now strobing in her eye line.

Tash sat down on the ground beside her and started to laugh. "I have to hand it to you — if you wanted to change the dynamic, you succeeded spectacularly." Tash rubbed Laura's arm and smiled down at her. "I've gone from wanting to kill you for being so bloody stupid, to wanting you to win your fight with a rake." She peered closer at Laura's face. "Although, by the look of it, I think the rake won."

Laura smiled up at Tash, then winced in pain. "I'm glad you were on my side," she mumbled.

Tash looked deep into her eyes and raised Laura's left hand to her lips. "Always," she said. "But shall we get you inside to assess the damage?"

Chapter Twenty-Eight

Back in the lounge, wine was still sloshing in glasses, condensation still running down ice-cold bottles of beer. Crisps in wooden bowls, nuts being cracked, socked feet stretched out, laughter peeling around the room. On the TV, somebody had found VH1 and they were screening an 80s music night — right now, Mister Mister were singing about Broken Wings.

The tension of earlier had dispersed in the air, settled onto the sofa, popped on the carpet, been pierced by the light fittings. In its place was an easy joviality between the six contributors, born of familiarity and being on holiday. Only TJ didn't meet the criteria, but it wasn't lost on anybody how her stretched-out body seemed to blend into the group.

Right now they had an air of inclusivity, of privilege, as if they knew something you didn't.

Abby's departure had been discussed and forgotten about within 15 minutes. Nobody was missing her — or Kat, come to that.

Tash and Laura had been briefly brought up, but after

a while their spat seemed to put a downer on the evening, so they too were escorted off-stage, their drama part of a different script.

Right at this moment the group wanted to star in a rom-com, something light and airy, nothing too taxing on the brain. The air with thick with talk of parties, nights out with the rich and famous, Champagne and fun. Tonight's unspoken remit was to not dwell on what was wrong in their world, but rather to celebrate what was right. They were sticking to their brief perfectly, skilfully skirting the less desirable corners of their lives. Tonight, time meant nothing and they were guarding their bubble fiercely.

"Did we tell you about that party we went to recently where George Michael was meant to turn up?" Darren swirled his vodka and coke so the cubes clinked pleasingly against the sides.

TJ's eyes widened. "You were at a party with George Michael? No way!"

Geri laughed and patted her shoulder from above. "Listen carefully — he said where George Michael was meant to turn up, not where he actually *did* turn up."

Geri had heard this story before but she knew the drill. Stu and Darren worked in PR and their world was made up of smoke and mirrors, of impressing others. The mere mention of a celebrity placed them at a party with them, whether or not the star showed up or not.

Geri knew that when TJ repeated this story, George Michael would probably have been there. And then three friends down the line, he'd probably have brought his guitar and given them a rendition of Careless Whisper on the spot.

Darren, ever the faithful PR, kept up the pretence. "He turned up later on but we'd already left — you know what these pop stars are like." Darren rolled his eyes. "But there were plenty of other famous faces, weren't there?"

Stu nodded loyally.

Darren leant forward. "And of course it was at a club in Mayfair and when we came out around 3am, they were turning Prince Harry's mate away!"

"Amazing!" said TJ, clearly new to this particular sideshow.

"It totally was!" Darren beamed. "I mean, we were almost tempted to go back in, but you know, 3am and we had to work the next day, so duty called."

TJ nodded. "Sounds incredible. We never get anyone famous around here." She took a swig of her beer and readjusted herself on the floor at the edge of one of the sofas. She'd shaken her head when Geri had patted the sofa cushion next to her, preferring to stretch out on the floor and lean against Geri's legs.

Geri didn't mind — she liked the warmth and the instant familiarity. TJ had clearly been a cat in a former life.

"Well, we get precisely no celebs round our way, either. Somehow that far east in London isn't a draw — no idea why," said Stevie. She was sitting next to Vic on the opposite sofa to Geri and Darren, legs touching.

"You'd think they'd be flocking to Limehouse, wouldn't you? Lovely basin." Stu smirked.

"We'll invite you next time we have a celeb party and then you'll have a story to tell, too," Darren said.

"Yes please!" Stevie grinned and gathered her feet up under her. "And can it be someone who'd impress my class, please? And I need photos for Facebook, Twitter, Snapchat..."

"Snapwhat?" Geri said.

"Snapchat." Darren rolled his eyes. "C'mon Geri, keep up with the kids. I hope you're not the youth liaison officer at your depot."

Geri smacked Darren on the leg and he yelped in pain.

"You know damn well I'm not the youth officer — and it's not a depot, Darren, we're people, not fucking lorries." Geri gave him a look that said 'I'm trying to impress someone here'.

Darren smiled. "Sorry, I forgot — you are a *detective sergeant*." He leant forward to catch TJ's eye as Geri stroked her shoulder. "She's very important, honest. The London policing community would fall apart without her. Probably already has, in fact."

Darren got another slap from Geri for his troubles and cowered into Stu.

"Domestic violence — you want to have a word with your mate," Darren said.

"You can call the police if you like," Stu replied. "Oh no, hang on..."

On the opposite sofa there was movement as Vic and Stevie drained their cups of tea and stood in unison, performing gymnast-quality exaggerated yawns in their bedtime play, graceful arms spinning like windmills.

"Much as this has been lovely, we're going to bid you farewell." Stevie put an arm around Vic. "Don't stay up too late, now."

"Have fun, girls — don't do anything I wouldn't do!" Darren shouted at their retreating backs.

He got a single middle finger from Stevie in return.

"And then there were four." Darren rubbed his hands together and heaved himself off the sofa. He eyed Geri and TJ. "You two fancy another or are you departing to bed too?" His eyes were bloodshot, his mood determined.

TJ looked up at Geri but their non-verbal communication wasn't that advanced yet — they may have had sex, but they couldn't tell what the other wanted through the power of glance.

TJ shrugged. "Up to you." She rubbed her ear.

Geri looked at her watch. It was already well past reasonable o'clock, and she had other ideas for filling the next few hours.

Geri smiled down at TJ with a wicked grin on her face. "I think we should go to bed, too."

TJ grinned right back.

* * *

It'd only been 24 hours since they made that same walk to bed together, but what a difference a day made. This time, Stevie was aware of every cushioned step, her twitching calves, her tense back. Her heart kicked noticeably in her chest.

At the doorframe Vic stood back and let Stevie in first. Stevie gave her a shy smile as she walked past her, far closer than was strictly necessary. Once inside, Stevie disappeared into the bathroom, switching on the light which seemed suddenly too bright. She'd got an attack of nerves, despite the fact Vic was the same woman — the only woman — Stevie had slept with in the past ten years.

Stevie pulled her face one way, then the other in the large, stage-lit mirror, wrinkling up her forehead even though she knew it wasn't good for her. She clutched the white sink with both hands and eyed herself full-on.

"It's like riding a bike, Wright," she told herself out loud. "Nothing to it — don't think, just do."

She nodded at her advice and grabbed the electric toothbrush, added toothpaste and was glad of the noise to cover her nerves, glad she had another two minutes to gather herself while the tiny bristles did their work. Molars, canines, incisors, wisdom. Stevie loved the order brushing your teeth brought, providing the end to your day.

For good measure, Stevie picked up the floss. She knew she was dragging her feet now and ordered herself to stop. She had to get out there and bring some normality back to their lives. It was just Vic. Just her wife. She could totally do this.

Stevie took a deep breath and walked back into the bedroom, bringing all the confidence she could muster into that one walk.

She needn't have bothered.

Vic was face down asleep under the duvet, already gently snoring.

SUNDAY

Chapter Twenty-Nine

The gentle rhythm of the sea below. The whir of the wind. The creak of a floorboard, the rattle of a pipe. Doors opened, toilets flushed, boilers cranked into life. A scurry in the loft. Water cascading onto naked bodies and white ceramics. Toothbrushes alert, body lotions slathered, razors scraped. The sound of the house coming to life.

Except, on this particular Sunday, it meant more than just cleansing, buffing and polishing. After the events of the previous night, the house was creeping back to life as if it knew nerves might be frayed, heads sore, emotions trampled.

The house had seen it all before. It'd been around for over 200 years and it wished it could put its arm around Tash this morning or stroke Kat's pounding head, tell them this shit wasn't worth sweating. Life was far bigger than all of this, all of them. Being perched on a cliff top, this house had a clear view of conflict. But always it remained in one place, always sober, always solid: observing, mindful, detached.

It'd seen plenty of internal conflicts, too, just like the scenes it had been privy to last night and those it was witnessing this morning. Every time it happened, the house wondered when humankind would learn to focus on what was important and discard the rest, because it was only noise.

If the house could write down all its wisdom it would be a rich house, but it could only communicate through creaks and cracks, quite apt right now. With every group that stayed here it developed another tick, another niggle. It was still waiting for the perfect guests where it might be able to rest for a weekend.

* * *

Kat opened her left eye, then shut it. Her eyelid scraped across her eyeball. She wiggled her big toes then flexed both hands — still there. She eased open her right eye. It was hard work. Was the lid bruised? Did she get punched last night? She had no idea.

She rolled over and groaned as she lifted her head. Her brain was rattling around in her skull with zero lubrication and she could almost feel it crashing against either side: a boat caught in a dry storm.

Kat placed her head gingerly back on the pillow and waited for the wave of pain to smash onto the breakers, then gently ebb away. It took ten whole seconds. She wondered how long she had till the next wave arrived but figured if she kept her head still, she had a better chance of damage limitation. She held her breath and, when nothing arrived, allowed herself to breathe. Then Kat opened her eyes again. Bad mistake.

Her mouth was dry and when she swallowed, she had to open her mouth to breathe out. Did she do drugs last night? Yes, she did — she couldn't breathe out of her nose and her mood had a dull, tainted quality to it. Paranoia and its good friend regret were also lurking on the window ledge, waiting till the most inopportune moment to pounce. *Why did she do this to herself again and again?*

She ran a hand up her arm and realised she was still wearing last night's clothes: jeans and her grey top. She'd bought it in the Christmas sales but had only just got the chance to wear it because the weather had been so bad. She wriggled her breasts from side to side then reached under her top and tried to unclip her bra — her body felt strangled. She couldn't do it without sitting up, though.

Kat braced before levering herself upright, her head slumping forward. Her brain slammed into the front of her skull and she grimaced. Arms up, top pulled off, raking her senses as it went. Then she was able to slip off the bra straps, followed by the rest of her clothes.

The tsunami of movement caused wave after wave of pain until she thought she might be sick. To combat it she lay still, flat and naked, feeling the soft duvet settle on her skin. Calm. She closed her eyes again.

After a few seconds her breathing was even and she felt cocooned — perhaps she could just stay here all day. Perhaps nobody would notice she hadn't come down for breakfast or dinner. Perhaps Abby would bring her breakfast in bed and they'd laugh about it, her girlfriend kissing her head, wiping her brow, bringing her Nurofen Plus. Perhaps.

Kat gently lifted her head to check for signs of Abby. She wasn't in the bathroom so she must be downstairs. How had she got home last night? Kat assumed — hoped — that it was Abby who had put her to bed, but she couldn't be sure.

Whatever, Abby was not going to be amused, and neither was her therapist. She hadn't taken her pills for the past three days, she'd been drinking heavily, and last night was a blank page.

"If you keep doing the same things and expecting different outcomes, that's the very definition of madness," her therapist had said. So clearly she was mad. Another achievement to add to her list.

Kat pulled the duvet up over her head.

* * *

Geri woke up sprawled across the bed, face down in her pillow, dribbling. Attractive. She turned her head right and saw TJ, which raised a smile. She moved her head left, reached out an arm and banged on the top of the alarm clock so it lit up. 10.10am. Ugh. Her neck creaked as she twisted back around and shuffled towards TJ. Geri kissed the top of TJ's head and rolled into her bed guest, her foot touching the back of TJ's knee.

TJ stirred and backed into Geri with a satisfied purr, reaching her arm backwards, twisting and pulling Geri in for a good-morning kiss.

TJ tasted of sulphur but Geri decided not to point this out.

"Morning gorgeous." Geri was keen to gain the upper hand. After coming to bed, Geri had finally got to touch TJ, taste her, feel her — and she was just as good as promised.

However, after allowing Geri to take the lead for the first part, TJ then proceeded to dominate Geri, sucking and fucking her until she could take no more, her whole body ragged, pulsing. Geri had never experienced a night like it in her life and was caught between being enthralled and not a little disconcerted at her passive role in proceedings. She had drowned in a sea of sexual desire and sleep hadn't done much to quench her thirst.

Geri was putty in TJ's hands and TJ knew it.

This morning was no exception. Before Geri could ask any pertinent questions about how she'd slept and what she thought of last night, TJ was on top of her, taking her hand and sliding into Geri, who couldn't remember the last time she was this turned on so early in the morning. TJ slid, ground, thrust, circled. She knew which buttons to press, had worked out Geri's PIN code in just one night. Soon enough, Geri was arching her back and seeing stars, just as she had the night before.

When Geri could take no more, TJ kissed her firmly

before swinging herself out of bed. She swiped her phone off the bedside table and padded to the bathroom.

Geri laid on top of her duvet, legs still spread and inert, trying to regulate her breathing and her thought processes.

Where had this woman come from? And why didn't they make women like this in London?

As she waited for her blood to pump back up to her brain, she entertained all kinds of scenarios. She hadn't met anybody she'd clicked with like this in a *very* long time. And, yes, she knew part of this feeling was lust, her body approving of what had just happened. But it was more than that.

TJ was on Geri's level.

She was around the same age, sorted, secure and, above all, sexy as hell. So much so, Geri was already working out the finer details of TJ visiting her in London, along with weekends spent in Devon drinking Rattler, dinner in the pub and then lying in TJ's arms under the stars.

Geri was already building a patchwork future for the two of them, which TJ had done nothing to discourage with her declarations of falling for her. Who had Geri turned into?

She heard TJ flush the loo, then the sound of the water hitting the basin. She smoothed herself down, arranged her limbs in a seductive pose and counted in her head to when the door would open, fixing her eyes firmly on it.

After eight seconds she heard the lock turn and TJ

walked in, shot her a wink and walked straight over to her jeans, steadying herself before sliding one leg in and then another. As she bent over, Geri noticed again a tattoo on the small of her back, some kind of Celtic symbol. It looked intricate, like it would have hurt. Another tick to add to TJ's pile — Geri had always found tattoos irresistible.

"You off?" Geri tried but failed to sound nonchalant.

TJ nodded as she turned and walked over to Geri. Her stomach was tanned and surfboard-flat, her breasts ample, her body fitting snugly into her skinny jeans. Her bare feet had flip-flop tan lines. TJ leant in and kissed Geri, then walked back to put on her bra.

"Don't want to outstay my welcome." TJ pulled her black polo shirt over her head.

Alarm crept through Geri's body. She hoiked herself up and into a sitting position, taking the covers with her, suddenly feeling exposed by her nakedness.

"You're not... *really*. In fact, I was hoping you might want to come back to bed and we could finish what we started." Geri poured every ounce of seduction into the last sentence, but TJ seemed unmoved.

Instead, she walked over and sat on the bed. She put on one of her socks, before turning to Geri.

"I should really go..." TJ stroked her chin.

"On the contrary, I think you should definitely stay." Geri dropped the covers to reveal her breasts.

TJ leant in and kissed one breast, then the other, before crushing Geri's lips with her own seductively, effortlessly.

Geri was lost for words again. She could happily set up home in that kiss and be just fine.

"You're very tempting but I think we both know it's best if I go. You're going tomorrow and I've got stuff to do today." TJ stroked a hand down the side of Geri's face lightly. "I had a great time."

But even Geri could see that time was now over and TJ's mind was elsewhere.

"Me too." And Geri had, only she'd like more. Now, later, ad infinitum.

But TJ was already up and gathering her watch, rings, wallet and phone, the last of which she checked, bit her lip, then stuffed into her back pocket.

Geri threw back the covers but TJ shook her head, grabbing them and covering Geri once more.

"You stay in bed, go back to sleep, one of us should." TJ looked at her watch as she put it back on and chewed the inside of her cheek. "I really have to go," she said. "I can see myself out."

Geri opened her mouth to speak but couldn't think of anything to say. She searched her brain for something.

"Will I see you at the pub later?" Geri asked, too high-pitched. She hated the tinge of desperation in her voice.

TJ shook her head. "Not tonight — I've got a family thing today. Easter, you know." She shrugged, then inched her way to the door and placed her hand on the handle before turning back.

"Happy Easter." She locked eyes with Geri.

This time Geri didn't care what she looked like or how she was perceived. She couldn't let TJ go without doing one last thing. She jumped out of bed, temporarily halting TJ with her naked body, then rustled in a carrier bag over by the cream wardrobe. She found what she was looking for, stood up and walked over to TJ with what she hoped was hot, naked swagger.

"Happy Easter to you too," she said, handing her a Smarties Easter egg. Then, with one skilled move, Geri grasped the back of TJ's neck and kissed her, sliding in her tongue and taking complete control.

TJ gave in immediately and kissed her back, pulling her in tight. Their mouths danced with sizzling abandon.

After a few seconds there was a dull thud as TJ dropped the Easter egg, followed by the beep of a phone nearby. TJ pulled back, fished her phone from her back pocket, then frowned.

Geri said it before she did. "I know, I know, you've got to go. Just thought I'd give you something to remember me by." Geri bent to retrieve the Easter egg and pressed it into TJ's chest.

TJ looked like she was about to say something, then changed her mind. A final, gentle kiss, a hurried smile and TJ was out the door and gone.

Geri watched her fade from view, the thud of the stairs, the scuttle of shoes, the swish of a jacket, the slam of the door. And then she was standing naked, heading back to bed, wondering if it had all been a dream.

She climbed back into the sheets and smothered herself in the soft bedding, her limbs aching, her body still throbbing. She touched herself and within minutes she was coming again, arching her back away from the bed, groaning and imagining it was TJ. It wasn't a dream. Her body remembered. She remembered.

* * *

Stevie woke up after one of her first nights of unbroken sleep in the past six months. She'd managed eight hours and had forgotten nights like this could exist, what it felt like to wake up after a stint of deep, unbroken rest. She felt refreshed, upgraded. This was first-class sleep and it was priceless.

She turned to Vic, still sound asleep, still none the wiser that she'd crashed out on Stevie's plans for a night of passion. Had she not made it clear enough? She thought she had, but maybe their signals were out of sync after so long apart. Or maybe Vic had just drunk too much. Whatever, the way she was feeling, today would definitely be the day. Stevie was sure of it.

* * *

Laura opened her eyes and was aware of the space between her and Tash purely because it was unheard of. Still, at least Tash was still in their bed and not sleeping on the sofa after last night. Then she felt the pain and put her hand to her face.

What the hell? She didn't remember getting into a fight last night, but her face was telling her otherwise. Was it Kat? It couldn't have been Tash, surely? Laura scoured her brain for an answer and then she remembered. The damn rake. She grinned, then immediately regretted it as her face began to sing a chorus of pain. This was no time for facial expressions, clearly. Laura winced and swung her legs out of bed to assess the damage.

The bathroom mirror was not in a friendly mood. Laura did a double-take as she switched on the light and gasped at her face. Her nose had a gash on the left-hand side where the rake had made contact, but it was her left eye that was the standout in this particular masterpiece. She counted purple, yellow, red and blue as her finger lightly traced the colours visible on her skin. They spread out below her eye and ran up around its corner and across her eyelid.

Laura was secretly impressed with the look — she'd always found black eyes cool. However, now she had one, she was less than impressed with the accompanying pain.

After a few minutes, Laura tiptoed back into bed. She'd just laid her head on her pillow when she heard her phone buzz on the table beside her and reached out to grab it. It was a text from Alex saying she'd been trying to get hold of Tash and it was URGENT, the final word in full capitals followed by seven exclamation marks. Seven. Laura doubted it was an actual 999-style emergency, but it was time they were both awake.

Laura rolled across the cold corridor of space up the middle of the bed and shook Tash gently on the shoulder. Tash woke far too easily, which told Laura she'd been awake and thinking about how to tackle the morning, too.

"Alex wants you." Laura draped her arm over Tash's body and dangled her phone between her thumb and index finger in front of Tash's face. "Said it's urgent. Probably a cosmetics emergency — cerise pink or electric blue?"

Tash let out a throaty chuckle before pushing Laura's phone away gently, hauling herself upright and rubbing her eyes. She grabbed her phone from the bedside table and pressed the On button. It juddered to life with its familiar jingle.

"How'd you sleep?" Laura was eager to gauge Tash's mood in a bid to know how to pitch herself this morning. Gauging it right could be all-important in the battle to win her round again fully.

Forgetting they'd been quarrelling, Laura reached out and stroked Tash's back underneath her T-shirt.

Tash, clearly also forgetting they'd argued, arched her back in response.

After around five seconds they both suddenly recalled their garden siege and Laura's hand stopped. There was silence, as Tash styled it out, pulling up her favourites on her phone and pressing the green dial button.

Laura lay on her back and stared at the ceiling as Tash connected.

"Hello, sweetheart — what's up?"

There was breathless gabbling at the other end of the phone followed by the sound of Tash's face cracking as she smiled. Her ginger hair was sticking up at the back and the freckles on her arm looked slightly more joined together after a day in the sun.

"Slow down — what does dad say?"

More chatter one end, some sighing this end.

"Well he's probably right then, isn't he?" Laura's ears pricked up. Tash was agreeing with Simon? This must be a first.

"No, I don't think he needs to ask your friend's parents what they're doing as I think I can guess. Look, I'm back tomorrow and we can speak about it then but you're 12, sweetheart, not 15."

The chatter got higher pitched.

"I don't think it's a suggested age — I've seen the posters and that's the age you need to be before you go. If you want to go then your dad has said he'll come too, otherwise you're not going."

The chatter reached a crescendo. Tash assessed her fingers then chewed a stray hangnail.

"Sweetheart, yes, it's not fair, and that's life. Now I'm going — have a lovely day with your dad. I'll see you tomorrow and we can talk more then. Is Taylor there?"

The chatter sounded sulky now, less animated.

"Okay, well give her my love. I'll text you later and we'll talk tomorrow. Love you."

Tash got the reply she needed, pressed the red button and hung up. She placed the phone back on the bedside table and twisted her head left to look at Laura.

"So was that comment aimed at Alex or at me?" Laura ran a tentative finger down Tash's arm.

"What comment?"

"About the fairness of life."

Tash shrugged. "You can't always get your own way, can you? And she certainly can't play me off against Simon while he's taken Taylor swimming." Tash rolled her eyes at her elder daughter's tactics.

"I'd give her points for trying, though — shows ingenuity." Laura's face cracked into a grin.

"Very true."

There was a pause as they both realised they were chatting normally about their life and their children. As if everything was normal, routine. So was it? Neither was truly sure, but they both knew this was their life. They'd thrown their lot in with each other, even if they hadn't committed to for better or for worse just yet.

Laura got the ball rolling. "So," she began, propping herself up on her elbow and turning towards Tash. "Are we okay this morning? Am I forgiven?"

Tash frowned but Laura could see a smile underneath it. "I think I need to make you suffer a while longer than this, don't I? I can't just forgive you straightaway. That's not in the rules of the game."

Laura leant over and kissed her girlfriend on the

mouth, softly, carefully, tearing up the rulebook with every step.

Tash kissed her back.

"I'm still pissed off at you," Tash said when she pulled back, slipping on her best scowl to emphasise the point. Within seconds though, she'd switched it up for a look of concern. "But I can't be too angry with you when your face looks like that, can I?"

Tash reached out a hand to touch it and Laura pulled back.

"I was just going to stroke your good side," Tash said, before doing just that. "Is it sore?" She winced as she said it.

"What do you think?" Laura gave Tash a half-smile so as not to hurt her face. "But it's true. You can't stay angry at this face for long, can you?"

Tash chuckled. "No. But I can't look at it too long, either. It's freaking me out."

* * *

Tash rolled onto her back, taking Laura's hand in hers. She went to say something, then stopped. Then she began again.

"I'm still pissed off with you though, despite the rake saving your skin last night. Not for sleeping with Kat — that was before me, you can do what you want — but for lying to me. I don't like to question us," Tash said.

"I know…" Laura replied.

Tash cut her off, shaking her head. "I'm not sure you do, but I hope you do. We've been together five years. *Five years*." Tash rolled to face Laura now, to ensure she had her full attention.

"You're woven into my life — but it's not just about me, it's about the girls too. I would never have got together with you, never have turned my life upside down and theirs too if I didn't think we had a future together. If I didn't think you were trustworthy." Tash paused before gathering her breath, licking her lips.

Laura went to speak but Tash put a finger to her lips.

"No, let me finish." Tash's eyes glowed with emotion. "You've never ever given me a reason to doubt that — *never*. You are that person — trustworthy, dependable, there for me and the kids always. Sexy, too." Tash smiled, before returning to her serious face.

"But any little chink in your armour, however small, makes me wonder if there's anything else. If this is really what you want. Would you rather be out there sleeping with the Kats of this world? Would you rather be going out drinking and clubbing, rather than sitting at home watching telly with me and the girls? Is this really the life you want?"

Tash ran her hand through her hair and exhaled a week's worth of breath. She knew there was a part of Laura that *did* want that life — and there was a part of *her* that would like to experience it, too. Not all the time, just occasionally.

"Something like this makes me question us, however briefly, and I really don't want to question us, ever. I need us." Tash ran a hand down the good side of Laura's face, her eyes brimming with tears. "I need us more than I've ever needed anything in my life."

And there it was, out there on the bed, emotions laid bare. But rather than feeling exposed, it was a weight lifted off Tash's mind. She felt unburdened, lighter, as if she was floating to the top of a surface she hadn't even known she'd been under. Her ears popped, light got closer, sunshine beamed in. She smiled as a tear trickled down her cheek, wondering just how ridiculous she looked to Laura right now.

Tash stared at Laura, unable to read her mood, unable to see what affect her words had made. After five years, surely Laura couldn't be scared away that easily?

Laura swallowed and started to speak, then changed her mind.

Not known for her patience, Tash blew out an exasperated breath.

"Well, say something. I put my heart on the line and you just sit there as if nothing has happened..." Tash had gone from elation to fear now. Were her worst fears about to be realised? Would Laura really prefer someone like Kat to her? If so, she'd been living the perfect lie for the past half-decade.

Tash sat up and crossed her arms defensively, shielding herself from her lover's words. Incredulity filled the lines between her freckles. Tash chewed a fingernail and waited for Laura's words to assault her. None came.

"Are you going to say something? Say anything, even if it's that you're leaving me for Kat. I mean, I'd understand, she's *such* a perfect catch..."

Bitterness was creeping in now and Tash was going down the line of insulting Laura's friends. This was not how this had ended in her head. In that version there were pronouncements of ever-lasting love and devotion. Now, the mood had soured and Tash knew that last comment was a big mistake.

"Leave Kat out of this, she has nothing to do with it — *nothing*. And she's going through a lot right now, so I don't think we need to blame her for *our* issues," Laura said.

Tash recoiled as if she'd just been slapped.

Laura was shaking her head vehemently. "This has nothing to do with my friends. *Nothing*."

How had things gone from Tash making declarations of love and lifetime commitment, to Laura almost spitting in Tash's face? Tash was baffled. She knew in her heart Laura was happy, that she didn't want Kat or anybody else. And that's what Tash had expected her to say.

So why were they sitting throwing daggers at each other across the bed?

Chapter Thirty

It was gone 11.30am by the time the first bedroom door opened. Darren and Stu tiptoed down to the kitchen, shrugging at each other when they encountered nobody. Darren was dressed in black shorts and a red T-shirt. He stabbed open a packet of Taste The Difference sausages. What did they taste different from exactly? Tyres? Cheese? Gloves?

"You think there's been some sort of mass-suicide pact?" he said.

"Bound to have been." Stu scratched his stomach and stretched, yawning as he did. "Quite likely Tash killed Laura and then Kat, but it seems a little excessive. Perhaps they're all just sleeping in instead?"

"Well, I hope Geri gets up soon because I'm gagging for some chocolate and she's the Easter bunny." Darren retrieved some foil from the drawer next to the sink and covered a baking tray, before arranging the sausages in neat lines.

"You're going to eat chocolate?" Stu pointed at Darren. "Did you get special permission because it's Easter?"

"Easter and Christmas I can pig out. After that, it's back to the regime." Darren flexed a bicep to demonstrate 'the regime'.

"I'm going to take a picture of you eating it and put it on Facebook."

"Don't you dare!"

Darren wiped his hands on a tea towel before neatly halving it and hanging it back on the oven door. His next job was to take a family-sized pack of eggs from the fridge. They were free range — he'd expect nothing less. These particular chickens probably had their own detached house, 4x4 and pool.

"Should we wake them?" Darren cracked the eggs into a bowl before placing the shells in the open food waste bin beside him. He flipped the lid of the caddy shut before whipping the eggs into a frenzy with a fork, watching the clear and bright yellow contents combine to form a milky, frothy shake.

"Maybe. Praps I'll just go and shout at them from the hallway?" Stu stood in the middle of the kitchen considering this option, one hand on hip, one hand on his chin.

"When you've stopped doing your Kenneth Williams impersonation, maybe yes," Darren said. "But stay like that as long as you like because it's amusing me no end."

Stu broke his pose, kissed Darren full on the mouth and walked out of the kitchen.

"Wish me luck," he said over his shoulder.

"Luck!" Darren filled the kettle before pulling the sticky yellow tag off the end of the bread and placing two slices into the toaster. He heard Stu take the stairs, heard him shouting, then heard him bounding back in, slightly out of breath.

"They coming?"

"They are now," Stu said.

* * *

First to the kitchen after Stu's wake-up call was Geri, flushed and sleepy, a pillow crease still visible on her cheek. She was wearing blue pyjama bottoms, a white T-shirt and was sans bra, her nipples clearly visible. Her hair was a mass of matted waves, still in its yet-to-be-straightened state.

"Alright boys?" Geri slumped over the table, her body and senses still alive and raw. She wasn't quite sure what to do with this feeling in front of her two best gay friends. Confess to the fact she was woozy from too much sex? Probably something they didn't need to know. She didn't want to commit the heinous lesbian crime of over-sharing.

"It's like dawn of the dead," Darren said, buttering toast and grinning at Geri. "Is it National Lesbian Strike Day and nobody told us?"

Geri put her head on the table, hands on top of her head and yawned.

"Where's TJ anyway? She gone already?" Stu placed a bunch of cutlery on the table beside Geri's prone form.

Geri covered her ears as they clattered to a standstill, before raising her head and rubbing her face.

"Yep — gone. Gone but not forgotten…" A knowing grin lit up Geri's features.

Darren held up a hand in protest. "Can we at least have a lesbian sex-free breakfast after I've cooked most of it?"

If Geri had the energy she would have shot Darren a look, but she didn't. Instead, she simply smiled wanly at him. "Sweetheart, if you wanted a lesbian-free anything this weekend, you've come to the wrong house."

Stu walked over to the table, carrying a second pile of hot, buttered toast, followed by some white side plates which he spread around the surface as if dealing a pack of cards.

"Are you seeing her again later?" he asked.

"TJ?"

Stu nodded.

Geri did the opposite. "Nah — she had stuff to do today." Geri put the 'stuff to do' in finger brackets and followed that up with a nonchalant shrug, even though she felt anything but. "Still, I got laid and she got an Easter egg, so everyone's happy."

Geri was interrupted by the appearance of Vic and Stevie, who entered the kitchen looking relaxed.

"What's this? You got laid?" Vic said.

"Was I the only one?" Geri asked.

Before Vic could answer, an ashen-faced Tash walked in and sat at the table.

"Morning lovebird — have you two kissed and made up after last night?" Geri asked her.

Before Tash could answer, Laura arrived in the doorway looking sheepish.

Geri could see everyone else's eyes swivelling to the door and widening, so she turned around too.

"Holy shit! What happened to you?" Geri's voice wavered. She looked at Tash, back to Laura, then again at Tash.

Tash held up her hands. "And before you all say it, no I didn't beat Laura up." She paused. "I wanted to last night, but I didn't." She tried a smile but the group of friends weren't budging.

"So how did you get that shiner?" Geri got out of her seat and walked right up to Laura. "It looks like *someone* thumped you in the face." Geri paused. "Wasn't Abby, was it?"

Laura laughed, then winced, putting her hand to her face. "Someone didn't beat me up. *Something* beat me up. A rake, to be precise."

"A rake?"

Laura nodded. "Yep. A rake. In the garden last night while I was grovelling to Tash. Some people would call it karma, I guess." Laura paused. "So that means something bad has to happen to Kat now."

Geri let out a strangled laugh. "Already taken care of." She looked around the group. "Abby left last night, went back to London."

Laura put her hand over her mouth. "No!"

Geri simply nodded.

Laura looked dazed by the news as she sat down next to Tash, who gave her a grim smile.

Geri noted the body language and frowned. She wasn't sure if she was buying Laura's story. She leant forward in her chair as she sat back down.

"So are you two okay now, despite rake-gate?" she asked them. "It was just a rake, right?"

Laura didn't respond.

Tash smiled weakly. "Yes, it was just a rake. And we've had a chat, working through," she said, glancing Laura's way.

Tash nudged her girlfriend, who returned her a look that could topple governments.

Just what had gone on last night? Geri watched the pair's emotions get tangled in each other's hair, up each other's nose, dangle on their ears.

She tuned back into the room again and heard laughter as Vic and Darren were making some rude sausage joke, Stevie and Stu throwing their heads back, too. Geri was sure it hadn't been that funny.

* * *

A minute later, the doorway was filled by Kat. She looked like she'd been in a boxing ring, her eyes puffy, her cheek bruised. She was dressed in her grey pyjamas and her efforts to remove her old make-up hadn't quite worked. Where everyone else looked tired, Kat just looked broken. She scanned the room once, then again, before addressing the table, a worried look spreading across her face.

"So — Abby's not here?" Kat asked.

The women around the table all winced, then shook their heads — all apart from Tash, who still couldn't quite manage too much sympathy for Kat.

Stevie got up and put an arm around her friend, pulling her in close.

Kat rested her head on Stevie's shoulder and sighed.

"She's gone, sweetie." Stevie hugged Kat closer.

"Gone? Gone where? For a walk?" Kat was grasping at straws and she knew it, but she wasn't quite prepared to admit defeat yet. Somehow, don't ask her why, Kat wanted to draw this out as long as she could.

Looks shot round the room but Geri took over, addressing Kat directly.

"She went home last night — back to London. She said she was going to text you — didn't she text you?"

Kat shook her head, her demeanour shrivelled, despondent.

"I haven't checked my phone yet, couldn't face the bright lights. My head's not so good." Kat paused. "Back to London? Did she drive last night?"

Geri shook her head. "Got a cab — she needed to leave. Speak to her, you might be able to patch things up when you get back."

Kat walked over to the table and went to sit down next to Laura. Then she remembered and changed direction, plonking herself next to Geri instead.

"Sorry, mate." Geri rubbed Kat's back gently. "But on the upside, the boys have cooked us a slap-up breakfast. And..." Geri's eyes lit up as she jumped up and sprinted from the room. The others looked bemused.

"Something I said?" Kat asked, slumping in her seat.

In the kitchen Stu fried bacon, a tea towel slung over his left shoulder. Beside him, Darren was proving himself an adept partner, popping open a tin of baked beans with the stainless steel tin opener that reminded him of his childhood, winding the butterfly key slowly. He emptied two tins into a small black-bottomed pan on the hob and swore as tomato sauce splashed up his forearm. He licked it off.

A minute later they heard footsteps bounding down the stairs and plastic rustling. Next, an out-of-breath Geri appeared brandishing a white carrier bag.

"Just call me the Easter bunny!" she said, holding the bag aloft. "Happy Easter everyone!"

Geri dished out the Easter eggs to happy faces. When she got to Kat she reached down and gave her a hug.

"That should put a smile on your face!"

Everyone knew it was going to take more than that to cheer Kat up today but right now, an Easter egg was the best it was going to get.

Kat gave Geri a wry smile.

"I'll put yours in your places," Geri shouted to the kitchen as if it was a million miles away and not in the same room.

Kat, Tash and Laura all clamped their hands over their ears at the screech.

"When did you become so loud in the mornings?" Laura mumbled at Geri, already tearing the foil off her egg and cracking into the chocolate.

"You'll ruin your breakfast!" Stu shouted from the kitchen.

"I bet I won't." Laura broke the chocolate egg and sucked on a piece, feeling it stick to the roof of her mouth.

Stu took out the sausages, which were by now golden and sticky, and shovelled them into an earthenware dish, followed by the bacon. He turned and carried it to the table borne aloft, as if it'd got sparklers and the group were about to celebrate someone's birthday.

"Cheers, boys!" Geri raised her coffee mug in appreciation.

"Eat, before it gets cold," Stu said.

"You're going to make someone a lovely mother," Vic said. "And thanks so much for taking over kitchen duties today — much appreciated."

Darren blew her a kiss in return. "Just our way of trying to make amends for last night — me and my big mouth." He paused. "I'm sorry, everyone."

Geri did a double-take: "Did you actually just apologise?"

Darren rolled his eyes. "It can happen, Ms Paterson."

Stevie leaned over and kissed Darren, while Tash murmured her thanks.

Laura stayed silent, concentrating on piling her plate with food.

* * *

Kat drooped at the table, not reaching for any food. Her eyes scanned the outside world: couples, solidity, health, happiness. She did a brief audit of her world: single, darkness, nausea, pounding headache.

She sat and took in the scene, a steadying hand on the white table top. Heavy eyes, smiling mouths, teas rippling as surfaces were broken. The sight of the food was more than she could bear. The room began to spin. She gripped the table tighter.

The details were suddenly grotesque, as if she'd stepped into some surrealist painting, as if Dali were warping the edges of her world. Kat saw grease glistening on lips, the yellow of the eggs too bright for her eyeballs, bean juice sliding down chins, bacon fat caught between teeth.

The walls of the dining room were dancing now, throbbing and stained. She took a sip of her tea. It was a step too far. The physical act of swallowing had opened up her body and digestive tract for business, and there was only one way it was going right now.

Kat's chair scraped on the floor as she got up, a small ball of vomit making its way up her windpipe. She lurched round the back of Geri, retching slightly, clamping her hand over her mouth in alarm.

Then her feet were moving fast and she was running to the downstairs toilet, vomiting over the sink, the floor, the toilet seat, not quick enough to save it for the toilet bowl alone. Kat's eyes were closed and she could barely focus as she gripped the sink with one hand and tried to steady herself, her breathing. Her brain was thumping inside her skull. She stayed still, hoping this moment would pass.

It did, but then it was building again, Kat's blood pumping stronger. In seconds, her insides bolted up through her throat and landed in the toilet. She hated this helpless feeling, the struggling to regain control of her breathing, her senses. The bowl was splattered with brown, yellow, even a hint of pink. Did she drink rosé last night? She didn't remember, but felt extra hatred towards herself if she had. If she was drunk enough to drink rosé then she was drunk enough for anything to happen.

On the toilet bowl were written the words 'Armitage Shanks'. Funny to think of a family somewhere, generations of the same family, their fortunes made from loos.

Kat grappled to get her breathing under control, swallowing down despite herself and wincing as she tasted her own acrid saliva. Did the Armitage-Shanks family get a feeling of sadness when they vomited on their own name? Or was that something you got used to?

The waves came thick and fast now. Kat heaved over the bowl, sank to her knees, knelt in her own still-warm sick. Thick sobs escaped her body as she hugged the toilet. She retched once, twice more, bringing up nothing except her own bile and self-pity, her whole body flushed with cold and shaking.

She stared at the walls in the downstairs toilet — they were purple, probably a paint called Aubergine's Breath. The slate tiles were cold as she slid into a sitting position. She leant back, the reassuring cool press of the wall at the base of her spine also touching the small of her neck where her hair was at its finest.

As omens went, sitting here in this aubergine cell among a pile of warm sick seemed apt for her life right now. Really, she should get one of her friends to take a picture so she could stick it to her fridge the next time she thought about having a drink.

Kat didn't want a drink now. Or drugs. Or, strangely, a girlfriend. But then her brain wasn't functioning fully so perhaps that was just the mechanics failing, some crucial node not attached. Her vision was blurred and her thought process, too.

On the plus side, the good thing about not having a girlfriend today was she didn't have to think about anybody else. Now, Kat could wallow in the mess she'd made of her own life, she could shower, ignore her friends, crawl back to bed and go to sleep because she knew from bitter experience that was the only thing that was going to cut it today.

So that was the plan. Sleep it off, get up, drink tea.

Tomorrow she'd drive her Beetle home. After kneeling in your own sick, the only way was up.

* * *

After Kat's vocal vomiting, most breakfasts stood untouched for a few minutes — more so for Vic and Stevie, who'd gone to help their friend up to bed. They'd shut the door on the toilet, declaring it out of bounds to the group.

But then stomachs had rumbled and hunger had galloped past any lingering doubts.

Darren leant back in his chair and grinned round the table before picking up his knife and tapping it lightly on his black-and-white mug.

Chatter stopped, heads turned, the only sound being Stevie at the sink refilling the kettle.

"So." Darren grasped the table with both hands. His chair scraped on the wooden floor as it shifted. "When I was in work very early on Saturday morning, I got to thinking about a beauty client we deal with in the South West."

Expectant faces stared back at him.

"Turns out they have a spa place down the road, so I pulled a few strings and I've booked us all in for a treatment this afternoon at two — you can choose between a facial or a massage, up to you. No Easter eggs from us but a half-day pass to the local spa. Seems fitting I do something for everyone else today."

This time, delighted faces.

"Have I ever told you that I love you and your freebies?"

Geri rolled her shoulder, which made something in her back click audibly. A massage sounded about perfect right now.

"Will we be seeing TJ again?" Stevie flicked on the kettle and walked back to her seat.

Geri shook her head casually, trying to pull off casual with aplomb. "Nah — it was a one-time only thing." Geri shrugged. "The Easter bunny can't deliver everything you want it seems."

"But it does deliver treatments, which sounds like a fine idea. Thanks, Darren." Tash raised her mug in his direction. "You've gone from being my least favourite person here to possibly my absolute favourite after breakfast and now this. You can tell you work in PR — that's brand management at its finest."

"And that is a PR mind wasted!" Darren drank the last of his tea. "If you ever find selling houses too dreary, give me a call."

There was a pause as the group assessed their coming day.

"You think Kat's going to make it?" Stu asked.

"I doubt it. If I was her I'd want to sleep and forget the world today. But I'll go and ask her in a bit, see how she is," Geri said.

* * *

Chairs scraped back and the first act of the day was done, their scripts open-ended until act two began at 1.30pm.

Vic and Stevie disappeared up the stairs to get ready.

Darren and Stu went through to the lounge to read the Sunday papers.

This left Geri and Tash to ferry ketchup, plates, mugs and condiments back to their natural habitat. Laura had scarpered straight after breakfast.

Geri was in charge of dishwasher stacking, slotting plates, placing mugs at angles, wedging bowls into unseen gaps. She hated anything to do with the dishwasher, so she wore a frown the whole time.

"Everything okay with you two now?" Geri was struggling to prize a dishwashing tablet from its packaging. "It's quite a shiner she's got."

Tension bubbled between them.

"I really didn't belt her." Tash caught Geri's direct gaze.

Geri relented. "I know, I know. It's just... a bit too obvious. I guess at least you didn't tell us she walked into a door." Geri tried a smile but Tash wasn't budging.

"I'd hope I could come up with something better than that." Tash leaned against the counter and sighed. "We nearly made up earlier, too. But then I said the wrong thing and we're back to square one, perhaps even further down the road than I'd imagined." She wrinkled her nose. "You know those days where you get up and would like to go back, erase it and start again?"

Geri slipped on her sympathetic face and nodded.

"Well, it's one of those."

Geri chuckled as Tash wiped down the side.

"If it helps any, been there, done that," Geri said. "But you'll be fine — you two are good together. And you know Laura when she gets in a funk — she needs time to get out of it. She'll be fine after a shower and a massage."

Tash sighed. "I know you're right, but why does everything have to be such a drama?"

"It's what lesbians do best."

Chapter Thirty-One

Upstairs, Kat heard the TV blaring, the dishwasher being stacked, the hum of chatter circling through the house. She was lying flat and naked again after a hot shower, her sick-stained clothes balled up in a carrier bag. The soft bed linen was caressing her skin, its lightness of touch appreciated today. Kat wished she was in her flat where she could convalesce — feeling this bad away from home was disconcerting, but she had nobody to blame but herself.

Her brain was casting around, trying to piece together scenes from last night, but all she could remember was eating the meal in the pub, drinking wine and then nothing. Blank. Darkness. Her right eye still felt like she'd been punched.

Kat picked up her phone again and squinted to read the text message that Abby had sent — short and sour.

'Had to leave, last night was all too much for me. Hope you'll be okay to drive the car back on Monday. I'll come by to pick up my stuff next week.'

No kiss at the end of the message, no term of

endearment, nothing. Just a statement of fact. She'd lost Abby, but there was no hot stab of regret. Rather, just an overwhelming sense that Abby had done the right thing. Why would she want to stick around a fuck-up like her? Kat was hardly catch of the day.

Her stomach rumbled but it would have to wait — Kat was in no mood to greet everyone's pity-filled stares right now.

She heard the stairs being taken two-by-two and knew it was Geri — nobody else bounded up them like her. Kat often thought it was her police training: she couldn't do anything half-heartedly, because in her mind she was always chasing the baddies. Kat knew what was coming next and, sure enough, there was a knock on her door.

"Kat?" Geri tapped again.

The gentle thuds hurt Kat's senses. She moved the covers up over her head.

More knocking, more ignoring.

The door handle moved. Honestly, she just wanted some peace and quiet. Then her duvet was being lifted and pulled.

Kat held on.

"Kat — can I come in?" *Bloody Geri.*

"I think you already have." Kat's voice was muffled. She pulled the duvet down and fixed Geri with her best glare.

"Had to come and check you hadn't vomited over your whole bedroom, too," Geri said.

Kat gave her a rueful look and pulled the duvet back up. "If you've got nothing nice to say, you can leave, thanks."

"Jokes!" Geri pulled the duvet again and held onto it so she could see her friend's face. "Seriously — you need anything?"

Kat shook her head and stayed silent.

"I take it you don't want to come out for a massage this afternoon?" Geri said. It was more a statement than a question.

Kat shook her head again. Her skin prickled. Today, a cocoon was called for.

"That's what I thought." Geri paused, looked around the room. "I think you got a better room than me, by the way." She assessed the crisp patterned wallpaper, the massive mirror at the end of the bed. "Nice mirror, too — good for sex voyeurism." Geri nodded towards it.

Kat felt bile rise in her throat.

Geri held up her hands in apology as she saw her friend turn green. She got up and began walking towards the door, before turning.

"Okay, I'm going to leave you in peace, no more talk of sex. But I shall return with vomit-friendly items — water, tea, toast — which you can do with what you will. And of course your Easter egg in case the chocolate mood takes you." Geri winked. "Back in a tic."

"Geri…" Kat began, muffled.

Geri turned back.

"I'll clean up the loo in a bit, just leave it..." Kat said.

Geri waved her hand. "Tash is already on it and I'm going to help her. Just try to hit the toilet next time, okay?" Geri shut the door.

Kat sunk into the bed in agony, silent screams ravaging her brain, her body floating.

Name one thing she had to live for. Her mind was blank. Kat saw the void, she saw it regularly now. It was impassable, she had no idea how to get around it, over it, through it. Her therapist had tried to help, Abby tried to help, but she didn't understand their language, didn't speak in rhymes.

Kat swallowed and winced; the toothpaste hadn't worked. She tasted her present and it tasted of failure, doom. She twisted her head left and looked at the alarm clock. 12.55pm. They should all be leaving soon.

Perhaps she could have a drink to take the edge off when they were gone. Her mind flailed as panic set in — did they have enough booze left? She didn't remember.

Kat scraped her eyelids closed over her eyeballs. They were studded with razorblades.

* * *

"You look nice," Tash said as Laura came back into their room. Laura was dressed in dark green jeans and a blue shirt that once fitted her perfectly but was now clinging slightly to her stomach. Tash knew better than to bring that up today.

"Thanks," Laura said. Her tone was cut from granite. Must try harder. "You do, too." Not quite an olive branch, but an olive seed at least.

"What you going for?" Tash's words were stilted like they were the first she'd learned in a new language.

"Huh?" Laura looked distracted.

"Treatment — massage or facial?" Tash smoothed down her hair and looked over her shoulder at Laura, who was trying desperately not to frown.

"Well, I can hardly go for a facial today, can I?" Laura said.

Tash looked at her girlfriend's bruised face and shook her head. "Good point."

"We might get a couples massage, imagine that," Laura said.

They stood looking at each other, searching for words, a clue to a routine they once knew. Both minds drew a blank, the only sound their laboured breathing.

Eventually, Laura broke the noisy silence. "I'll see you downstairs then." She pointed a thumb over her shoulder to give direction.

Tash nodded.

Chapter Thirty-Two

"This looks fancy," Vic said as her tyres rolled over finely colour-matched gravel.

Darren's 'spa place down the road' turned out to be a five star, white-bricked stately home that oozed grandeur. The car park was studded with foliage and set within pristine gardens and, in the distance, a lake shimmered invitingly.

"I know, it's gorgeous. Sometimes I think I might run off with Darren," Stevie said, taking in the opulence. "Would you be upset?"

"Might put a dent in my day," Vic said. "But I'd get over it."

Stevie laughed and leaned across to kiss her.

"God, you two are sweet but nauseating at the same time." Geri was sat in the back seat, where she'd taken the opportunity to check her emails during the drive. "Good job it's only me in here and not Kat — she might just have vomited all over your shiny interior."

"I wouldn't have allowed Kat inside the car today," Vic said. She unclipped her seatbelt and it whizzed past her earlobe.

* * *

Moments later, Laura and Tash's silver Renault pulled up beside them. In the passenger seat, Tash's face was the colour of sludge.

Stu and Darren had their faces at the window as if they were the family pets. As soon as Laura cut the engine, they hopped out of the back, gasping for air.

"Is this ace or what?" Darren grinned broadly at his handiwork. It was as if he'd got up that very morning and built the place from scratch.

"Stevie's already threatened to run off with you, just to warn you," Vic told him. She dug her hands into her jacket pockets.

Darren put an arm around Stevie. "You can run off with me anytime, darling. So long as you bring one of those fake cocks you lesbians are so fond of. I can't cope without one."

Stevie rolled her eyes and poked Darren in the ribs.

Darren let out an almighty squeal.

"Can we try to behave?" Stu's voice rose as Tash and Laura got out of the car and joined the group.

"Yes miss," Stevie told him as they made their way across the car park to the main hotel.

Inside, the grandeur continued with sweeping archways, intricate stone staircases and open fires. Several staff smiled their hellos and they were directed down a long, regally carpeted corridor towards the spa to get changed into their white robes. Everybody had plumped for the massage and it was agreed that they'd regroup in the relaxation room afterwards.

"Now remember, nobody's allowed to run off with their masseur — not unless he or she is really good-looking," Darren said as they signed in.

"I might do if you don't shut up," said Stu. "I thought I took your Duracell battery out this morning."

"It's all that chocolate," Darren replied, showing off his Colgate smile. "I'm fucking wired!"

"See you on the other side, ladies," Stu said.

* * *

The changing rooms were impressively huge with acres of wooden pegs, flowers, fresh fruit and cubicles dotted about for the more modest. Banks of hair dryers with theatre-lit mirrors lay ahead, along with gallons of complimentary moisturiser and lotions.

"This is what I'd like our bathroom to be like when it gets redone," Tash said.

"Sure. And I'll get you a slice of the moon while I'm buying it," Laura replied.

"Anybody going for privacy or are we going for a full-on show?" Vic hung her jacket on a peg and sat on the wooden bench below to take off her trainers.

"Nothing any of us haven't seen before, so let's do it," Tash said.

Geri sat down on the bench and bent to undo her

trainers, feeling an ache in her groin still from this morning — she'd no idea what muscle TJ had brought to life but she wasn't complaining. Geri smiled as the fresh memories landed in front of her eyes.

Stevie broke the spell with a nudge to her elbow. "Hey — isn't that TJ?"

Geri's gaze followed the line of Stevie's outstretched arm. She blinked and did a double-take, her mind saying the woman putting on her jeans at the far end of the changing rooms couldn't possibly be TJ — but it looked a heck of a lot like her. Just then, the woman bent over and Geri saw the tell-tale tattoo she'd kissed only that morning. What were the chances?

"I think it is." Geri gazed in TJ's direction. Perhaps this was a sign.

Stevie nudged her again. "You gonna go and say hi?"

The question hung in the air blinking and Geri wasn't sure what the right answer was. TJ had made it abundantly clear their liaison was a one-night thing, their parting final. And no matter how much Geri would like the situation to be different, playing it cool seemed the right option. Even though every sinew of her body wanted to go up and kiss that tattoo just one more time.

"I don't think so." Geri gave Stevie a wry smile.

But Stevie wasn't buying it. "Come on!" Stevie got up and dragged Geri by the arm. "Let's just go and say hi. I'm not suggesting you propose."

Geri didn't put up much of a fight — she knew it was

Stevie's mission to find true love for all. As they advanced down the changing room, Geri checked her hair in one of the many mirrors and tried to ignore the red flags her mind was waving.

Stevie had pushed Geri into matador mode.

"Hey TJ," Geri heard Stevie say, alarmed at how easy the words slipped out of her mouth. Geri had been wondering what her opening salvo should be, but her mouth had dried up at the thought. Stevie had saved her the trouble. Geri's heart was in her throat, every sense on high alert.

TJ spun round, jeans fastened but topless. Her jaw dropped so fast when she saw the two of them that Geri swore she heard it hit the floor and bounce down the changing room, quickly followed by TJ's bravado.

Something wasn't right. Soon enough, Geri discovered what.

A tall brunette walked across Geri's path and up to TJ before putting a hand on her back and whispering something into her ear.

TJ laughed in response and kissed her cheek.

Then TJ's eyes met Geri's again over this woman's shoulder.

Geri looked into them and saw a world of panic.

Time slowed, the rest of the changing room faded out and the camera panned round to a different angle of this meeting. This time though, it was Geri who held all the power. However, now she had the upper hand, Geri was less than sure she wanted it. Goddamn it, why hadn't she just stayed sitting down?

And then the tall brunette turned and addressed Stevie. "Hey! How are you — having a good weekend?"

Geri looked at Stevie, confused. This woman knew Stevie? Geri could see panic flooding Stevie's eyes now too, although the smile on her face didn't betray it.

"Hi Grace — yeah really good thanks, the house is amazing. We just came over to say hi to TJ after we met in the pub last night — this is my friend Geri," Stevie continued, as if this was the most natural conversation in the world.

Grace shook Geri's hand warmly.

Geri's blood stilled in her veins.

"Grace owns the house," Stevie explained to Geri, nodding to confirm the point a little too much.

Grace gave Geri a full-on smile, before bending down to retrieve her make-up bag from the bench.

TJ took the opportunity to slip on a red T-shirt hanging on a hook in front of her, not stopping to put on her bra first. Clearly, nakedness was something she'd rather not introduce to this increasingly delicate situation.

"Well, it's Tom's actually," Grace said, running a hand through her long hair. "Old family heirloom. Your granddad built it, didn't he?" she said to TJ.

Blocks of gritty reality slotted into place in Stevie and Geri's mind, neither daring to look at the other for now.

Tom. TJ was Tom. Tom was not a man. Tom was a woman. Tom was TJ.

Geri saw a muscle in TJ's jaw click as she fixed her with a gaze.

TJ had come back to her own family house and fucked her. For once, Geri was lost for words.

TJ, however, had no such qualms. "Yep, clever man my granddad — the views are amazing, aren't they?" TJ styled it out with aplomb, staring Stevie straight in the eye.

Bizarrely, Stevie found herself following suit, agreeing with TJ and Grace. She commented on the views ("astounding"), the kitchen ("light and airy"), the wooden floors ("really bring warmth and character").

And then there was quiet, a gap in the conversation, an assessment of where they were at. And while it was clear Grace wanted to get to the mirror to do her make-up, the other three just wanted to get away and pretend like this had never happened.

Geri in particular wanted to wind back the clock to this time yesterday, before they'd even arrived at the pub.

"So glad you're having a good weekend," said Grace. "We'll be at the pub later if you're down. But we better get a wriggle on if we're going to make lunch..." she said to TJ, glancing at her watch before kissing TJ on the lips.

Geri's heart plummeted. She stepped back into the heat of Stevie's sympathetic gaze.

Grace was still smiling, holding up her make-up bag in her left hand. Something sparkled under the changing room lights. On the fourth finger of Grace's left hand.

Her wedding finger. She was wearing an engagement ring *and* a wedding ring.

Geri dropped her gaze to TJ's left hand and saw what was not there last night: a wedding ring. In fact, TJ had no rings on last night. But Geri remembered her putting some on that morning when she'd been hurrying out of her bedroom. After she'd just spent the previous night having sex with her.

The room span slightly. *Didn't stuff like this only happen in films?*

"Anyway, we better get off for our treatments. Good to see you again," Stevie said, indicating over her shoulder with her thumb as if she was hitching a ride.

"You too," Grace said. Chatty, friendly, good looking… just what Geri didn't need her to be.

"What are you having?" Grace asked Stevie.

"Massage," Stevie replied.

TJ was frozen solid beside Grace, a smile slapped in place.

"Oh you'll love it, they're amazing here, the best. This was my Easter present wasn't it, gorgeous?" Grace snaked an arm around TJ's waist.

Geri wanted to turn away, but she couldn't stop staring. TJ and Grace were married.

Grace continued: "And she surprised me with a naughty chocolate egg this morning when I got back. Not good for the waistline, but you know." Grace patted her impossibly flat, tanned stomach and kissed TJ on the cheek one more time.

Grace's words winded Geri, already bruised by their

connection. Geri would bet everything she owned that Grace had been given a Smarties egg.

"Have a good lunch." Stevie grabbed Geri's arm just as she had a few fateful minutes earlier.

"Good to see you again," TJ said, her face stoic.

Geri turned on her heel, feeling the cool of the tiles beneath her feet and propelled herself back to her group. The others were all swamped in their robes and slippers when they returned.

"Where'd you go?" Vic asked. "We were all chatting and then you wandered off."

Geri looked over her shoulder, saw Grace laughing at something TJ had said and shook her head.

"Nothing — just a case of mistaken identity," she told Vic, fixing Stevie with a stare that told her 'not now'.

Stevie muttered to Vic she'd fill her in later.

Vic was confused but left it. "Get changed, it's nearly time." Vic led the others to the door. "See you at reception?"

Stevie and Geri nodded in unison.

With the others gone, Stevie and Geri concentrated on getting changed — as well as not turning their heads in a certain direction. Having something to focus on was a welcome distraction and within minutes they were stripped, robed and ready to go.

"You okay?" Stevie rubbed Geri's back lightly.

Geri gave her a rueful smile. "Just swell," she replied.

"Look on the bright side," Stevie told her. "At least you're not married to her."

Chapter Thirty-Three

Back at the house, Kat was vertical and on the move. She'd eaten the two slices of toast Geri had brought to her and could now stand upright without wanting to vomit. Things were definitely looking up so it was time for an adventure.

Kat put a foot on the stairs, her knuckles white as she gripped the bannister. *She could do this.* She made it to the bottom and cursed — she had no socks on. She saw Stevie's slippers by the pile of shoes and slid them on — not only were they luxuriously furry inside, they were still warm.

She stuck her head around the lounge door and noted its calm, its quiet. She walked through the hall and stared at the bizarre artwork on the walls which looked like somebody had just thrown the dregs of their paint pots at a canvas and then rolled around in them. They probably cost a fortune but Kat didn't get modern art; didn't get much art, come to that.

Sure, Kat had been to a zillion gallery openings with her job — correction, her former job. She'd drunk the free

Champagne and eaten the free canapés, but it was all a charade, a lie that Kat had created.

She caught sight of herself in the hall mirror. Puffy eyes, cartoon hair, black bags, spots sprouting. Her old paramours, of which there had been many, would run a mile. Or perhaps, like Abby, they'd see Kat as a project, one they could swoop in and save.

If Abby were here now she'd be trying to flush Kat's system with water and tough love. Kat felt a faint pang of loss, of missing Abby's voice, her lips, her smell of expensive body creams — L'Occitane, Decleor, Bliss.

Kat tore her face away from her reflection and forced herself back to the moment. No point living in the past — Abby was gone. Kat's lip trembled. She ignored it.

The kitchen had also been left pristine — Kat marvelled at the tidiness of her mates. That they'd all deserted her wasn't lost on her, either.

Maybe Abby had been right. Perhaps her friends *were* all too wrapped up in their own lives and their own problems to care about her. *Well, fuck them.*

Kat opened a number of cupboards before she thought to check the fridge and hit the jackpot. Wine and vodka heaven.

She grabbed a wine glass from the cupboard and placed it on the counter-top, unscrewing the top from the bottle of Oyster Bay — she could count on her mates to get good wine. She heard the liquid hit the glass and smiled. Then Kat took the lid from the bottle of Smirnoff:

it was blue, not the usual red, and she wondered if that meant it was stronger. She felt a twinge of excitement. Kat swigged, winced and blew out hard as she felt the vodka slide down. Only then did she smile as she felt the familiar buzz seep into her system.

The bottles were cold against Kat's bare arms as she carried them into the lounge. She put her goodies on the wooden side table and set herself up looking out over the ocean. Kat raised her wine glass in a toast to Jesus, it being Easter Sunday and all. Then she downed half the glass in one.

Kat wasn't religious but her family were. This morning would have been a church date to give thanks for Jesus's uprising, singing hymns out of tune beside crumbling parishioners. Her mum, sister and three nephews all in a row, her mum having polished her shoes especially for the occasion, her nephews' faces sullen.

Kat closed her eyes before downing the rest of her glass of wine. She followed it up with another slug of vodka. She twisted the bottle round in her hands, condensation wetting her fingers. Somebody must have brought this back from their travels — probably Darren. He'd be annoyed with her for drinking it, seeing as it was the least calorific option available. Kat smiled wryly.

She tipped the bottle and took another slug for good measure. Her blood warmed, her body relaxed. She was two steps closer to normal but more booze was needed. Perhaps some snacks too, just to give it the edge of civility, to take the focus away from the fact she was drinking alone mid-afternoon.

But she wouldn't be alone for long. Soon her friends would be back to take care of her and they'd all laugh and have a drink, too. Then she'd be normal again, a social drinker in a crowd. Perhaps she should have some of her pills, too — she hadn't taken them for a few days and her doctor would be cross.

Kat refilled her wine glass and gulped it down in four healthy swigs. She wanted to get to the edge now, this was her unconfirmed plan. The smooth liquid coated her throat and danced on her tongue. For a brief moment, Kat was utterly content.

Chapter Thirty-Four

Knots tangled, muscles sore. Limbs pummelled, skin smooth. Lavender, jasmine, geranium. Panpipes in the air, the fake sound of the ocean breaking on the sands. Long, warm beds with hot towels. Candles, relaxed breathing, eyes flickering open, then closed. Footsteps shuffling in, out, around. Sounds muffled, oil slick.

* * *

Geri's head was pressed into the massage bed's hole — white leather, like looking through a giant polo. She shifted her forehead until it was comfortable and then tried to relax. Easier said than done.

Her masseur told her she felt tense.

Geri wasn't the least bit surprised. He'd feel tense too if he'd had the day she'd had.

Geri saw TJ's face, felt her lips, the shape of TJ inside her. She shifted on the bed and the therapist asked if she was okay. Was he pressing too hard?

Geri mumbled no. She tried to shake her thought process but it was stuck rigid like a high-speed train, never leaving its track and slicing through everything in its path.

Geri could see TJ's wife clearly, too. So happy to be with her today, an Easter treat. Chocolate, massage, dinner. They were having identical days, only TJ fucked Geri in the morning and it was Grace's turn in the evening.

Geri closed her eyes and blew out. She could not quite get over the fact she'd given her an Easter egg and fallen for her lines. What a fucking idiot.

Geri tried to block it out, to engage with the hands on her, to feel and not to think. Her mind had other ideas. She'd known in her heart this couldn't work out, of course she had. Geri lived in London, TJ lived in Devon. But a wife? That took it to a whole new level of deceit, of cunning.

It also made Geri spectacularly morose — not just for herself, but also for Grace and for love. TJ had ignited her romance gene and now she'd have to package it up and put it in the loft. Who knew when she'd be bothered enough to go up there again?

As for Grace, she thought she had a fantastic, thoughtful wife. Looks can be deceiving.

* * *

Stu was too tall for the bed and his feet hung over the edges. He was used to that. His therapist was called Ringe, a young woman in her 20s from Scotland. Was Ringe a common Scottish name? Stuart supposed it might be. The woman had short, dark hair, a slim waist and a determined smile which made him think he was in for a rough ride — wimps need not apply. Luckily, though, Stu loved massage and the harder the better.

He also preferred female masseurs — he enjoyed the difference of feeling a woman's hands on him for a change. Smaller, more intricate, yet still firm. Conversely, he knew Darren would be crying into his bed if his masseur turned out to be a woman — Darren was a man's man.

* * *

Tash slipped off her robe as her therapist made herself scarce — she didn't need to, Tash wasn't shy. She found it daring to be naked in such a public place — naked all except for the paper knickers that Juliet had given her to put on. These places may be posh, but paper knickers? So very 70s.

Juliet stepped back in — she was wearing too much foundation and Tash tried not to stare. Juliet's manicured nails ran down her checklist as she quizzed Tash. Yes, no, yes, hard as humanly possible without breaking any of my bones please. Juliet laughed.

Tash placed her head into the hole on the massage bed, shifted her body and waited for calm to take over. So this weekend hadn't quite gone according to plan just yet, but Tash was hopeful it could get back on track soon. She just had to wait for Laura to come out of her funk.

The problem was that everyone wanted a piece of Tash and, sometimes, just sometimes, she wanted all the pieces for herself.

She heard mixing and the music got slightly louder, then there was oil on her skin, hands, movement. Tash opened her eyes to stare at the beige floor, sighing when Juliet's feet became visible and she began work on her shoulders. Tash felt the tension of the weekend being scrunched in her capable hands, sharp points and harsh angles being softened, tamed.

Tash thought she might like to marry Juliet. Especially if Laura turned her down, which was more than likely right at this moment. How was Laura doing with her bruised face squashed into this hole? Her masseur would have to get creative.

* * *

Next door, Stevie was trying to relax but her mind kept stumbling back to the changing rooms' showdown. Poor Geri. She couldn't believe TJ had turned out to be Tom, married to Grace. Also, she couldn't help equating the situation to her life. But she was over that now, right? Stevie had moved forward. Hadn't she?

But could Stevie ever really? Was that how Vic had behaved at her office party, erasing Stevie from her life for one night, focusing solely on the other woman? It made her sick to think about it still. She didn't want to either, not today, not when they'd nearly sorted so much out. Not when she wanted to make it work. She twisted her wedding ring. It was cold on her finger.

Stevie hated to think of Vic's hands on someone else, *inside* someone else.

Then there were hands on Stevie, kneading her lower back, moving onto her bum. Stevie told herself not to be so stupid, to forget about the past, to think about the future.

It wasn't that easy, though.

Chapter Thirty-Five

Kat stumbled down the stairs, pills in hand, grabbing the bannister again. Wooziness was taking over. Did she feel better than when she'd woken up that morning? Yes, but that wasn't difficult.

She arrived back in the kitchen and grabbed another bottle of wine along with some Minstrels — Easter was a celebration of booze and chocolate, after all.

Kat bumped the fridge door closed with her bum, hearing the bottles in the door clinking as it shut. She shuffled across the kitchen and retook her sea-view seat in the lounge. She drained the remains of the first bottle of wine in one swift move and then took another healthy slug of vodka. Kat was beyond wincing now, just opening her mouth to let some air in.

She looked at her watch: 2.30pm. They were probably all getting massaged now, not giving any thought to her, purely to their own needs and desires. Selfish idiots. Kat unscrewed the cap of the second bottle and poured the wine into her glass, purring with satisfaction at the reassuring glug, glug, glug.

She shook some Minstrels into her palm, ate three and lined the rest up on the arm of the sofa neatly. This was the life, at least that's what they told her. Kat swirled more wine inside her mouth before swallowing, tasting the pleasing mix of it with the chocolate. She always thought it was red wine that went with chocolate, but it turned out white wine did the job just as well.

Chapter Thirty-Six

Darren insisted on Geri coming back in their car so he could extract the gossip, and Stevie encouraged that wholeheartedly. Geri wasn't nearly as keen as everyone else but she didn't have much say as she was shovelled into the back seat, Stu and Darren sandwiching her neatly with eager faces.

For her own sake, Geri was just glad to be in the car and out of the spa. She'd been a bag of frayed nerves as everyone was getting ready to leave in the changing rooms, even though she knew TJ had probably scarpered soon after they ran into each other, just as eager to escape the scene as she was.

Had Geri detected something in Grace's expression at the end, some recognition the meeting might not be so innocent? How many times had Grace thought that and how many times had she been right to? It was probably best not to contemplate.

"So — what happened?" Tash asked while she twisted in her seat. Not for the first time this weekend, Geri found herself the subject of interrogation in Laura's Renault.

There was no point fighting it, though, and she gave in easily, explaining what happened in the changing rooms between her and TJ.

For once this weekend, her friends were stunned into silence.

"Married?!" Tash shook her head. "Well, I didn't see that one coming. And it's her family house? That's just too weird."

"I know," Geri replied. "Imagine that being your ancestral home and doing *that*." A shiver ran down Geri's body. "If I'd known, I would *not* have gone there."

"I guess that's why Stevie wanted you to discuss it in this car and not theirs. Bit too close to home." Stu lowered his passenger window and drank in some fresh countryside air. He put his hand to the back of his neck and winced as it came into contact with some oil — he'd wanted to have a shower at the spa but was hurried out, his friends telling him they had to get back for Kat. Stu was sure she could have lasted another 15 minutes.

"Well, she's not going to be able to avoid some discussion later," Darren said. "This is *big news*, after all." He twisted round to look out the back window at the car behind and saw Stevie and Vic in what looked like relative harmony. All quiet, for now. He turned back to face front.

"It's just so fucking depressing," Geri continued, one hand on the back of Laura's driving seat. "I mean... back in the day we couldn't get married and that was bad. Now we can get married but we're also cheating and having affairs. Makes you wonder if it's worth it: does marriage really work for anyone?"

"True," Tash said. "But some people also live happily ever after. And some people make a mistake and try to get over it, like Vic and Stevie. It's the same for everyone and there will always be people like TJ, straight or gay." Tash patted Geri's hand, adding kindly, "It's not all doom and gloom."

"It is if the woman you just shagged this morning turns up three hours later with her wife," Geri said.

The whole car winced.

"Was she ugly at least?" Laura asked from the driver's seat without turning her head.

Geri shook her head. "Nope — friendly, tanned, good-looking and she had an impossibly flat stomach."

"Fucking bitch," Laura replied.

* * *

Laura pulled into the drive around five seconds ahead of Vic, swinging her Renault round nearest to the garage, giving Stevie enough room for her Fiesta. Kat's Beetle sat in the same place they'd left it earlier. Abby may have vanished but Kat was going nowhere today.

Doors slammed, feet crunched, then the seven of them were jostling around the porch, eager to get in the house and waiting for Stevie who had the keys. They were reinvigorated now and tonight was their last hurrah before returning to their real lives. They were determined to spend it wisely: food, drink, friends, good company. The entrance hall was as they left it, too, coats and shoes obediently stationed, the house silent.

"I can't hear anything — maybe she's still asleep?" Stevie hung up her jacket on one of the white pegs. She slipped off her shoes and frowned. "I'm sure I left my slippers there," she said to nobody in particular.

"Old age, darling," Vic said, hanging up her jacket. "They're probably still in the bedroom." She gave Stevie a kiss on the cheek and headed to the kitchen.

"I'll go see how Kat is." Stu kicked off his trainers so that one hit the skirting board and left a mark.

Darren tutted loudly.

Tash and Laura followed Stu upstairs to their room, closing the door softly behind them.

Stu rapped his knuckles on the door lightly at first. No response. He knocked louder. "Kat?" No answer. He rapped again before trying the door handle, but walked in to see an empty bed. Stu left the room and picked up his pace as he descended the stairs, heading straight for the kitchen where he could hear chatter.

"Kat's not in her room," he said.

Geri, Stevie, Vic and Darren looked up from where they were standing in the kitchen.

"What?" Geri had her finger suspended under a stream of cold water from the tap. When she was satisfied with its temperature she filled the glass she was holding in her other hand and took a gulp.

"Kat — she's not in her room," Stu repeated.

"Then where the fuck is she?"

Geri's stomach lurched and she was already walking past Stu, through the doorway and into the lounge. There was something in Kat's eyes this morning, a desperation, but Geri had thought she'd just sleep it off. As soon as she walked in Geri saw some feet resting on the footstool encased in Stevie's slippers. She let out a breath she didn't know she'd been holding.

"Kat — you gave us a fright," Geri began, smiling as she walked round the sofa. But then her face dropped when she actually *saw* Kat.

Eyes closed, skin papery, colour ghoulish. Her face was unnaturally slumped — it shouldn't be that way. Geri was already screaming for everyone before she took in the empty wine bottles, the vodka bottle, the pills.

Geri knelt over Kat and cradled her face, saying her name over and over again and stroking her cheek. She sensed an audience behind her and turned.

"She's still breathing but we need to get her to a hospital — she's out cold. Fuck. Fuck!" The alarm in Geri's voice was mirrored in everyone else's faces.

Darren was first to react. "We need to find out where the nearest hospital is. I'll get my iPad." He twisted one way, then the other, eyes wild. "Where the fuck's my iPad?" he asked Stu.

They both raced out the door to find it, leaving Stevie and Vic to gawp, helpless.

Stevie moved the wine bottles — three in all — and the vodka.

"Should we try and put her in the recovery position or something?" Stevie asked.

Geri nodded. "Good idea — can you..." Geri held up one of Kat's limp arms.

Vic and Stevie helped shift her around the sofa so she was on her side and curled appropriately. Vic gently wedged a cushion under Kat's head and when they were sure she wasn't going to fall, they all stood back, hands on hips.

"What if she'd choked while we were out..." Stevie shook her head and put a hand to her mouth.

"Don't, babe..." Vic put an arm around her.

"She didn't, that's the main thing," Geri said. "And now if she does we're going to be here. I just hope the boys get some reception soon — her breathing's shallow and she's put a fuckload of booze down her."

Geri squatted in front of Kat and smoothed back her brown hair. "What were you thinking, Kat?" she whispered. "What were you thinking?"

Her friend at least felt warm, if clammy. However, up close she smelt putrid, the remnants of recent drink and drug debris lodged in her system and seeping out of her skin and airways.

Geri shook her head — she should have stayed this morning, helped her shower, offered a friendly ear. Instead they'd all left her and now she was nearly dead.

A tear slid down Geri's cheek and she wiped it away quickly before standing up. The effects of the massage had worn off now, knots reassembling and guilt seeping into every muscular nook and cranny.

"She told me yesterday a bit," Geri told the other two, not looking at them. "She told me about losing her job, about being depressed. I should have known she might have been on the edge but I thought she'd just be too zonked today. It's my fault..."

"It's nobody's fault..." Stevie replied.

She was cut off as Darren reappeared clutching his iPad, looking wired.

"Nearest hospital is in Torbay which is about 20 minutes away," he said. "We've got the postcode, so let's put it in the sat nav and get going. Who's driving?"

Vic immediately volunteered and Darren walked over, followed by Stu to ferry Kat to the car.

"Careful," Geri said.

Darren ignored her.

The men lifted Kat gently, cradling her head and supporting her body. Neither Stu nor Darren would admit it, but they both took a lot more care and effort with this lift than they had with drunk Kat the previous night. They shipped her out of the lounge, over the hallway, through the main door and into Vic's car without a single word or bump. With almost funereal silence, Stu and Darren laid Kat across the back seat, tucking her feet in, her head cushioned in Geri's lap.

"She can vomit all over me, I don't care. Just don't die, Kat. *Don't die*," Geri said.

Her words hit home and Vic and Stevie took a breath before getting in the car.

Geri smoothed her friend's hair against her head and simply stared.

"We'll see you there," Stu told them, leaning in the open passenger window.

Stevie, Vic and Geri all nodded grimly.

"Don't forget to grab Tash and Laura," Stevie told Stu.

Stu clicked his fingers together and nodded. "I'll get them now." He tapped the car roof with his right hand in farewell.

* * *

Vic clicked, ignited the engine and twisted the sat nav.

"Well, this is an eventful weekend, isn't it?" She looked over her shoulder and reversed, before heading out of the drive. "When I joked that we could try to outdo the last reunion, I didn't actually mean it."

"I'll second that," Stevie replied. She looked lost in thought, her arm propped on the car door and her head leant against it. She looked at her wedding ring and nervously twisted it.

The sun had come out fully now, the few morning clouds burnt away to reveal a gorgeous spring day. As the car glided along country roads ably assisted by the sat nav, they passed a host of daffodils and blossom, the grass impossibly green, the sky crystal blue. Weather-wise their weekend had taken a turn towards the French Riviera. Events-wise, it had gone down the route of a Danielle Steel novel– and everyone knows that in Danielle Steele world, someone always dies before the happy ending.

Kat was still out cold and Geri kept feeling her wrist to check for a pulse which wasn't the wisest idea. Despite the fact Geri had been in the police for nearly two decades, she'd never been great at checking pulses, which was a bit of a fail. She felt Kat's forehead — still clammy, still alive.

"How long did it say it'd take?" Geri asked from the backseat.

"About 20 minutes — says 15 now on the sat nav so we're on the right road." Vic glanced at Geri in her mirror.

Stevie turned to look at Kat from the front seat, her face etched with worry.

"I can't believe she drank so much — when did she start to drink so much?" Stevie asked nobody in particular. Her bleached hair looked stark against her skin, which had turned red and blotchy.

"She told me yesterday but I didn't think she meant three bottles of wine in a couple of hours. I think Abby leaving must have tipped her over the edge," Geri said.

"But drinking that much when you've just been sick — it makes me feel ill just thinking about it," Stevie said.

Vic stopped at some traffic lights and flipped down her sun visor, squinting as she looked ahead.

"You're not inside her head though, are you?" Vic leaned over and put her left hand on Stevie's thigh. "If you were jobless, depressed and your girlfriend had just walked out on you, maybe you'd drink three bottles of wine too. I know I might."

Chapter Thirty-Seven

The hospital turned out to be a sprawling grey concrete structure, built in 1925 by an award-winning architect named Charles. He may have been lauded back then but none of the group could see the gold standard much today. The outside resembled a grim council building where lilac-shirted civil servants decided on parking regulations over weak coffee and stale Custard Creams.

Inside wasn't much better. The waiting room felt like an incubator for MRSA, rows of gnarled blue plastic chairs, dead skin and hair floating across the floor. All around them, nurses strode past looking hassled.

The staff rushed Kat in with a mixture of concern and judgement, given the amount of booze she'd drunk at this time in the day. Still, at least it wasn't midnight as Geri pointed out, where drunks would be queuing up. Right now, Kat was standing out from the crowd.

"And that's meant to make us feel better?" Vic looked at Geri like she'd gone mad.

Geri shrugged and went to get a cup of coffee from the

vending machine. Curiously, it tasted of goat's cheese, so she decided against drinking it. Instead, she followed the signs to the hospital café. She reappeared 15 minutes later with a selection of sandwiches for everyone, along with an array of fizzy drinks and coffee. They were hungrily set upon by an appreciative crowd.

"Isn't this how you imagined today going?" Vic sat down and handed the carrier bag around. "A luxurious massage followed by lunch in a hospital waiting room."

"Don't," Stevie whispered.

The group ate their lunch in silence, registering the concern etched on every face around them. A middle-aged man sitting in the corner had been clinging onto his can of coke for over ten minutes without drinking a drop, just staring into the middle distance with bloodshot, rheumy eyes.

Meanwhile, a couple of rows back, a young woman sat clutching her stomach, doubling up in pain and moaning every few minutes.

After they'd been waiting for over an hour and a half, the group were starting to get restless.

Darren stood in front of a noticeboard a little further down the corridor trying to establish how long some of the posters had been here — his guess was at least a couple of months.

There was an advert for a family fun fair coming up on May Day. Another was for a group for people who wanted to quit smoking, imaginatively called Smoke Free.

Weight management, depression and alcoholism were also covered, although Darren couldn't help but think that if people were in A&E already, these help groups might be too little, too late. He turned on his heel and headed back over to the group.

"D'you think we should go and ask what's happening?" he said, putting both arms above his head and yawning as he did so. He could feel the muscles in his back clicking as he performed this motion, still aware of the recent pummelling they'd had from his masseur, Rico.

"I'll go." Geri sprang up from her seat eagerly. "I was getting pins and needles in my leg anyway."

* * *

Geri walked away from the group towards the front desk, shaking her right leg as she went. The corridor was short, dotted with squares of bright lights indented into the ceiling, which were covered by metal grills. The cream walls were lined with a thick wooden divider running horizontally across their centre. The decoration was functional at best, institutional at worst. Running the length of the floor was a green line. Geri had no idea where it led.

The reception staff were polite and efficient, which went against everything Geri had heard about the NHS. Ten minutes later and she was back with the news that Kat was awake and steady, her vitals having been brought back to normal, her stomach pumped.

"Thank God," Vic said. She sighed with relief.

"Or the wonders of modern medicine?" Stu replied.

"You know what I mean."

"So can we see her?" Stevie chewed at her right index fingernail — it was the only one left with anything to chew.

Geri nodded. "Yep, but she's still pretty zonked out. They want to keep her in overnight as a precaution and do a mental health assessment in the morning."

This surprised nobody.

Geri led the way as the group walked down the too-bright corridor to the line of beds surrounded by off-white curtains. The young female doctor with glossy black hair recognised Geri and took them to Kat's cubicle, her black rubber-soled shoes squeaking on the shiny floor.

When the curtain was drawn back they were all relieved to see their friend with a vague semblance of colour in her cheeks, propped up by a mass of pillows, an IV drip attached to her arm. She still looked drained and dazed, but a few hours earlier, they'd all have taken this outcome.

Now, at the very least, Kat looked like she wouldn't die at any second and they were all grateful for that.

Chapter Thirty-Eight

They arrived back at the house just after 7.30pm, massage oil now sticky on all their bodies, having been warmed up and cooled down throughout the day. Dirty nails, coffee breath, emotionally drained. The house looked somehow different as they pulled in, more menacing, shadowy. It had turned from an emotional haven into something sharp and barbed. The only sensible option was to reclaim it as their own with their final night, their planned takeaway now acquiring more significance, their final meal now with two empty spaces at the table.

* * *

Back at the hospital, Stu and Darren had kept Kat amused with tales of their massage, Darren laying on his Rico crush in thick, doorstop layers that even managed to break through Kat's thin veneer of consciousness, provoking a tentative smile.

The group had stayed in various formations, chatting to Kat when she was awake and sitting staring into space when she wasn't, still venturing to get hospital coffee in the vague hope it might suddenly take a turn for the better. It hadn't.

Kat was transferred to a ward and kicked them out just after 7pm. She looked relieved and had both eyes closed before they'd even left her bed.

* * *

After a reinvigorating shower, Vic bounded down the stairs Geri-style and into the lounge. She had to hand it to Kat: some people tried to kill themselves in some dismal multi-storey car park with a car exhaust, but Kat attempted it, intentionally or not, in a beautiful house with a wraparound view of the sea.

Vic crossed the room to the table beside the fireplace which held the brochures for local services. She fingered a few through the clear plastic ring-bound wallets before reaching the Indian takeaway menu she was after. Tonight they were going to finish their holiday with curry, which had been a major star of their university weekends. She walked through to the kitchen where the others were already busy filling bowls with crisps and nuts as well as lining up icy cold bottles of beer on the work surfaces.

"Fucking Kat drank nearly all my vodka, so I guess this means I get a free pass to have a couple of beers with all of you tonight." Darren spoke the words without an ounce of shame.

"Darren!" Stu chided.

"What?! She's not dead, is she? And she did neck my vodka." He paused before breaking into a trademark Daz grin. "But I forgive her because that's the sort of bloke I am — and that's why you love me Stuart," he said, pointedly saying Stu's full name. "But if I get fat from drinking this lager, you have to promise you'll still love me. D'you promise?"

Stu's response was to grab the bottle from his hand and take a long swig himself before setting it down on the counter-top.

"If you don't want it, I'll drink it. And if you get too fat, you know the rules..." he grinned.

Darren's revelry broke the sullen mood and, as if given permission, everybody relaxed and cracked open their own beers.

"To Kat," Geri said, holding up her bottle. "You're a stupid fucker but we love you anyway." They all chinked bottles and the night swung into gear.

* * *

Stevie took charge of organising the table, with everyone else her willing helpers. Placemats wiped, cutlery assembled, wine glasses buffed with tea towels. Red wine breathing, white wine chilling, snacks resting.

"Feels like I'm in the army," Darren grumbled as he blew hot breath onto a wine glass and rubbed around its edges. However, even though he was moaning, he had to admit to taking some pride in performing his task.

He, too, loved a shiny glass and sparkling cutlery, totally understanding Stevie's attention to detail.

"You should go on The Apprentice, you know — you'd whip some of those young idiots into shape."

Stevie laughed. "Vic says that every time it's on." She chewed a mouthful of carrot. "The only problem is I might kill them before I whip them into shape — they're all so detestable."

"Which is exactly why you should go on there, to show you don't have to be that person to succeed in business," Darren said.

"Nah, I'm too old for that shit. Now maybe if you'd said it 20 years ago, I might have done." Stevie paused and put her hand to her chin. "But you know what, scrap that." She gave Darren a dismissive wave of her hand. "I'd have been far too busy being up my own arse to apply for something like that back then."

* * *

Outside, Tash and Laura had slipped out into the garden to watch the sea slither to grey. The sun had long since departed, with them having spent most of their afternoon under fluorescent strip lighting instead. The pair sat on the garden bench opposite the one they'd occupied the previous night, but this time they sat together, bodies fused, hands clasped. This time, they were a united front rather than two parties at war.

"I'm sorry," Laura said. She squeezed Tash's hand.

Tash squeezed back.

"And I agree with everything you said this morning, it's just… it kinda went off and I couldn't pull myself back. Even though I wanted to." Laura glanced shyly at Tash.

"I know." And Tash did. She knew how Laura worked after five years together, knew she'd needed time to cool off, reconsider, get things clear in her head. It didn't mean to say she liked it, but she knew.

"And I didn't help by bringing Kat into it. What's done is done; I was just being stupid." Tash sighed to emphasise the point, before kissing the back of Laura's hand.

"But look," Tash said, sweeping her other hand expansively. "We're in Devon, we're on holiday with friends, we've got a beautiful view and we love each other. Let's look at the positives."

Laura chuckled. "And I've got a multi-coloured face the kids are going to love to poke tomorrow." She turned to face Tash, kissing her hand this time. "You know I love you, though, right?" Emotion welled in Laura's eyes as she searched Tash's face for confirmation.

Tash wasn't leaving anything hanging in this conversation, leaving nothing to chance. She gently reached over and touched the good side of Laura's face, pushing her dark hair back behind her ear.

"Sweetheart, I know. I knew this morning. Or at least, I was 99% sure this morning." She leaned over and kissed Laura gently, with just enough pressure to let her know there was more to come. When she opened her eyes, she saw Laura's face crack into a grin, then a grimace. When would she learn?

"What are you smiling about?" Tash asked, eyeing her girlfriend with suspicion.

Laura smiled again, but this time she put up with the pain, before sliding off the bench and onto one knee. When she looked back up at Tash from her new vantage point, Tash's mouth was open, her mouth forming a tiny letter 'o'. Her forehead furrowed into a line of questions but she stayed silent.

Very slowly, Laura took Tash's left hand in her right, making sure she had Tash's full attention, her eyes telling Tash all she needed to know.

Tash's eyes were wide and welling up. Her heart was thumping in her chest, her face flushed and she was glad she was sitting down. Holy shit, was this what she thought it was?

"Natasha Jade McWilliams, I love you," Laura said. She was grinning madly, dealing with the pain. "I love you, I love your children, I love us. So will you do me the honour of being my wife?"

A tear tracked its way down Tash's cheek as she slowly nodded her head. "I would love to, my black-eyed girl," she said.

Laura drew herself up from her knees and kissed away Tash's tears, then pressed her lips to her wife-to-be. That was the kiss that signalled the rest of their life together as a family. Just the four of them.

* * *

From the lounge, Geri could see Tash and Laura's heads close together, sitting on a garden bench. Unlike last night, Tash was now leaning into Laura's body and accepting her arm around her.

Geri was glad they'd patched up their differences because it was a stupid argument in the first place. Plus, with everything that'd happened since, last night seemed like a lifetime ago.

Last night, Geri had sex with someone who turned out to be married. In Geri's long sexual history she'd never slept with a married woman — *had she*? She supposed it was possible some of them might have been married, to men as well as women.

Geri was no saint, as Stevie could attest, but in the past ten years her cheating track record was blemish-free. She just hadn't met the right woman who she might want something more with. Until last night. But apparently the right woman might already have the right woman for her. Life sucked like that sometimes.

Geri watched Laura and Tash embrace, kissing each other deeply. If she was up closer she'd be able to hear their tongues clicking. She turned away, not wanting to be confronted with it, going back into the kitchen to sit at the table with the other four.

The fact this was TJ's family home made tonight even weirder for Geri than she could have possibly imagined.

TJ had probably sat at this very table for Christmas dinners, made countless cups of tea for her and Grace. Heck, they'd probably had sex in this very kitchen.

Geri abruptly took her elbow off the table and sat back. "So this feels like a murder mystery weekend now," she said. "I'm just glad I'm single — which couple's going to leave tonight?"

"More importantly, will the crime be committed in the hallway or the library?" Stu asked, swigging his beer.

"Seeing as we don't have a library, I'd say beware of the hallway later."

"And the downstairs loo, too — it still has a certain odour of vomit about it," Darren chipped in.

"Eugh!" Stevie let her gaze flick around the group. "But talking of disappearing couples — where are Tash and Laura? Have they gone to properly make up?"

Geri nodded. "They're being romantic and snogging overlooking the ocean. It was nauseating, I had to leave the lounge."

"Have some food, gorgeous." Stevie leant over and squeezed Geri tight with her arm, before placing a bowl of crisps in front of her.

Geri loved Stevie for that. "I need a beer too after today."

"I'm sure Kat would concur," Vic said.

Agreement all round the table.

"Yes, I know, but you know what Ally McBeal said." Geri eyed her friends.

"That karaoke cures all ills?" Vic said.

"Wattles are great?" Darren added.

Geri laughed. "She probably did say all of those things, but she also said that my problems are bigger than anybody else's because, well, they're mine. So yes, I know objectively that Kat drinking a vat of booze and nearly killing herself is worse than what happened to me, but it doesn't alter the fact that I got fucked over last night so I'm feeling sorry for myself. And yes, I'm a bad person, clearly."

"Does that mean you don't want to go down the pub in a minute?" Darren asked. "You, TJ, Grace, nice Easter drink. Awkward!" He said the final word in a sing-song voice, as if he was starring in a West End musical.

"I thought you were being nice today, Darren?" Geri said. "Or was that just this morning?"

Darren waved a hand in her direction. "I can't keep it up all day, woman," he said. "Jeez..."

The group laughed and then fell silent for a few seconds, the day's events being digested and churned.

"Did you say TJ was short for Tom?" Stu piped up eventually. "Whoever heard of a girl called Tom?"

"First time for everything," Geri said.

"Not for me — I went to school with a girl called Tom. Short for Thomasina," Stevie said.

"I blame you, then — you should have warned me!" Geri pouted.

"My fault, totally," Stevie agreed.

"I wonder what the J stands for." Stu sat back, looking thoughtful.

"Jezebel?" Stevie said, which drew laughter from everyone.

Geri shook her head again. "I still can't quite get my head around what she was thinking, though. It's just too surreal. Okay, your wife's out of town so it's an opportunity to fuck someone else, I get it. But to fuck someone else who you know is renting out your *family house* for the weekend? It's too odd for words."

"Agreed," Stevie said. "It's like something from the pages of The Sun." She shrugged. "But life is often stranger than fiction."

Geri saw Vic eye Stevie and she hoped this wasn't going to throw a spanner in the works of their reconciliation. Stevie was twisting her wedding ring again, a look of intense concentration on her face.

"And you certainly couldn't make this shit up." Darren scraped back his chair and crossed the room to the kitchen, opening the fridge before popping his head back around it.

"Everybody want a refill?" he asked. They all held up their near-empty bottles in response, so Darren dutifully ferried the drinks before standing behind his chair and performing three consecutive sets of squats, breathing out as he propelled his body upwards.

Stevie noted his knees didn't click as they bent and felt a wave of envy. Perhaps she should start doing squats at every given opportunity.

"You do know that isn't normal behaviour, don't you?" Vic leant over Stevie and helped herself to some crisps.

Darren shrugged. "Normal in the world I live in. Besides, I'm just trying to spread the word and do a public service in the process — you too could have thighs like mine if you did a few sets of squats a day."

"Call me old-fashioned but I do my squats in the gym, not while drinking beer."

"Old-fashioned!" Darren trilled, before sitting down and grabbing some carrots from the bowl.

"Anyway, you know the other thing I thought about today that we haven't done?" Geri ran her thumb up and down her fresh beer bottle.

"Group sex again?" Vic cocked her head to one side. "I thought we had enough of that last time."

Geri rolled her eyes in response. "I was just thinking we haven't posted any photos on Facebook. At least, I haven't."

"Because everyone who cares is here, so what's the point?" Vic replied.

"Tut tut, showing your age," Darren replied. "We should be videoing each other's drunken moments, posting selfies, all of that."

"Yes but we're not 21, I think that's the point," Vic said. "And I for one am glad. Can you imagine if we'd posted last night's happenings? Rows, collapses, walk-outs, shagging..."

"Now that would have been awful," Geri agreed, rubbing her hands up and down her face. "At least I didn't update my status to 'In A Relationship' in a lustful moment. Thank goodness for small mercies."

"And you didn't record yourselves having sex, either?" Darren asked.

"That's strictly a third-date thing."

"Should we take a picture now?" Stu retrieved his phone from his pocket and held it up to eye level. "Squeeze in you three," he said.

Stevie dutifully put an arm around Geri and Vic, and the three women smiled their best cheesy grins. There was no click and no flash, but after a couple of seconds Stu looked satisfied.

"Lovely," Stu said. "Give me a minute and I'll make it look even prettier." He paused, fiddling with his phone. "We could really do with Laura and Tash, too, though, get one of everyone... well, nearly everyone."

* * *

Half an hour later the curry arrived and Stu collected everyone's tenners before opening the door to a 20-something man in a branded Tandoori-Hut Mini. In London, Stu was used to harassed delivery drivers balancing food on scrawny mopeds but clearly, in Devon, only the latest car model would do.

The man was dressed in jeans and was trying to cultivate a beard but Stu wasn't convinced he'd ever get the growth he wanted, his current effort being too wispy. Stu took the two brown paper carriers from him and tipped him almost 20%. The delivery guy looked amazed and dashed back to his car before Stu could change his mind and demand the money back.

On Vic's instructions the curry was to be served on the kitchen counter to save any nasty stains on the white table — even though it wasn't her house, her house rules still applied.

"On the contrary, I think we should smear curry up the walls just to piss them off," Stu told her.

"I second that emotion," Geri said.

"Think of the deposit," Stevie replied.

Chicken bhuna, lamb tikka, garlic naan. Onion bhajis, tarka dhal, chicken balti. Plates piled with rice, rich pools of curry, poppadoms and mango chutney. Grins as they settled to eat, no prayers said here. A brief cheers and everyone tucked in, nobody realising quite how hungry they were. The curry didn't last long for anyone — today had been hungry work.

"This really is a reminder of university life, isn't it?" Stevie said. "Friday nights down the curry house, Stu and Laura finished before everyone and polishing off all the poppadoms. You want mine Stu?"

Stevie held up half a poppadom from her side plate and Stu leant over for the exchange.

"There are differences, though," he told her, spooning mango chutney onto his plate, along with the hot chilli sauce that only he and Laura liked. "I mean, we wouldn't have proper wine glasses for a start, would we? Or napkins."

"Or wine for more than three quid a bottle," Geri added.

"Three quid bought you some top quality plonk back in the day." Stu waved his index finger to underline the point.

"Yeah, but didn't we used to buy that terrible table wine in plastic bottles? Vin de Table?" Geri shuddered. "Doesn't bear thinking about."

"It all made sense at the time," Stevie said. "And now here we are, 20 years later, drinking wine that costs more than a fiver out of shiny wine glasses. I think that means we've evolved."

Stevie looked around the table at this group, these people who knew so much about her and had seen her through so many times. She swallowed down as a lump began to form in her throat, heat searing through her body as she blinked away tears.

Stevie had seen this enough in films, heard it sung about in songs, seen it written down in print to know this was one of those special moments, the one you wish you could capture –its smell, its vibrancy, its taste, its touch. It seeped into her bones and she knew when she looked back on this weekend, it would be this last-evening glow she'd remember most, the roses not the thorns. This weekend had pulsed with so many emotions, but when

Stevie looked back, the overriding one she'd remember was their abiding friendship and love.

"I think we deserve a toast, don't you?" Stevie refilled her wine glass with the rich Malbec that Vic had selected earlier, then waited until the wine had seduced everyone's glass before standing up and raising hers. Tonight, she was their self-appointed matriarch.

"To us, to our friendship and to us all making the wise decision that perhaps a 30-year reunion isn't totally necessary." Stevie watched everyone toast and then stop, registering her last bit, looking mildly perturbed.

Darren was the first to object.

"I know I wasn't at university with you, but I'd be gutted to miss out on the 30th. Perhaps you should go for a 25th instead?" Darren said.

"You're still planning on being around for that, are you?" A smile creased Stu's face.

"Course!" Darren flashed his boyfriend a killer smile.

"Thirty years? Really?" Geri laid her knife and fork on the side of her plate. "Don't you think these weekends are somewhat tinged with drama and doom? You really want to risk it all again?" She looked like she'd just about had her fill.

The group were startled by a tapping sound of spoon on glass and their gaze shifted to Tash. Attention gained, she took a deep breath out and went to say something. She opened her mouth, then closed her mouth.

"What?" Geri asked.

Tash and Laura both cast their eyes down, grinning.

"What? Come on, spit it out!" Geri said.

"Well we... we had a talk outside and we've... we've... you say it," Tash said, nudging Laura in an uncharacteristically bashful moment. The group's attention was piqued now, jaws hushed, chewing aborted.

Laura cleared her throat. "What with everything that's happened this weekend, we've decided that yes, these weekends are times when major life events happen — people get together, have sex, break up, break down. But what we also decided was that they don't always have to be negative. So you should all know that this weekend will be remembered not only for Kat nearly dying on us, but also for being the weekend we got engaged."

There was silence around the table as this new information sunk in, all seven holding their pose, curry in mouth, wine glasses still as if they'd just been told by their primary school teacher to "stop what you're doing right now!"

Five, four, three, two, one. Brains processed, eyes lit up, arms outstretched, screams released.

"Did I hear that right?" Stevie asked, not trusting her own ears on this one.

Laura and Tash nodded. The newly erected grins on their faces looked like they'd hold fast even through a hurricane.

"Oh. My. God!" Stevie said. "You're getting married! I'm so excited!"

Stu was up, around the table to join in the group hug already being rugby-scrummed by Vic, Stevie and Geri.

"Mind my face!" Laura shouted as faces crushed hers and arms squeezed her body. Nobody was listening. "Face, people, face!"

Vic hugged Laura's shoulders and tapped her head sympathetically.

Stu and Darren tacked on either side, flankers in their own right. Stu hugged someone's body, someone's arm, gripped someone's waist. It was a mass of female flesh, which was terribly novel in their world. After around 20 seconds they came up for air, Stevie in particular having played the role of second row was looking rather flustered.

"Who was it squashing my face? Seriously..." Laura moaned, rubbing it tentatively. Everybody ignored her again.

"So when did you decide this? In between wanting to kill each other this morning? Over the disgusting hospital goat's cheese coffee? Or was it the hospital strip lights that made you come over all romantic?" Geri asked.

Tash ran her hands through her ginger hair and leant back in her seat as the rest all returned to theirs.

"We were just sitting out in the garden, watching the sun fade and we just got to talking," she began. "And then Laura just... came out with it." She leant across and kissed her fiancée on the lips. She tasted of promise, of their future.

"Even after she beat you up. You must love her," Darren told Laura.

He was rewarded with the look that comment deserved.

"Did you get down on one knee?" Vic asked.

Laura nodded. "Of course. Gotta do it properly."

"And have you got a ring?"

This time Laura shook her head. "We'll go shopping for some in Southend — get a discount down one of the pawn shops."

"She's thought of everything, my darling wife-to-be," Tash smiled, drinking some wine.

"Well this calls for something fizzy — but we don't have any do we?" Stu asked, looking at Darren.

"I think there's a bottle left for just such an occasion." Darren got up and walked to the fridge, before prising a bottle from the door and raising it high above his head in triumph.

"Thank your lucky stars that Kat doesn't do Prosecco. You shall go to the ball, Cinderellas," he said, bowing as he returned to the table.

"Thanks, Darren." Tash smiled and nudged Laura, who simply glared slightly less at him.

Stu and Vic got Champagne flutes and poured the Prosecco before Stevie raised her glass.

"Toast number two!" She looked around the table. "To Laura and Tash — congratulations! May you have many happy years together. Cheers!"

Chapter Thirty-Nine

Kat opened her eyes. *Where the hell am I?* Cream walls, white blinds, rough sheets.

Who have I gone home with this time? And where's Abby?

She swallowed and winced. Her throat was on fire. She moved her head to the right and saw a white curtain — a hospital white curtain.

Of course. I'm in hospital. And there is no Abby.

She shuffled higher up the bed — her body was in a world of pain, from head to toe.

So this is what it felt like to have nearly died. She didn't recommend it.

Kat sat up further in the bed — somebody was in pain nearby. She had no idea how many people she was sleeping near, but it felt uncomfortably public having to close her eyes and drift away.

She opened the chipped wooden side cabinet beside her bed and found her mobile phone inside. She pressed the On button and stuffed it under her pillow to avoid the start-up sound waking anyone up. She had no idea what time it was and couldn't see beyond her curtains to check.

Right now, reality was breathing in, standing still.

Kat brought her phone out from the covers and the bright glare of its screen made her wince, the wrinkles around her eyes bunching up. 9.23pm. Not late at all. The others would be tucking into their last-night curry, getting on without her, without Abby.

She had no texts, just a few new emails. The first was from The Guardian, attempting to make her subscribe to its online format. At least The Guardian cared.

The second was from a company she'd once bought her brother-in-law a tie from. He'd been dead two years.

The third was from Sainsbury's, informing her she had a healthy balance of £64.30 on her Nectar card. *I can buy a case of wine with that.* Or maybe not.

Kat hadn't been trying to kill herself. At least, she was fairly sure she hadn't. No, she'd just been feeling sorry for herself and got carried away. It was a Bank Holiday, after all, no work tomorrow. Weren't millions of people up and down the country doing exactly the same thing, just not on such a grand scale?

She read Abby's texts again, typed her a short one back saying she hoped she got home okay and was having a good Easter Sunday. It had to be better than hers at the very least. Then she texted Geri saying she was awake and feeling better. She didn't really feel much better in truth, but Kat knew that sort of talk cheered people up no end, so she gave them what they wanted to hear.

Kat shifted the covers further down her body, fighting

to get them off. She placed her feet on the shiny linoleum floor, right, then left. Her brain throbbed in her head. She steadied herself on both arms and pushed herself upwards. The room span. She steadied, focused and moved forward. Out of the curtain and into the semi-light.

She was in a small ward of six with a large window to her right looking out onto the hospital grounds. Her bed was by the double doors, both shut for the night. She could see a TV flickering behind a curtain beside the window, heard its occupant snort at something funny. TV would be good to take her mind off things. TV, tea and something for her headache. She pushed through the double doors in search of the loo.

Chapter Forty

Stevie and Vic had just finished clearing up the dinner dishes, the others having all disappeared. Now they were staring at each other in a way they hadn't managed to do at the same time and in the same place for over six months.

"That was quite some announcement tonight." Vic licked her dry lips.

"Laura and Tash? I know." Stevie smiled. "Remember when you proposed to me all those years ago?" Stevie folded the tea towel she'd been holding and put it on the counter-top.

"No, remind me," Vic said, smiling.

"You haven't got dementia yet."

"Not quite yet." Vic paused. "Course I remember. Paris. At that crêperie at the bottom of the Eiffel Tower. You had that massive jug of cider that you hated but drank anyway..."

"...And then vomited up later." Stevie's laugh lit up the room.

"Never a more romantic proposal evening had by

anyone in the world." Vic paused and the kitchen seemed to take a breath. "And I wouldn't change it for anything."

Stevie saw her wife now as she always had — strong, dark and beautiful, tufts of her brown hair sticking out at the sides of her head where the arms of her glasses had trapped them. Her eyes were slightly bloodshot, tired from the weekend's exertions. However, her skin was still smoother than her 39 years, her demi-butch poise still evident.

If quizzed after the event, Stevie wouldn't be able to give you reasons for her actions. Just that the house was quiet and desire was thumping through her veins. Then suddenly she was in the moment where it was just her and Vic and nobody else's crap. After months of letting her head rule her thinking, she finally let her heart take over.

Stevie propelled herself towards Vic, pressing herself against her wife's body. It felt like home.

* * *

Vic's head was spinning: Stevie was snogging her — full-on, honest-to-god pashing. It was like they were at some teenage party and someone had a stopwatch going, with honours to the couple who could snog the longest. They were going for gold. Vic had forgotten what it was like to hold her, to feel her body this close, to breathe in her skin. Right now, it was a house of full-on love.

They kissed for what felt like hours, their lips clinging to each other, their tongues probing until they weren't sure where each one started and ended. Because in that moment, they didn't. They were one.

Vic could feel their future being rewritten before her, draping itself over her like a magic cloak; she could taste it as she swallowed the information down. It tasted like honeycomb, like freshly squeezed sunshine. It tasted like she always knew her life was meant to taste.

Vic heard a door slam and it broke the moment with Stevie, who stepped back, grinning shyly. She was still holding on to Vic, whose mouth was curled into a smile.

"So." Vic held her wife's gaze.

"So."

She pushed Stevie back slightly and held out her hand in greeting.

"Vic, nice to meet you."

Stevie took her hand which, as usual, was freezing cold. Stevie shivered, which made Vic smile.

"Cold hands, warm heart," Vic offered.

"Cold hands, freezing wife more like."

Vic gazed up into Stevie's deep green eyes, noting the flecks of yellow and blue painted through them. She touched Stevie's face, angled her head and they kissed again, their lips fused, Stevie's shoulder clicking slightly as she leant down to Vic's mouth. The chemistry was instant, had never left. Vic lost herself in the kiss of her life.

"Ahem," a deep voice said.

Vic and Stevie jumped away from each other.

"It's okay, I mean, carry on — *please* carry on," Stu

said. "I just didn't think I should come in here and get a drink and pretend like nothing's happening." His eyes widened as he clapped his hands together.

"Because this," Stu continued, indicating the space in front of Vic and Stevie, "this is very good news, isn't it? You're kissing, soon you'll be shagging and then all of our futures won't have to be rewritten like in Back To The Future! I can't tell you how relieved I am. I had visions I was going to be erased and have to go back to one of my past lives, like as a waiter or something. This is *great news*!"

He came in for a group hug, taking both bemused women in his arms. "I love you guys but most of all, I love you guys together. All is right with the world again!"

When the hug broke, Vic stroked her chin. "Do you mind just... running all that Back To The Future shit by us again?" she said. "Because it may have been stewing in your brain for a while, but you have to understand this is all new to us."

Vic and Stevie were standing apart from each other now, staring up at Stu.

"All new Stu, all new," Stevie nodded. "So am I Marty McFly?"

Stu threw his hands up in the air. "You're both Marty McFly!" he said. "And now we all get to live again!" He paused. "You did have us worried for a bit, though..." Stu stopped and took a huge gulp of air.

Vic and Stevie took in his words, which was difficult as there were so many and they were all still bouncing around the kitchen, sliding off work surfaces, oozing across the floor. There was a noise and they all looked up, turning towards the door as Darren came in.

"What did I miss? Why are you all looking so weird?" Darren walked over to Stu, who beckoned him in.

"Group hug, group hug!" Stu gathered everyone up together. "Vic and Stevie are kissing again and everything is great. I love you guys!" he said into the huddle, looking down at everyone's socked feet.

"And you tell me I speak a load of rubbish," Darren said.

Chapter Forty-One

Tash and Laura were laid in bed holding each other, their thoughts spinning madly above them. Both hearts were racing, minds blotchy, skin clammy. They were both carbonated with love, both thinking about their lifetime ahead of sleeping with each other and nobody else. It felt comfortable, warm, right.

"So when are we going to tell the girls?" Laura's hot breath bounced off Tash's cheek and back at her.

The corners of Tash's mouth turned upwards. "Really? That's the best post-coital talk you've got? I thought I trained you better than that."

Now it was Laura's turn to smile. "Sorry," she said. "You were hot. It was amazing. You're the best I've ever had. Shall we do a reality TV show?"

"Now we're talking..." Tash turned to her.

"Sure-fire ratings winner," Laura said. "And I'm sure the girls would love it."

Tash shook her head, closing her eyes with a smile. After a few seconds, she opened them again and tilted her head up towards Laura. "But seriously, I think we just need to sit with it a while first, work out our reactions and how we want to deal with it. Not put more pressure on us than we need to."

Laura made a face. "I don't want to lie to them..."

"We're not lying to them." Tash reached out and smoothed down Laura's hair, which was static after recent exertions. "But we don't tell them everything we're going to do in our lives straightaway, so why should this be any different? Let's get used to it ourselves first, then we can sit them down and tell them, tell the rest of the family. I'm talking days and weeks, not months and years."

Laura stroked Tash's face. "I guess you're right."

"I'm always right, sweetheart — you really need to learn this, especially since we're getting married," Tash said. "And then, once it's out there, we can burrow a trench in the back garden and sit there for about a hundred years until everyone's stopped asking us what we're wearing, what's the theme and how big the cake is. Deal?"

"Deal."

Chapter Forty-Two

When Vic returned from the bathroom Stevie was lying under the covers with a seductive smile on her face. As she walked across the bedroom Stevie raised and lowered both her eyebrows in quick succession, which made Vic laugh.

"You okay sweetheart? Having a fit?" Vic sat down on the bed and tugged off her jeans.

Stevie pursed her lips. "I'm giving you my come-to-bed eyes."

Vic looked over her shoulder. "Looks more like come-to-bed eyebrows."

Stevie wafted her hand through the air and rolled her eyes. "Lost on you," she said, giving Vic a mock scowl.

Vic placed her glasses on her bedside table, then swung herself under the covers and round to face Stevie. Their faces were now inches apart as she leant in for a kiss before taking Stevie in her arms, joining their bodies together: lips, breasts, thighs, feet. Vic ran a hand over Stevie's body and pulled back, giving her an amused look.

"You're naked," she said, smiling. In contrast, Vic felt like a prude. She hastily pulled her T shirt over her head and wriggled out of her pants, throwing both on the floor beside the bed.

"Good work, Sherlock. Ever thought about going into police work like Gimps?"

"I wouldn't want to show her up." Vic rolled on top of Stevie, the pull of their two naked bodies slotting back into place drawing low moans from them both. Vic soaked Stevie in before opening her eyes and planting another kiss on Stevie's mouth.

"I forgot how good you feel," she said.

Stevie simply nodded.

And just like that a lock turned, the door was thrown open and the past six months crumbled to nothing. The force field between them was now replaced with magnetic love, wrenching them together, refusing to take no for an answer. Tonight the question and the answer were simply: yes.

Stevie licked her lips, kissed Vic, slid down to her neck. Vic swallowed hard and clung on tight as the longing became a tornado rolling through her. She circled her tongue around Stevie's nipple, kissed down her body, slid hands down her back, squeezed her buttock.

In return, Stevie nibbled, licked, worshipped. Vic was taut and firm beside her and she felt herself clawing at her skin, wanting it all at once, not able to get enough in one go. They rolled together, primal instincts taking over, hands sliding between legs, thighs between thighs, teeth grazing skin.

Then Vic was on top, taking control. Stevie's eyes flashed with wanting, she knew what was coming next: the pop of the lube, the aching want, her legs spread.

Stevie arched herself into it, ached for it, dug into Vic's back as she steadied herself. The slam of her head into the pillow as Vic entered her, the feeling engulfing her. Her whole body sizzled with want — she'd missed this, needed it, craved it. Stevie let the sensation overtake her and fell with abandon. After a few minutes, Stevie felt an orgasm rip through her body from her very core as she spread her legs wider, revelling in its glory. A few seconds to recover and then...

Then they were both at it, grasping, rhythmic, poetic, glorious. Mouths fastened, clits hardened, words whispered in ears. Both reaching for each other at the same time, finding angles, lubing up, sliding in with no finesse. Fingers filling, backs arching, sweat glistening.

Then just when Vic could take no more, Stevie slid down and applied her tongue, gliding through liquid heat, working it like a pro. Knuckles whitened, grips tightened, edges toppled, stars circling. Vic swore loudly as she was sent spinning, her body taken to a new dimension.

Moments later they were still, touching, together. Eyes glazed, brains woozy, kisses softer, bodies fused. They were both floating now, wrapped in a cocoon of sex. I love you. I really fucking love you. Repeat to fade.

MONDAY

Chapter Forty-Three

At the front of the house Geri was wide awake. *Why couldn't she sleep in anymore?* If this was what she'd got to look forward to in the coming years, she had every right to feel depressed. Soon she'd be standing in front of shops waiting for them to open, tutting at the young shop assistants because they were 20 seconds late.

Still, for some reason Geri was smiling as she woke up today, refreshed by sleep and ready to take on the world. She was more than ready to leave this supposed idyll, get the hell out of Devon and back to London. Yes, London had its fair share of cheating dykes, too, but at least she knew what they looked like. Clearly, her radar had completely failed in Devon.

Geri heard voices in the corridor, the gentle brush of the stair carpet, the creaky stair that was two up from the bottom. A pause, then the front door closed and the sound of feet running up the gravel of the drive, onto the path, Darren laughing at some joke Stu had just told him. The boys were off for a morning run and she felt a pang of envy — she wished she'd brought her running gear. It would have been a fine way to say goodbye to the cliffs, the sea, the breeze tickling her ears.

There was nothing stopping her walking it, though. Geri made the decision and jumped out of bed, throwing on her clothes, eager to take in as much sea air as she could. Within hours she'd be back to the rough smog, congested crossings and black bogeys, after all.

* * *

Vic heard Geri get up and rolled over to check her phone. 8.12am. Her mind flicked forward to the day ahead and she knew they should get moving. Beside her, Stevie was snoring gently. Vic left her wife to dream and padded down the stairs in her pyjama bottoms and T-shirt.

She went into the kitchen and poured herself a glass of water. It wasn't quite cold enough but she drank it anyway. Hadn't she read somewhere that lukewarm water was better for your system than cold?

She opened the fridge and surveyed its contents — cherry tomatoes, six bottles of beer, fizzy water, margarine, milk, jam. They'd run down their supplies smartly, so today's breakfast would be continental — all the basic food groups so long as you weren't a stickler for the rules. She popped a couple of tomatoes into her mouth and they exploded on her tongue, juicy and sweet.

This morning, Vic felt renewed, alive, victorious. This Easter weekend, Jesus wasn't the only thing to have risen from the dead — her marriage had, too. Easter could well become her favourite holiday from now on, seeing as you got two days off work and no pressure from your family to visit. It was a mystery to her why it wasn't lauded more.

Vic wriggled her butt cheeks as she leaned on the side and thought about last night, grinning. She was back where she belonged — rather, love had lifted her up where she belonged. She let out a snort as she realised she was quoting cheesy song lyrics to herself. Way to go Vic, way to go.

Out of the corner of her eye Vic saw something scurry across the floor. She tiptoed over towards the back door and saw a tiny mouse sitting next to the white skirting board. It looked up at her, wondering what she was doing in its kitchen.

Vic took a step forwards, pushing her glasses up her nose. However, the mouse wasn't taking any chances, shooting left through an unseen gap and away. Vic let out a long breath.

At home she'd be freaking out, already planning where to buy mouse traps, disinfecting everything in the kitchen. But somehow, in this rural setting, mice seemed acceptable, almost as if they should be here. There was an almost poetic quality in Vic's mind about Minnie Mouse paying a visit. She smiled to herself as she put the kettle on.

* * *

"So, did she text you back?" Stu asked.

"Yep — midday, she reckons."

"Did she say anything else?"

Geri shook her head. "Not really — it was brief. She's seeing a doctor this morning, that's it. After that, she can go."

"Okay. Well, we've found her car keys, so we'll go get her and drive her back. I take it you're still getting the train?" There was toast stuck to Stu's front teeth but Geri didn't point it out.

"Yep, you know I can't do long car journeys without vomiting. But I'll definitely come to the hospital with you and make sure she's okay. And I want to be out of this house before TJ and Grace turn up to get the keys and play happy families."

Stu nodded. "Roger that."

Beside him, Darren's cheeks were still glowing from his run, his hair freshly washed. Even Darren, the city boy, was making noises about being sad to leave Devon this morning. It was only Geri who seemed happy to be heading east and not staying put.

"Shall I toast the rest of this bread — anyone interested?" Stevie got up from the table, freshly showered and perky. She got enough mumbled interest and so set to work darkening squares of bread, slotting them into their caged straightjackets. This morning looked like their last of the long weekend, everyone imbibing carbs, their possessions stacked up on the end of the table as if they were getting ready for a car-boot sale.

"So, are we doing this again?" Laura's face was coming along nicely, her bruising a fresher shade of purple and yellow this morning.

"I hope so, I really like this jam," Darren said, studying the label.

"Ignore him, Laura, I do." Stu rolled his eyes. "He's had far too much fresh air this weekend. You were saying?"

"Are we going to do a 30th? Or a 25th? Did we decide in the end last night?" Laura sipped her coffee.

"I think we were going to but then your news kinda trumped it," Stu said, stroking his bald head.

Furrowed brows all around as the contents of the last 20 years of their joined lives spilled onto the table in front of them, bouncing around like those tiny rubber balls Geri used to buy so many of when she was a kid.

Geri sipped her tea and spoke first. "I seem to recall we all agreed we love these times — they're original and dramatic, to say the least."

"The very least," Darren said.

"So I think a 25th would be a good idea. Silver anniversary. We can buy each other silver rings and swear allegiance to our gang by chopping the tops of our thumbs off," Geri said, smiling. "It'll be just like Stand By Me, but with less leeches." She paused. "Only I'm not sure it's wise for Kat to come along — her track record isn't the best at these events."

"There is that," Tash agreed. She looked far more relaxed than this time yesterday. "But who knows what'll have happened by the time five years have elapsed? Let's wait and see. It's not like we have to plan it tomorrow."

"You'll be married by then for one thing — have you set a date yet?" Stevie said.

All eyes turned to Tash and Laura.

"Not yet," Tash said. "We're going to take our time — set a date, then tell the girls and our families. So this is top secret till then. Nothing on Facebook, okay?"

Murmurs of consensus all round.

"That includes you Darren," Laura added.

Darren feigned shock, but mimed zipping up his lips and throwing away the key.

Vic got up and slotted another capsule into the Nespresso machine. She was definitely going to see how much they cost when she got home — she'd fallen into coffee love.

"I still think we should agree to another meet-up in principle," Vic said, rolling her neck. "I know we see each other in between times, but this is a commitment to this. It's important to me at least." Vic pointed at her chest.

"Agreed," Geri said. "All those in favour say 'Aye'!"

Geri held up her mug towards the centre of the table. All seven of them slowly, deliberately raised their mugs, Vic having to lean over the table, letting her gaze creep around the group. They weren't to be put off, they were coming back for more.

"Aye!" they said as one.

"I knew you couldn't resist," Darren grinned.

* * *

Laura was wiping down the kitchen sides and doing a final tidy-up when Darren walked in, glass of water in hand. He stopped, thought about walking out again, but then decided against it. He wasn't going anywhere, she wasn't going anywhere, so maybe it was time to sort this out. Try to for now, at least.

"Hey you." Awkwardness settled on him as he washed up his glass at the sink and set it down in the drainer.

"Hi." Laura's face told Darren she was about to bolt.

"Look, Laura." Darren cleared his throat. "I really am sorry about the other night — I didn't mean to make things worse for you, my mouth just ran away with me." He held out his hands, palms upstretched.

"It's a familiar story for you, isn't it?" Laura was giving him nothing.

Darren sucked it up. "True. But look, I'm not going anywhere here. Me and Stu... we're... something. So I just thought we could... try to make amends." He paused. "Or rather, I could try to make amends."

Laura looked at him questioningly. "Is this an apology?"

"And a truce," Darren said. He held out his hand to her. "What do you say?"

Laura studied Darren for a moment, but then gave in and took his hand. They shook on it.

"I was half-expecting you to have one of those electric

shock toys attached to your finger then," Laura said, snatching her hand away anyhow. You couldn't be too careful.

"They'd sold out in the shop," Darren told her, winking.

They smirked at each other as he dried up his glass.

Chapter Forty-Four

Wardrobe doors slid on their runners, opening smoothly, shutting abruptly. Toothbrushes abducted from their temporary homes, silently screaming. Shampoo lids tested once, twice. Wash bags zipped. Shirts halved, quartered, laid. Doors open, left ajar. Hallway walls scraped. The bump of suitcases on the stairs. Final drinks, a temporary feel in the air, of closure and of new beginnings.

Darren and Stu were the last down the stairs, Darren with his Louis Vuitton bag over his shoulder, Stuart with his Debenhams case on wheels. Darren had changed his top since breakfast, Tash noted. He jumped the last two steps and landed theatrically in front of the group, the noise making Geri look up from her phone.

"Shall we have a last picture? Out in the garden?" Darren asked.

He was the only one looking enthusiastic.

There was no way Stevie was traipsing all the way around the house and back again right now. She'd had her final wee, she was ready to go. Besides, it'd been raining.

"Let's just do it at the front of the house instead, shall we? We haven't got any there yet." Stevie was using her best teacher's voice so nobody would argue. It worked.

They all dutifully trooped outside the front door. As they did, the sun was just peeking through the clouds and a rainbow was presenting itself in the sky above.

"Will you look at that!" Darren beamed upwards.

A warmth spread through the group as they all looked up and then around, smiling at each other.

"It's a sign — God loves the gays!" Stu hugged Geri tight as he said it.

"Rainbows are so beautiful. Just like my wife," Vic said.

Geri and Stu both made retching sounds.

"Please!" Geri said. "Just because you were up half the night getting laid."

"It's true, that was cheese on a stick," Stevie told Vic.

Vic simply shrugged and smiled.

Darren insisted on taking the picture, so they all squeezed together in front of the porch, the sun's rays slanting directly into their eyes.

"One, two, three, blue vein!" Darren cried.

Everyone grinned widely.

When they looked back on this photo in five years' time, they wouldn't remember Darren's puerile joke. They'd just see their huge grins and think about that long weekend in Devon, time sanding the edges of emotion so that all that was left were black-and-white emotions, no room for hangovers, sugar spikes and tiredness. They'd all think they must have had a good time judging by their faces. All apart from Kat, who was elsewhere.

"It's a good one," Darren said. "I'll post it on Facebook later along with all the others. I thought we'd wait till we showed Kat first."

Stu shot him a surprised but impressed look, dangling Kat's car keys in his right hand. He walked forwards and lifted the boot, inserting first his and then Darren's bags inside.

There was a chorus of slamming boots and then they reconvened and formed a huddle on the drive.

"Same time in five years, then?" Laura said to nobody in particular.

"Yep," Geri agreed. "But we'll see you at that lezza night next month first, right?"

Laura nodded. "Promise — we really will make it this time."

"Yeah, yeah!" Geri waved a hand. Laura and Tash had been promising for the past six months.

"We'll definitely be there, whatever." Stevie leant in to hug Geri, squeezing her friend extra-tight.

Vic followed suit, her pat on Geri's back light.

Tash, Laura, Darren, Stu. Kisses one cheek, two cheeks, lips.

"Drive safe, sweet cheeks!" Laura told Vic, pressing firmly on her back.

"You too, fiancée," Vic smirked.

Laura stuck her tongue out at her as she walked towards her car.

Vic ran back to the porch to leave the keys, realising they were still in her pocket. Then she dashed back to a waiting Stevie, already drumming her fingers on the dashboard.

"Let us know how Kat is — drop me a text. Tell her I'll give her a bell tomorrow," Stevie shouted towards Kat's car.

Stu waved his acknowledgement back before disappearing into the driver's seat, Darren getting into the back with Geri riding shotgun.

"Wagons roll?" Stu asked.

Geri settled in her seat and turned to grab her seatbelt, which Darren was already thoughtfully holding out for her. Geri gave him a strange look.

"Wagons roll," she replied.

Chapter Forty-Five

Tash leaned over and turned the volume up, belting out the chorus as loud as she possibly could.

"Hey baby, I think I wanna marry you!" She was grinning across the car at Laura, who was driving with a smirk.

"Bruno? Is that you?" Laura glanced to her left.

"I sing it way better than Bruno, you know that..." Tash replied.

Laura shifted in her seat, trying to find a more comfortable position for her back. They'd been on the road for over two hours and they still had another four to go. Still, at least it wasn't raining and they weren't arguing anymore.

The weekend had been surreal — Laura wasn't sure what was in the water at these events but they never failed to enthral. This one had topped the lot: they'd nearly broken up and now they were engaged to be married. Plus, she looked like she'd done five rounds in the ring with someone. Laura glanced in her mirror and saw her colouring coming along nicely.

"What you thinking about?" Tash reached over and stroked Laura's left thigh.

Laura felt Tash's touch run through her entire body and smiled. "Just how this weekend has been a whirlwind and how I'm now the luckiest woman alive to have you as my fiancée." Laura smiled at Tash, then winced. Yep, her face still hurt.

"Back at ya, sweetheart," Tash replied.

Chapter Forty-Six

"So how far have we got to go?" Stevie got back into the purple Fiesta, her knees clicking audibly as they bent in under the steering wheel. She'd just eaten a tuna sandwich at the services and had a half-drunk cup of coffee in her hand, which she wedged into her cup holder.

Vic propped the map on her lap and traced the line of the M4. "Well we're at Leigh Delaware, so I'd say at least three hours. And that's providing we don't get stuck in traffic."

"Are you not even going to turn the sat nav on?" Stevie arched an eyebrow.

"Nope." Vic's tone was defiant. "It was the sat nav's fault on the way here, so I'm relying on me and my map. Never let me down before..."

"Can you put on a sexy voice like the sat nav at least though?" Stevie asked, grinning. She looked left and saw that Vic was smiling too.

"Whatever makes you happy, baby," Vic said, lowering her voice and wiggling her left eyebrow. "We've got three hours to go until I can get you home and ravish you..."

Stevie threw back her head, laughing. "I'm definitely going to put my foot down now."

Vic leant over and kissed her wife, before buckling up her seatbelt and stowing her coffee cup too.

"You ready?" Stevie asked.

Vic nodded.

Stevie cracked the engine and they were off.

Chapter Forty-Seven

Geri waited at the station, looking up at the departure board: her train was due in two minutes, bang on time. She was glad she'd upgraded her ticket to First Class on the way back — it was only an extra tenner and after the weekend she'd had, it seemed a wise decision. She felt like she'd been away on Mars and was looking forward to catching up with the world on her way home.

To her left on the platform were a family — mum, dad, two small boys. The kids were carrying buckets and spades, both with a small rucksack on, while the parents were weighed down with cases and bags. Their faces were flared hot.

To Geri's right, a young woman with far too much fake tan was staring intently at her iPhone, scrolling with her thumb. She was wearing blue suede shoes, though, which impressed Geri. Just along from her was a man in his early 20s, an archetypal surfer dude. His blond hair was tussled and his stubble was a few day's growth. He was also wearing shades, presumably to cover tired eyes.

Has his Easter been as eventful as mine? Geri doubted it.

The announcer told Geri the train was due and she saw its grey hulk hoving into view, sliding along as if propelled by magic. She watched the First Class carriages slide by and began walking down the platform in their direction, matching or bettering the train's speed. Geri's bra cut into her body as she walked. She'd have to double her running schedule this week.

The train hissed as it halted and Geri picked up her pace, slinging her holdall over her shoulder and arriving at the door of her carriage just as the train doors opened. She made her way to seat C14 and found it was on a table of four, the other three mercifully empty for now. She hoped it stayed that way.

She lifted her bag with both hands, slotting it onto the overhead metal railings. She took off her leather jacket, smoothed back her brown hair and sunk into her First Class seat, tapping her pockets to check for phone, wallet, tickets. Check, check, check.

Geri sighed as she relaxed for what seemed like the first time today. She heard the train doors lock, felt it lurch and within seconds they were out of their concrete surrounds and dropped into green fields, the train unzipping them at nearly 100mph.

Geri's mind meandered and it arrived at Kat.

When they'd arrived at the hospital, Kat had been waiting on a bench like she'd just finished a work shift. Stu had insisted he drove home and she'd given in fairly easily, still looking drained from her ordeal and lack of sleep.

They'd agreed Kat would move in with Geri for a bit, just until she got back on her feet. Well, Stu and Geri had agreed, with Kat frowning at the plan.

But tonight, Stu and Darren would drop Kat back at her flat and stay until Geri came to get her later. None of them wanted to leave her on her own, despite Kat's protestations she'd be fine. Recent behaviour suggested otherwise.

Kat had just rolled her eyes and got in the back seat, before closing her eyes.

And now here Geri was, determined to make the most of her last time on her own, leaning her right ear on her headrest. It was that weird almost carpet-like material they seemed to favour for train and bus carriages — it made her ear itch and she rubbed it absentmindedly.

Geri closed her eyes and a semi-naked TJ popped into her head. She opened them immediately and shook her head in a bid to erase the image. It half worked.

The buffet car was in the adjacent carriage, so Geri got up and headed that way, looking out through the window as the South West countryside flew by. Near the door was a man in his thirties reading his Kindle, which meant Geri couldn't do any in-depth analysis on his character, one of the snags of the Kindle generation. He was wearing a Ralph Lauren shirt and loafers, so she decided he was probably reading some high-powered business biography.

Geri pressed the illuminated button on the doors at

the end of the carriage and stepped into the next one, eyes down and not looking where she was going. Consequently, she walked into a woman just leaving the buffet car.

"Sorry," Geri said, flicking her eyes upwards.

"No problem." The woman flashed Geri a smile that made her stop in her tracks.

Geri thought she recognised her, but then she didn't. Geri frowned, then smiled.

The woman gave her an amused look.

Geri's heart sped up and she could feel her face turning scarlet.

The woman was holding Geri with her eyes, almost willing her to say something else — but Geri was lost for words. The woman's deep blue eyes were penetrative, her smile electric.

"Sorry again," Geri muttered, blushing and squeezing past her in the narrow aisle. She heard the woman press the button, heard the doors hiss open and then shut. Geri shook her head. She always hoped that when she met an attractive woman these days, she would act differently than she had when she was 25. Apparently not.

Geri got her coffee and sandwich and walked back through the carriage, grabbing a headrest as the train lurched one way and then the other. She arrived back at her seat within minutes and was surprised to see the woman she'd just nearly run into sitting on her table of four, coffee and sandwich in hand.

"Oh — hi again." Geri put her deli bag down on the

table and shifted across to the window seat. She could feel another blush waiting to pounce as she sat down.

"Hi." The woman was smiling at her, still amused. She had short cropped black hair and was wearing a simple black T-shirt that worked amazingly with her olive skin. She pinged Geri's gaydar immediately.

Geri took out her coffee, sandwich and biscuits, not daring to look up, not trusting her words. Plus, she must look a state after the weekend she'd had. Tired, puffy, spotty. She wished she had her sunglasses. When Geri did eventually look up, though, she found the woman's warm, interested gaze on her.

"Snap." The woman indicated that the two of them had exactly the same lunch.

Geri smiled, making sure it was as wide as she could muster.

"Shall we try this again," said the woman. She wiped non-existent crumbs from her fingers and held out her right hand.

Geri took in short fingernails and long, slim fingers. Geri's heartbeat got louder still.

"Rachel," she said. She took Geri's hand and shook it warmly, fixing Geri with an intense stare. It had the required dazzling effect.

"Geri." If she was feeling giddy, at least Geri's voice sounded normal. She decided she could chance speaking again. "So is it any good?" Geri pointed towards the sandwich Rachel had already taken a bite of.

Rachel made a face. "It tastes like a train sandwich." She paused, cupping her chin in her right palm. "I think it might need a while to warm up." Rachel smiled, revealing teeth so straight she must have spent her entire teenage years in braces.

Geri smiled right back. "My friend Tash says all these sandwiches taste like fridge. It's an acquired taste. I don't think I'll ever get the hang of it, though."

At this, Rachel nodded, holding Geri with her unwavering gaze. "Me neither." She blew on her coffee before pausing, then took a sip. "At least the coffee's not too bad." She flicked her eyes upwards. "But then, I'm a chef, so I'm hard to please." Her smile lit up her face once more.

Geri sat up in her seat and took a sip of her coffee. "A chef?" A slow smile ploughed across her face. "Whereabouts do you work?"

"I've just opened up my own place in Islington. You probably don't know it," Rachel said.

"Try me," Geri replied.

THE END

Want more from me? Sign up to join my VIP Readers' Club and get a FREE lesbian romance, ***It Had To Be You!***
Claim your free book here:
www.clarelydon.co.uk/it-had-to-be-you

Also by Clare Lydon

London Romance Novels

London Calling

This London Love

A Girl Called London

Other novels

Nothing To Lose: A Lesbian Romance

Twice In A Lifetime

The All I Want Series

All I Want For Christmas (Book 1)

All I Want For Valentine's (Book 2)

All I Want For Spring (Book 3)

All I Want For Summer (Book 4)

All I Want For Autumn (Book 5)

All I Want Forever (Book 6)

Boxsets

All I Want Series Boxset, Books 1-3

All I Want Series Boxset, Books 4-6

All I Want Series Boxset, Books 1-6

A Note from Clare

Clare Lydon lives in London with her wife and precisely no pets (what a terrible lesbian she truly is). She's from a huge Irish family who like to sing at any given opportunity, and she bakes a mean banana cake. Even her mum says so, and *she knows cake.*

Clare's absolute favourite things in life are (in no particular order): bourbon, Curly Wurlys, stationery shops, sales in stationery shops, music, shoes, beer, signage, roast chicken, Christmas films, road trips, coffee, bananas, slow Loris videos on YouTube, red wine, karaoke, bus countdown apps (life-changing), tea, line-dried laundry, mustard mayo, musicals, lists and those Salted Caramel Puddles from Hotel Chocolat. Try them. You'll never look back.

If you fancy getting in touch, you can do so using one of the methods below — I'm most active on Twitter, Facebook or Instagram.

Twitter: @clarelydon
Facebook: www.facebook.com/clare.lydon
Instagram: @clarefic
Email: mail@clarelydon.co.uk
Web: www.clarelydon.co.uk

THANK YOU FOR READING!

Printed in Great Britain
by Amazon